i

Auction Block

Louise Furley

Auction Block

ISBN- 978-1-7369376-2-4 (Paperback)
ISBN- 978-1-7369376-1-7 (eBook)

Cover design by Pixel Mischief Design

Isle of Orainn

Anastasia

Auction Block

The Kissing Number

Cini and the Beast

The Poser

Wrath of Wolf

Auction Block

Chapter One

"Please Beks," Queenie Benani implored her younger stepsister. "You have to tell them you took it. You know Father said if he catches me in his wallet again he'll send me away. I will be locked up in that God-awful boarding school. You're used to it, I'm not. I'll die there without my freedom!"

To herself, Rebeka Benani thought, *yeah, and without your drugs and your men and your jewelry and your-*

Queenie's impatient grunt interrupted Rebeka's thoughts. Rebeka regarded her beautiful sister with faint envy. Their parents always extolled Queenie's beauty.

She had natural red hair but enhanced the bit of dullness with highlighting, just as she augmented her hazel eyes with contacts making them emerald green, and fringed them with the longest thickest eyelashes money could buy.

Father had paid a fortune to shorten her nose and enlarge her breasts boosting her AA cup to double D's to balance her height and robust bottom.

Rebeka on the other hand, squashed under a heavy parental thumb, was kept humble as the parents told her there couldn't be two beauty queens in one family, therefore Rebeka mustn't aspire to being one.

They said, well, Queenie's mother said, that one of the sisters had to be the plain one in order to be a foil so the other can shine brighter.

Since Rebeka was so petite next to Queenie's larger-boned model height, Rebeka held down the homely side of the sisterhood.

Rebeka pinched her flaxen curls in a tight bun and kept her curves stashed under loose clothes. Her small upturned nose had only a sprinkling of freckles on her fine-boned face, unlike the heavy peppering Queenie spent a lot of money on makeup and facials to keep hidden.

Queenie's thinner lips were often flattened into a straight sullen line when she chastised Rebeka for letting her tiny lush lips curve up in friendly smiles. Queenie said it made her look doltish and stupid.

She'd schooled the younger girl to keep the smiles, the friendliness concealed, that if they looked down on others, they would be treated more like royalty, it was the way the world worked. Yes, the sisters couldn't be less alike, in looks or behavior

"But, Queenie," Rebeka implored, "then I'm the one to be in trouble. You keep doing things and tell the folks it was me and then I'm the one that pays for them. I've only just returned home after being shunted off to that deplorable boarding prison."

At her sister's mulish expression, Rebeka begged her, "Please Queenie, since I was three I've barely spent a few weeks over the years at home. I've been tucked away in that prison of a school. I don't want to-"

"Oh for God's sake, Beks," Queenie snapped. "You whine like a baby. I'm the one in trouble here, not you. They won't be as hard on you as they will on me." She deliberately softened her tone. "Please Beks, please, I really need your help here."

Although Queenie was wrong, they were always harder on Rebeka than her, Rebeka could never say no to anyone. She hated to see people hurt or in trouble.

Seeing the girls she had lived with at the school receive daily lashings tore at her soft heart. Sure, she was whipped as well, but it was easier to take it herself then to watch her friends writhing and screaming in agony.

Well, Queenie was her sister, stepsister, but still, they were blood. They should look out for one another. Rebeka gave her sister a short nod with a heavy sigh. "Sure, okay, I'll tell him it was me."

"Oh Beks!" Queenie chortled, "You are the best sister ever!" She ran over, gave Rebeka a shoulder-breaking quick hug then danced out the door.

Rebeka stood there watching her go, chagrin biting at her gut. Queenie had talked her into it again.

They had grown up mostly apart. Rebeka's mother died shortly after her birth. Queenie's father had run off with another woman, so Queenie's mother, Isabelle, chased after and finally caught Rebeka's father, Garrison Benani.

But Isabelle didn't want a reminder of Garrison's beloved first wife around, so she'd shipped Rebeka off to an all girls' boarding school in a country so tiny it barely registered on the map and managed to keep her there.

Rebeka came home for infrequent holidays and was treated as an unwelcome intruder, like a stranger.

But, it was better than being trapped in the old convent type of structure half buried in a scantly populated wilderness, with cruel mistresses eager to use a belt or a stick or anything they could get their hands on to keep the girls in line, or just for their own sadistic fun.

Queenie, on the other hand, lived in luxury at home basking in her mother and stepfather's love. And wealth. Queenie had always been a spoiled, troublesome child.

As she grew older she became more unmanageable, often bringing the law to their front door. At his wit's end, Garrison had started punishing her by sending her off to the boarding school for a month or so as punishment.

It didn't make a dent in Queenie's misbehavior. Because she knew her mother would badger Garrison until he relented and let Queenie return home.

Sighing, Rebeka tromped down the stairs. She decided to take a walk down the street to the shop and gather some items to bake something. She felt better when she was baking.

She picked up her purse and headed out the door. Having finally completing two years of college at the boarding institute, she had been searching for scholarships for the past year or more so she could continue on with her academics without being under her father's thumb and she could finally come home and stay there.

Her VISA only allowed her to attend school in the very rural mountains in Kapistan near Russia where she was boarded, so she was unable to work.

Now, she had been applying for universities in her home state of Oregon when her father just recently brought her home.

She was dying to go to a university where she could earn a higher degree and finally be free and on her own. But she had no money, and the town they resided in was so small it was desperately hard to find a job.

No matter how good her grades, the private boarding school was not accredited, therefore she wasn't winning any scholarships.

Her father decided he would have Rebeka marry his friend the mayor's son maybe next year to strengthen their political solidarity, so he felt she didn't need an education to be a politician's wife.

Garrison never considered Queenie for the position because, even Garrison was well aware of Queenie's…indiscretions, the many, many, indiscretions that kept her solidly on bi-yearly birth control shots.

For now, Garrison did the same with Rebeka although there was no need to. Home so infrequently and now for only a short time, Rebeka reveled in it and seldom left the house.

Due to being tucked away in the rural mountains with only females, her experience with the opposite sex was almost nil. She had put all her time and effort into her schoolwork. The only things she knew about men were what the other girls gossiped about the fleeting times Rebeka wasn't in class or otherwise inundated with her studies.

Garrison paid for Queenie's high-maintenance and had Rebeka go along for electrolysis treatments.

Because Rebeka had no interest in makeup and clothes and the trappings of females, Garrison was trying to inch her into getting used to the lavish, fancy things that would make a politician's wife look polished.

Rebeka had zero interest in marriage. She wanted to go to school but didn't have the funds, and couldn't get a loan without a co-sign, and Garrison refused to do it.

The only time Rebeka left the house was to job hunt or go to the market. She was having no luck getting hired. People had told her they assumed she was as wicked as her sister and did not want to take a chance on her.

Trying to keep her flagging spirits up, Rebeka strolled quickly down the street to the market.

She was almost at the door when a man rushed up to her and grabbed her arm, stopping her.

Rebeka gasped, "Curt McCain, what are you doing? Let go of me."

The handsome young man only held onto her more tightly. He had attended the same high school as Queenie and saw Rebeka with her one day in the store. He had hit on her the few times he'd run into her since, but she had rebuffed his advances.

"Rebeka, come on, I have something at my house I want to show you," he started pulling her down the street.

Rebeka tugged on her arm protesting, "No, Curt, stop it, let go of me, I'm not going anywhere with you."

He had to be near six feet tall, his grip was solid. Shiny dark hair matched his dark eyes that at the moment were lit with anger and undisguised lust.

He stopped and glared in her face. "You fucking bitch," he snarled. "You deny me again and again to go out with me. I've had it. You're coming with me now and we're gonna fuck whether you like it or not. I tried to be gentlemanly. I'm done with that shit. You're Queenie Benani's little sister, you have to be at least half the slut she is. Quit playing so hard to get. Come on," he jerked hard at her arm pulling her.

"No!" She wrenched her arm from his grasp when he turned. "You leave me alone or I'll-"

He suddenly gripped her jaw and jerked her head up to his. "You'll what? Go to the police? You even think of doing that and I'll kill you. You understand me? I will fucking kill you. Now, you're coming with me right now," and he started dragging her down the street.

"Curt! Stop! No!" she yelped, trying to dig her heels into the pavement. *Was she suddenly living in a lawless land that a man could just grab her off the street?* Not a car driving by stopped to help her.

Her heart slammed against her ribcage, he meant it, and he was strong enough he could do what he wanted with her.

Rebeka punched at him shouting, "No! Let me go!"

He ignored her protests and dragged her faster, ruthlessly, not caring that she stumbled as he held her in an iron grip.

Then, a man stepped out of a store and called out, "What's going on out here? Why all the yelling?"

He took in Rebeka's frightened flustered face, Curt's harsh grip on her arm and his fierce expression, and the shop-owner strode to the walk.

"See here now, let her go. You let go of her or I'm calling the cops!" Behind him, a woman with a broom came out. She moved to stand beside him, the pair glowered at Curt.

Under his breath, Curt snarled, "You bitch. You're gonna pay for this, I can't have you I'll take Queenie. I'll fuck her up and it'll be your fault." He released her so suddenly she toppled backwards.

Without another look at her he stomped off down the street.

Chapter Two

Over the next week, Rebeka struggled with whether or not to tell her father about the incident. She did warn Queenie but her sister had laughed her off.

Queenie told her if she told Garrison about Curt's threat, he would undoubtedly send them both back to the wretched school. So, Rebeka kept her mouth shut, keeping the turmoil and anxiety stuffed inside.

She hadn't been back outside, terrified Curt would come after her, and this time no one would be around to stop him. She-

There was a disturbance at the front door. A wailing crying and then the door flung open and Queenie staggered inside. Breaths gusting hard, she trod crookedly across the room, then fell to her knees at Rebeka's feet.

Rebeka shrieked and knelt beside her. Queenie's dress was torn, she had blood on her face, she was sobbing into her hands.

Rebeka gasped, "Queenie, oh my gosh, what happened?"

Queenie just sobbed and sobbed. Rebeka didn't know what to do, their parents were out of town, the maids weren't there today.

She sat beside Queenie on the rug and pleaded with her sister, "Queenie, sweetheart, please, tell me what happened, please."

A few more chest rattling sobs, then Queenie looked up at her sister with tear-flooded eyes. "A- a man, Rebeka, a man...he- he raped me!" She wailed and flung herself into her sister's arms.

Rebeka's stomach plummeted like a rock. "Was...was it Curt, Curt McCain?"

Through the river of tears Queenie looked at her, asked, "How did you know? How could you know that?"

"Oh Queenie," Rebeka cried in despair. "Remember I had told you about Curt's attack on me and what he had threatened."

"So," Queenie sobbed, "this is your fault. This is all your fault! How could you, Beks, how could you let this happen to me?"

"But, no, but, Queenie, I tried to warn you, you wouldn't let me, you wouldn't listen, you made me promise not to tell Father, I-"

Queenie swung on her sister, the red fury on her face marring the simulated beauty, "This is not all about you, Beks. You should have made me listen, then this wouldn't have happened. It's all your fault that I'm...ruined." She staggered to her feet.

Rebeka bit back the words *you already were*, but said instead, "No, please Queenie, what can I do to help?"

"I hate you, you've let them hurt me!" Queenie wailed and fled out the door.

Rebeka stood flabbergasted. Queenie was right, it was her fault. Curt had wanted her, she should have given in. A shiver raced through her body at the thought.

She hated him, he scared her. He was rough and mean and crude. But, still, her own sister had suffered due to Rebeka's own cowardice.

How could she fix this? How can she make it up to Queenie?

A few days passed, her parents were still out of town. Queenie stayed somewhere else making Rebeka feel even more guilty that her sister didn't stay home so that Rebeka could take care of her, make up for what Curt McCain had done to her.

At the very least let her take her to the hospital, make sure she was okay. But Queenie refused to go to either the hospital or the police station and file a complaint. Rebeka called the police but they advised Queenie would need to come in and press charges in person. Rebeka hadn't been present during the assault so she was not a witness.

She just finished frosting a cake she planned to bring next door to Mrs. Lowe. The poor dear elderly woman had spent the past few weeks in the hospital and was finally back in her own home.

Rebeka was about to put the cake in a Tupperware when someone knocked at the front door.

It was so quiet, so lonely in the huge mansion with no one else there, Rebeka was eager for company even if it was only the mailman.

Wiping her hands on a towel, she untied the apron around her skirt, set it on the counter and hurried to the front door. She peeked through the side window and frowned. There was a man there she didn't know.

She stepped back from the door unsure if she should open it.

"Hello?" The stranger's voice came through the door sounding friendly yet worried. "Um," he said, "my car broke down and my cell died. I was hoping, please, if I could use your phone to call for roadside assistance?"

He sounded normal, nervous, nice. He needed help. Rebeka opened the door.

Suddenly there was a second man there, and now the two of them looked huge and downright sinister.

Rebeka rushed to shut the door and lock it but the first one stuck his foot in the doorway preventing her from closing it.

"No, honey," his voice dark and hard, he said with an unpleasant smile, "we need to talk." He shoved the door open forcing Rebeka to lurch backwards with a yelp of surprise. The two men barged in.

The first man, tall with short brown hair and eyes, was built like a boxer in a sweater and jeans. Thick scruff covered his lower face, he said gruffly, "We're looking for Queenie Benani, you her?"

Rebeka backed away, her eyes darting from one man to the other. "W- why do you want her?"

The second man had thin blond hair that hung over his pale eyes but didn't cover the pockmarks pitting his ashen face. Taking a step towards her, he said belligerently, "We ask the questions, girl, not you."

Rebeka moved back further.

The first man, the boxer, softened his voice, he said, "It won't hurt to say why, Paddy," he said to his friend, then smiled more benevolently at Rebeka.

"If you're Queenie Benani, then you already know what you did, honey. You slept with King Martin and while he was asleep, you fucking stole a kilo of smack from him. He wants to talk to you. We're going to take you to him."

Her mouth dropped. "But- but, I- I," she stammered, trying to think. Queenie was in trouble. Rebeka needed to tell these scary men that she wasn't her sister. But, if she did that and they waited for Queenie to come home, oh dear, they might hurt both of them!

Maybe if Rebeka could talk to this Mr. Martin and explain that she would make sure Queenie brought his property back to him. Queenie could be stubborn, Rebeka would need time to convince her-

"Well bitch?" Paddy snapped at her. "You Queenie or what?" He glanced at his friend. "Fuck, Neil, I think we should take her to Martin anyway, whoever she is."

"Wait! Please, I-" before she could say another word the two men pounced on her.

Last thing she saw was Neil's big fist coming at her.

Chapter Three

*H*er jaw ached, head pounded, Rebeka felt like hell. The faint jostling of her body only made her headache worse.

"Ahh," groaning, she went to put her hand to her jaw- and couldn't move her hands. "What-" she jerked her arms trying to move her hands, but she became aware that her wrists were tied together behind her back.

Her eyes felt swollen, too painful to open, she went to sit up and found her ankles were also bound. Her movements made her head pound harder and pain shot to her jaw.

Then, she heard people talking. All around her, male and female voices. Some loud and boisterous, some whimpered, she heard crying.

With a hard forced move, she pushed herself to sit up with her legs curled to the side. Waiting out the spell of dizziness and nausea that overcame her, she cracked her sore eyes open.

What on earth?

The jostling she felt was due to the rumbling, cranking train car she was in, the clank of metal wheels grinding on metal rails sounded below her.

A few cracks around the edges of the tin box she was in let in meager light. People were crammed inside with her, bound as she was. They stopped talking as they gawked at her.

"Huh," a man grunted, "the princess awakens." A few of the people snickered.

Struggling to shuffle back to lean against the side of the boxcar, Rebeka squinted around at the crowd of people. She wriggled to move her skirt lower to cover her thighs.

"I...don't understand. Where am I? How did I get in here?" Her gaze traveled the room of men and women of all ages, races, tied up just as she was, staring at her.

Some of the women sneered, chuckling amongst themselves. A couple of men nearby looked at her sadly, others with avarice in their debauched eyes blatantly stared at her breasts and legs curved gracefully to the side.

One of the women close to her sighed.

The woman appeared to be in her late thirties with ash blonde hair to her shoulders, and dull brown eyes. It was hard to tell because she was sitting, but she seemed at least average height but maybe thirty pounds overweight.

She wore a tight shirt that revealed her pudgy belly and pointed breasts, and short-shorts. A hard life had angled her plump face. "Hell girl," she said, "you have been out of it for a long time. You missed the entire plane ride."

"Huh," a man grunted, "didn't miss nuthin' on that bucket of bolts in the fuckin' cargo hold, Jackie. Stuffed in like fuckin' cattle."

Everyone jerked and jostled back and forth as the train chugged on with sounds of the engine grumbling and the unending clanking grind of steel wheels rolling roughly on old steel rails.

Jackie skewed narrowed eyes at him. "Yeah, well, Sam," she turned to Rebeka and said to her, "you were lucky to have slept through it. Neil musta really packed his fist into you before he drugged you."

Her gaze fell to the purple bruise on Rebeka's jaw. "Anyways, you, we, are all on our way to Nikolai Łizhiní's famous, or infamous as it were, auction block."

Rebeka blinked her bewildered blue eyes at her. "I don't understand, we're going where? And why would we be-"

"Listen girlie," Sam interrupted. He said rudely, "Don't pretend any innocence here, we are all the same." He nodded around at the crowd.

They looked like normal people to Rebeka, except, the closer she peered at them, the more she saw the same tough, immoral cast in their eyes that Queenie carried, like a brand.

The way they held themselves, heads tilted slyly, lids lowered to conceal their dissolute depravity, shoulders rolled in as if to hide their iniquity.

Jackie studied Rebeka then shook her head. "No, she's not like us, Sam. You can see crystal clearly that she's…as pure as the un-driven snow." The laughter at her words rang around the tin car.

"Don't matter," Sam sniffed, "she's goin' to the same fate."

Her blues wide and fearful, Rebeka asked anxiously, "Fate? What are you talking about?" Her head swung around at the other people then back to Jackie.

Everyone was staring at her.

Not understanding the pity creased around Jackie's eyes and turned down mouth, Rebeka asked, "What do you mean not like you?"

Jackie smiled sadly. "Honey, I'd tell you to calm down, say it'll be okay, but you will only plunge back into fright when you get there and find out it's true. That it will never be okay again. Nothing…will ever be okay again."

"What's true?" Rebeka's voice shook, her wrists hurt, her jaw throbbed, her fingers were numb.

A weary sigh wobbled from the older woman. "Ah, well, the auction block. We," she motioned with her head to the others, "all of us, we are," she sighed again. "Thieves, prostitutes, druggies, traffickers, some even killers." Her sad smile widened at Rebeka's disbelief.

"It's true hon. We're all bad, we've all done bad things. The word is that you stole King Martin's dope and it's already been cut and out on the streets, the cash spent, so he sold you to get his money back."

Jackie's gaze stroked down Rebeka's slender form. "Anyways, we are going to Nikolai Łizhiní's auction house to be," she shrugged, "auctioned off. As slaves. The men will be bought by those that will send them to work in mines, dig fields, migrant pickers, anywhere they will be unpaid labor for miserable hard labor."

Terrified to ask, Rebeka's voice squeaked out small, "And…the women?"

Jackie's lips pulled in, she looked around at the others. No one was laughing now.

"Uh, yeah, we women. Well, the older, more unattractive ones will be sent as slave servants, or to work fields, things like that. The younger, the pretty ones will be bought by…brothel owners."

Still blinking rapidly, Rebeka relaxed a hair. She could get help, escape then. "So, I, I would be sent to work farms or maybe to clean houses?" She flinched at the coarse laughter that broke out around her.

Even Jackie's mouth twitched before it fell in sorrow for the girl in front of her. "No, hon. You will definitely be sold to some sort of brothel, or massage parlor. You're too beautiful to be put on the streets and truck stops to hook cheap like some of them will be, like me probably."

Resigned to her own fate, Jackie shrugged one shoulder. "I'm still attractive but getting long in the tooth, ya know?"

"I- no," Rebeka shook her head. "I don't have any looks a man would really want, pay money for." Sure, Curt had wanted her, but who knows what drove that sick man. He had told her she must be a slut like Queenie so he obviously wanted easy sex.

"If I'm to be sent to a field, there's a chance of my," Rebeka couldn't believe she was tied up, on a train heading for hell, and believing what this woman was telling her, and she was thinking of how she would escape.

Seeing how her mind was working, Jackie's sigh was heavy with compassion. "You're going to fight it, I can tell, you're that kind. Not like the rest of us resigned to accept our fate as recompense for our misdeeds. But, believe me little girl, this is all real. Very real."

Sam said, "You're going to be put up on a block, a stage, you'll be lucky if they allow you to wear anything at all, and if they do," he made a huffing sound, "it won't be much."

"And it won't be staying on anyway," someone said.

A few snickers circled the room.

Jackie continued, "The owners of brothels and such from all around the world will be there and they will bid on you. Top bid will purchase you, and, trust me this is the truth, you will be put to work, as a prostitute, for the rest of your, well, as long as you last. And," her smile bleak, "there will be no escape. Ever."

Jackie's lips pinched, then she went on, "The girls that try, trust me, they are always caught. The first time they try to run they are beaten, whipped within an inch of their sorry-ass lives, the second time they try, they die. The owners can't have it known that anyone could think to ever escape them."

"Yeah," another woman joined in, her voice rough from years of smoking and drinking. "They use the whip to train you in the first place if you are, let's say reluctant to work. But, if you try to run, they will catch you," she moved to reveal an arm covered with ugly scars.

"They will take as much of your flesh that they can and still be able to sell you, day after day, night after night. There are no weekends, no holidays," her bleary eyes blurred with tears of hopelessness.

A woman across from Rebeka told her, "I was sold once. My pimps were murdered for trying a takeover, so I was snatched away and am now on my way to be resold. But, I mean," a faint blush colored her gaunt cheeks. "It was my fault. I had, have, an addiction. I used to sleep with prominent men, politicians, then blackmail them to feed my habit."

Her eyes wide, Rebeka's face expressed her sympathy for the hapless woman.

"Eventually," the woman continued, "livin' the hard life with drugs and booze you lose your looks and, well," she chuckled ruefully, "you end up doin' the dangerous streets and the grungy truck stops. A pimp scoops you up, there's no gettin' away from them. So, this really ain't gonna be no hardship on me like it will on a youngin' like you."

Rebeka's stomach rebelled at what these freaky people were telling her. Sell her? To work as a- no, she shook her head. She could not believe it. She was only there to give Queenie time to return what she took.

As soon as Queenie heard what happened she would do it. Then of course Rebeka could go home. In maybe one day, two at the most.

Her body bouncing and rocking, she looked around but there were no windows. It may have already been one day judging by what the woman told her about being passed out on a plane.

Fortunately she was terribly dehydrated likely from the drug they'd used on her so she had yet to require the facilities. Wherever they might be. And with her hands tied, she didn't know how she was to manage it anyway.

She had no idea how long she had been on this train. Leaning forward, she asked, "Miss, um, Jackie, where are we going? Where are they taking us?"

A plane, a train, she'd been in the northwest, they could be anywhere in the United States.

Jackie and the other woman shared a look. Jackie's lips pulled in then pursed out. "Uh, I hear tell it's in South Africa this time-"

"No," Sam cut in, "Israel."

"No, no, that was last time," someone else said. "This one is near Turkey, they move the very private auction so it can't be busted. Only those rich enough get invitations."

"We're headed to Pakistan-"

"Arabia!"

People blurted out more different locations.

Tears stinging that back of her eyes, Rebeka whispered, "We aren't in America anymore?"

"Huh," Sam scoffed, "haven't been for about 16 hours or so."

Rebeka fell back against the metal wall. Her head spun with confusion, disbelief, terror. She grew quiet, letting the voices drift around her. She thought adamantly, they had to let her go home tomorrow.

Of course they would, she told herself sighing out some of the tension in her shoulders. They can't hold someone against their will, sell them, it was against the law.

If Queenie doesn't come through, Rebeka will tell the leaders her real name and they'll have to let her go. How she'd get back to America would be a problem. Well, she'd call her father and he'd find a way to get her home.

To the tune of squeaking, rumbling, and chatter, her lids grew heavy and drifted closed.

As she drifted off again, she thought, *when I wake up again, for sure I will be stepping out in the sunshine* at a train station in Colorado or Texas or maybe New York.

Yes, those people were making up stories just to scare her. They were certainly still in the U.S. How could they smuggle a group of people out of the U.S. and into a foreign country? No way, that's how. Heck, she didn't even have a passport.

Rebeka shifted to lean more comfortably, or as best she could with her limbs restrained. She wondered why they were tied up.

Maybe, because as Jackie said, they were bad people and they were being protected from each other.

Chapter Four

*H*er body tossing more roughly back and forth woke Rebeka.

The train was slowing.

Thank goodness, they were finally stopping. Her feet and arms were numb, her back and jaw and head ached.

Conversations and snoring rambled around the car. Voices hushed as the train came to a rattling, whistle blowing stop. The car creaked and rocked then stilled.

No one moved or spoke, they just waited.

After quite some time, there was sound outside the big door.

More metal ground against metal as the door slid, slamming open with a resounding grating clank. In both directions up and down the line, Rebeka heard the same jarring sound.

Several men appeared in the open doorway. From inside the dark car, people squinted out, the men were only shadows with the blinding early morning sun as a backdrop.

One of the men jumped up into the car. He wore some type of uniform, looked military. He barked at the drowsy occupants, "Okay people, last stop, everyone off."

Since the prisoners were bound, the soldier bent and grabbed the nearest person, and jerked him to his feet.

The man swayed as his numb legs tried to come to life and hold him up.

The soldier cut the ties at his ankles leaving his wrists restrained, and gave him a shove to the door and told him to sit in the doorway.

When he awkwardly lowered to sit down at the edge, two men outside reached up and caught his arms and pulled him roughly out of the car. Then they did the same to everyone else, one at a time.

When the soldier reached Rebeka, a slow leer creased his weather-beaten face. While freeing her ankles, in accented-English, he said, "Ah, *yah*, you're gonna fetch a fine fee little honey." He bent and hauled her to her feet.

Her legs buckled. He grunted, "A soft one you are, you ain't gonna last for shit, girl." He scooped her up in his arms and carried her to the door.

Crouching, he lowered her, shifting her into the arms of one of the men waiting outside.

The man took her with a scowl. Snarling under his breath, "Frail," he set her on her feet and held her momentarily while she gained her balance. "Get with the others," he ordered, also in an accented voice.

Rebeka glanced around. The train cars were all being emptied of their human cargo. Fifty, maybe more, prisoners were being corralled into one huge cluster that continued to grow as others joined them.

Awkwardly moving her stiff legs, she slowly propelled herself to enter the murmuring crowd.

Men wearing uniforms of olive green with red collars and cuffs, combat boots, carrying automatic weapons

22

surrounded the prisoners. They aimed the weapons at the prisoners and ordered them harshly, "Get into a line, go."

The soldiers maneuvered the prisoners into several lines then they cut the binds at their wrists. No one was going to try to run or fight with all those weapons trained on them.

The area was soon alive with people talking, soldiers shouting, ordering, threatening, while moving people around to form a line. The prisoners rubbing and shaking out their arms to get the blood flowing.

One of the men with the soldiers trod down one line and up another glaring at each prisoner. Not in a uniform, he wore a black t-shirt and khakis.

Built like a bull with a sandy buzz cut and angry blue eyes, he looked like a Marine but with his accent he obviously was not. He barked at those that weren't standing neatly in line, suddenly raising his weapon he slammed the butt into a man's head.

"I said get the fuck in line!" he yelled, as the man staggered backwards, his hand to his bleeding head.

When the big guy was satisfied with the lines, he stood back so he could see them all. The other soldiers kept their guns trained on the prisoners.

Her heart in her throat, Rebeka surreptitiously scanned the land around them.

They were standing on hard-packed dirt and sparse grass. Rows of rusty beige barracks lined both sides of a large square building. Jeeps and trucks were parked off to one side.

Knots of smaller, separate buildings bunched all around the camp. Soldiers strode back and forth patrolling.

Fields of thicker grass and scattered trees bordered the site. Way in the distance loomed a foreboding barrier of gabled mountains like impregnable sentries.

"*Bine*, okay, listen up," buzz-cut said with an uncommon accent. "I am Captain Ving Lankov. You all know why you are here. You count your lucky stars that you are here and not rotting in some squalid foreign prison."

The prisoners remained silent and blank-faced. A few wriggled and moved their feet, but none strayed out of line.

Captain Lankov said, "The auction will be held on the ninth. Anyone that does not cooperate, does not do as they are told immediately, tries to fight or run, will be shot, or beheaded," his mouth slid up in a smirk, "whatever we are in the mood for at the time."

He trod back and forth while he spoke, eyeballing the prisoners with a hateful demeaning glare. "All of you will be housed in module barracks, the males and females will be kept in separate sets. Co-mingling between genders will be limited."

The male prisoners hugely outnumbered the females.

"He means sex," one of the other soldiers snorted with a laugh.

Women who weren't prisoners filtered amongst the soldiers. A couple hung on a few of the soldiers, the others stared with rapt interest at the prisoners.

The women's sleazy attire, their super tight skirts or pants and blouses cut low or unbuttoned, along with the slatternly smiles on their heavily made-up faces made Rebeka think they were like groupies. Some kind of soldier-jungle-groupies.

Her lip curled, she quickly dropped her eyes so no one could see her judgmental thoughts.

Lankov said, "That goes for between prisoners and soldiers as well. Too many times a female has been torn up while being used by men, some have died. That can be a big financial loss. Any of you choosing to have consensual sex will ask permission from the Zăffe himself."

He paced a few steps glaring at individuals. "Additionally, you may bring your requests to me or another captain. There are four captains, the other men in uniform are soldiers and will be addressed as Sir."

His eyes narrowed at the men. "Any rape or attempted rape will result in the attacker losing first his balls and then while we sit around watching him bleed out for a while, he will lose his head. Am I clear on this?" He looked around at the group of solemn nodding heads.

Rebeka stood partially behind two women with her head down and her eyes lowered. Her body was frozen with shock, so anxious she could scarcely draw a breath. Where in God's name was she?

She had to be deep in a nightmare she could only hope she was about to wake from. Peeking up briefly she quickly dropped her eyes. Besides the criminals she was lined up with, all around them stood stone-faced men, some muttering in differing accents, their guns aimed at them.

Sweat prickled her temples, she struggled to keep her shaking legs from collapsing. Where was the Calvary? How long will it take for Queenie to come through and rescue her?

Surely, when her father asked where Rebeka was Queenie would have to confess and then they'd contact the police.

The captain came to a stop, his hands clasped behind his back, legs rigidly akimbo. "Now then. You will be examined to verify you are either a man or a woman. There will be no trannie shit here. We see any of you looking like one gender and then we find out your sex doesn't match, you will be disposed of. It will be a kind death, quick, you will be shot."

There were collective gasps from half the audience. The other half just didn't care.

Lankov explained, "We can't put you on a block to sell you to a buyer and have your gender in question. These people are paying good money to get what they want. And, we will not have any mixed toilets, you are either clearly a male or a female, or you die today. Now-"

The sound of a truck approaching from the opposite direction of the mountains came around the train. Everyone turned their attention to it.

Lankov smiled. "Ah, here is our Zăffe now." He broke from his place in front of the prisoners and strode over to the truck as it parked.

The passenger door opened and a man stepped out, he and the captain nodded to each other. Several soldiers piled out of the truck and went in different directions.

Lankov and the man walked towards the crowd. When they stopped, a handful of groupie-women hurried over and gathered around them. One hung on one side of the new man, and another clung to his other side.

"*Bine*, prisoners, this is Zăffe Jephunneh Kajic. In English, he is called Chief Kajic. He is in charge of this operation. He is the law." His hands clasped behind his back he looked to Kajic.

Rebeka couldn't help sneaking a swift glance up at the man, she blanched, her stomach pitched. She thought she was going to vomit, not that she had anything to throw up. But the man was so…terrifying.

He was huge, like Lankov, but instead of khakis and a T, he wore a long-sleeved buttoned down shirt and black pants. His enormous shoulders corrugated with muscles pressed against the material of his shirt, huge biceps bulged, and his chest rippled with strength when he moved. A gun holstered at his hip hung low on his lean hips.

The indomitable expression on his hard face was ghastly along with the scars carved at one temple, his cheek, and his neck, where a tattoo was visible.

His dark hair waved to his shoulders, black scruff looked like it would always shadow his tough jaw no matter how closely he shaved it. Black brows lowered heavy over a masculine ridged brow.

Lids hooded over crocodile eyes that to Rebeka, looked black as night, dark with a cruel Satanic glint, completely void of compassion or mercy. The orbs, blank as enamel, glittered at the crowd. They briefly flashed with arrogance and power, and penance.

Kajic nodded once to Lankov.

Lankov said, "*Bine*, all right men, start the examination."

Soldiers kept their weapons trained on the prisoners while one of them went to the beginning of the line. When he reached the first person, a man, he said, "Take down your pants."

The man hesitated for only a second before doing as ordered. The soldier stuck a finger in his underwear, pulled it forward and peered down.

Letting the underwear go with a snap, he said, "Fine." Beside the soldier another had an iPad, he asked the man his name. When the prisoner responded, the soldier recorded it and they moved to the next person.

Each person was treated the same. Including the women. The examining soldier would order them to lower their pants and they complied. Then, if they wore any, the soldier would pull open the underwear and check before saying yes they were okay, or no, they were not.

If they were recorded as a no, they were roughly pulled from the line and shoved to the side. Some of the women wore dresses. The soldier would order they unbutton their blouses and lift their skirt and he would examine them.

He reached Rebeka. She was gaping at him in horror, her arms rigid, her hands clasped tightly down the front of her.

"Open blouse," he ordered.

Rebeka glanced over at the man they called the Zăffe.

The huge blond man with the buzz-cut had said Zăffe meant chief. The woman next to her muttered Zăffe meant leader, boss.

One of the girls standing beside him had locked her mouth over his and was trying to kiss him but he didn't seem to be interested.

The girl on the other side was pawing at the bulge behind his fly.

What a pig he is, Rebeka thought then her eyes flashed back to the soldier in front of her.

"Blouse," he snapped.

Keeping her arms over the front of her body as if she could protect herself, Rebeka lowered her eyes but didn't move.

"Blouse, bitch," the soldier said louder.

Still, she remained motionless.

"Goddammit," he cursed, stuffed his gun in his holster, grabbed her blouse and ripped it open.

Rebeka shrieked, pulled it closed and stepped back.

He had seen she had breasts. His cheeks stained red at her resistance. "Skirt, lift skirt, woman." His eyes gleamed in anticipation of seeing her bared sex.

Refusing, "No," she shook her head and took another step back.

"Bitch," he spat and stomped to her, grabbed her skirt and jerked it up, when he went to snatch at her panties, a heavily accented, coarse voice said with bored curtness, "You are wasting time, Soldier, she is obviously a broad, move on."

The soldier paused, looked over his shoulder. The Zăffe's eyes were narrowed at him, but he didn't look at Rebeka.

Scowling, the soldier let her skirt drop, gripped her arm, jerked her back into line then went on to the next person.

Rebeka peeked at the Zăffe under long lashes.

He had his arm across the girl who had tried to kiss him, his hand covered her breast. Playing with it, he shoved the other girl that still pawed at his manhood away, his glittering gaze now speared straight at Rebeka.

Rebeka felt icy chills race up her back. He had the dead eyes of a monster.

One slow blink, then he turned his head to murmur something to the girl he was feeling up, and moved his hand up under her shirt to grope her braless breast. While he fondled it, she leaned against him with a sultry moan.

The other girl stood with a frown and mumbled something barely audible, something like, "Me, I'm next, Zăf, me," and stuck her faux breasts up for his perusal.

The barest hint of a smirk edged up the corner of his harsh mouth at Rebeka's look of disgust before Kajic turned his attention to the female sucking at his face that he was groping.

When everyone had been examined, several soldiers gathered around the small group of people they had pulled to the side that failed the inspection. They were transgenders or cross-dressers, or something else. Whatever they were, they were signaled out.

The inspecting soldier said, "*Bine*," and nodded to the soldiers around the prisoners, "take them."

"No!" the small group yelled. Half burst into tears, they pleaded, begged for their lives. But the soldiers rounded them up and started forcing them with their shotguns nudging them to move through a grove of trees.

"What is going on?" Rebeka whispered to the person next to her.

The woman answered with no inflection in her voice, "They are trannies, transvestites or whatever, they are being taken to an empty well where they'll be shot and dumped. I know a few soldiers here, they told me the gist of it."

The cries of the people being led away roiled through the air, their wailing and pleading and sobbing was even louder as the rest of the prisoners lapsed into silence.

"No!" Rebeka yelled and ran to the small group, long blonde curls flapping behind her.

She implored the soldiers, "My God, they are people just like you and me. You can't just- just kill them because of…I mean you just can't!"

The lead soldier backhanded her hard, knocking her to the ground. She fell with a cry and lay stunned, he raised his rifle about to smash the butt into her head.

"Soldier," the Zǎffe said calmly from several yards away, "you plan on damaging my property?"

Everyone looked over at him. He stood with his hands in his pockets, the two girls no longer beside him, a few feet away they hovered with pouts.

He started walking across the grounds towards the commotion. The prisoners about to be executed were crying, the soldier scowling. Rebeka lay dazed with her legs bent and braced on a forearm.

Kajic sauntered across the dirt and grass to them. He stopped a few feet from Rebeka.

Still stunned, her head reeling, she put a hand to her face where the soldier had hit her and peered up at him. "Please," she licked her lips, her throat dry with fear and the horror of the entire situation. "Please don't kill them, they are human beings just like the rest of us!"

The soldier snarled and pulled back his boot to kick her.

Kajic commanded, "*Na.*"

The soldier halted, then stepped to the side glaring at Rebeka.

"Get her up," Kajic instructed him.

The soldier snapped his heels together then bent, grasped Rebeka's arms and roughly hauled her to her feet.

Still half-dazed, she tripped. The soldier held her firm, his fingers deliberately squeezing, pinching her slender arm hard enough to bruise her.

Lowering his gaze to the soldier's grasp, Kajic said calmly, "I cannot get top dollar for damaged goods."

The soldier blinked, pulled in his lips and let go of her.

Kajic's eyes drifted down to Rebeka's open blouse, traveling boldly over her exposed rounded flesh then up to the red blush that brightened her cheeks.

Swaying on unsteady legs, she jerked her blouse closed.

His strong jaw covered with dark scruff made him look like a dangerous thug, his cheeks hard angled, one had a scar across it. The scar at his temple beat with the vein under it.

He looked so…unscrupulous, big and brutally menacing, Rebeka struggled to hold in the shivers so violent they threatened to split her body in two.

She fought to keep her eyes level at his. But her body shrank from his powerful bulk and hard face. Sheer lethality radiated from his dark, heavily hooded eyes.

31

He towered over her petite form. Looking down at her under those scary hooded lids, he said "Ah, little girl," his words so heavily accented she had to work to understand him. His voice was as hard and coarse as his face. "You wish to take their place? Those transvestites, the transgenders? Die for them?"

In the harshly sculptured face, his full mouth chiseled in cruelty, quirked up as the color drained from her face leaving her skin so pale it was almost translucent.

Rebeka blinked rapidly at him holding back the panicking tears, she swiped a hand across her face to stop them from falling.

The soldier raised his gun at her movement as if she was going to be a threat.

Kajic glanced at him, his arched brow mocked him for insinuating the slip of a girl could be a danger to him.

Clearing her throat to gather her bravado, Rebeka sucked down the knot in her throat that clogged her windpipe.

Taking a deep breath, tremors of terror rippling through her soft voice, looking directly at him, she said, "What you plan for me is death anyway. Yes," her faint words shook out, "spare them. Kill me instead of them." Her head lowered, she was too frightened to maintain eye contact with the heathen.

His black brows jumped in a surprise then dropped over the black enamel eyes. His gaze raked her body from head to toe. He said, "Unfortunately, girl, you will be worth too much for me to slaughter without better cause."

He gestured to the soldier and told him, "*Bine*, soldier, note their names and put them back in line. We may have a category for them that bidders will like. Take her," he raised a hand to signal the soldier and took a step to Rebeka.

Auction Block

Still dizzy from the hit and starving, she looked up at the hulking promise of death, thinking she was about to die, her brain shut off in terror and the world went black.

Chapter Five

"What the fuck," Kajic growled and caught her up in his big arms. Lifting her to his chest, the shirt he wore tightened over huge carved muscles. He looked down at her.

Her skin ghostly pale, plush lips parted, tears glistened on child-like round cheeks.

The people who were about to be killed were identified technically as all males.

To the stunned soldier, in a foreign language, Kajic ordered, "Get those people into gender appropriate clothes and house them with the men. Ask them what they consider themselves to be, then label them on the record, there might be a market for them. Get all the prisoners into their assigned barracks."

He turned and stomped across the dirt and tall grass with Rebeka held up high, hard against his chest.

He strode past the prisoners, the curious soldiers, the camp whores who glared at the girl in his arms, at the long blonde curls wavering over his arm as he walked. He kept going until he reached a small building.

Reaching under her, he opened the door, stepped inside and kicked it closed behind him with a heavy boot.

He looked down at the young woman in his arms, at her soft face, long flaxen lashes curled on pink cheeks, lips like puffy rosebuds.

Her natural wildflower scent surrounded his senses, like a perfumed missile it shot straight to raise his dick already hardening from holding the soft female in his arms.

Shaking off his odd reaction, hell, he was only holding her, he lowered his gaze to her plump breasts half-exposed in the open shirt.

Her head hung over his arm, causing the creamy mounds like big scoops of vanilla ice cream to rise higher. Completely unconscious, his prize was helpless to cover or protect herself. He bent his head and put his mouth on one of her irresistible breasts cupped in a silky peach bra.

First, like a dog, he licked her soft skin then he sucked. He sucked hard until a red mark rose. Looking down at it, his dick straining at his pants, he licked the mark then moved his mouth to between her cleavage so both breasts hugged his face, and licked the center valley of them.

He opened his mouth to suck her flesh, bite it. He nuzzled with his chin to unearth and taste a nipple, when she stirred in his arms. He paused and then lifted his head. He laid her on the bed.

The door opened. He looked from the woman on the bed to the man in the doorway.

The soldier said, "We're getting them into the barracks and on lockdown until we're ready to travel. What about her?"

The soldier moved to the bed and looked down at the unconscious girl. His hand on his belt buckle, with a leer, he asked, "We taking our shots at her before we put her with the others, or," he gave his boss a sly look. "You keeping her in here with you to fuck until we leave?"

On her back, she lay slightly curled, brilliant hair waving around her head. Her hands were up by her head as if in surrender making her appear strikingly vulnerable, the blouse fell wide open.

Both men stared at her plump breasts rising and sinking with her breaths.

Standing next to Kajic, the soldier said, "Yeah, she's the damned finest we've ever taken in, makes the rest of them look old and haggard, built like sticks or blow up dolls. Let me get her warmed up for you." He moved closer to the bed tugging his belt open.

Kajic shoved him away, snapped, "You know the rules. We do not do the prisoners. Just get the others settled, I will bring her when she comes to."

A sheen of lust misted the soldier's face as he stared at the girl with greedy eyes. He said eagerly, "Shit Boss, I'll be quick. She's so fucking hot, a few pumps and I'll be done. Let's see those primo titties," he reached for her breasts.

"Do not make me say it again, Soldier," cold, hard tone, the chill froze the soldier.

Without a word, the soldier trod to the door buckling his belt.

When he left, Kajic watched the girl for a moment then he saw her lashes flutter, her lips pulsed.

Slowly her eyes opened. When she saw him standing there staring at her, she gasped and sat up. Her woozy head spun, she put a hand to it and tried to move to the side, away from him.

"Get up," he told her. Standing like a threatening, arrogant bear, his gaze rolled over her blonde hair, to the plush lips then down her front.

Seeing him staring at her chest, she lowered her eyes and saw the red mark on her breast then looked up at him. Staring at the mark, he wiped his mouth like he'd just done it.

Getting to her feet, she snapped her blouse together and said angrily, "You are a horrible man, not even a man, you are a despicable base beast." Shaking off the dizziness, she stepped away from him.

"*Yah,*" his smile crude and cold. He moved to close the distance between them then swung around in irritation as the door opened again.

The woman that he'd had his hand up her blouse stood in the doorway.

"Zăffe Kajic," she said, stepping inside. A purr gurgled from wide crimson lips so glossy the light reflected off them. "Chief, you have been gone for weeks, you must need," brown eyes framed with thick fake lashes flapped as she glanced at the girl.

Long brunette hair swayed down her back as the blowsy woman moved her voluptuous body closer to Kajic. She simpered, "I can quench your needs, Zăf, much better than that skinny infant." Her disparaging gaze swept the younger woman, and dismissed her as unworthy of attention.

"Patrisia-" Kajic's stony dark eyes flicked from the woman then to the girl.

Saying quickly, "Zăf," Patrisia hurried to stand between him and the girl. She set a palm on his chest, and cupped one of her huge breasts.

Squeezing the mound of flesh in her hand, she purred, "I can satisfy you. Get rid of the," her gaze ripped down then up Rebeka with a sneer, "*puta,* she cannot take the rough ride you will give."

Rebeka didn't know too much about other languages, but she watched television, she knew when she was being called a whore. "Hey," she retorted to Patrisia.

A mild smirk on his harsh face, Kajic held a hand up to Rebeka. "*Na, níshka.*" His voice more of a growl, he frowned at the other woman.

"Patrisia," an undertone of pissed off steel threaded his deep voice. "You know better than to come to my room uninvited." His eyes dropped to the hand on his chest, he said coldly, "Get the fuck out."

Rebeka's eyes rounded at the coarse way he spoke to the woman. Patrisia appeared to be in her mid-twenties.

Her big lips pursed, Patrisia looked like she'd been slapped. Whining, "*Zăf,*" she dropped her hand from her breast but kept the other splayed on his powerful chest.

"You call that bitch 'sweet honey?' She is nothing but a *puta* for the block. I am not a prisoner like her. Please, send her away, you know you want this," she moved both hands to mold under her bosom, and smiled hugely up at him.

Kajic's eyes tapered at her. His dark voice low and deathly silky, he said, "You question my words? You make me repeat myself?"

Her face on the squarish side whitened. Patrisia stepped back, lowered her head. Shooting a nasty look to Rebeka, she stalked to the door and left.

Kajic didn't watch her leave, he said to Rebeka, "Let us go, *níshka.*" He reached out, strung his long fingers around her slim arm and walked her out.

As they started across the grounds, yanking at her arm, Rebeka said, "Get your hands off of me, I can walk to wherever we're going. I obviously can't run very far with all your...*soldiers* around."

He didn't respond, and he didn't let go of her.

They went a few yards and one of his captains standing in front of the main big building waved at him.

As soon Kajic acknowledged him, Rebeka snatched her arm from his grasp and kept walking, keeping an arm's length of space between them.

He looked down at the top of her blonde curls, the side of his mouth lifted with a cold smirk.

He guided her to the women's barracks stopping at the door.

Kajic nodded to the soldier standing guard then said to Rebeka, "Woman, I can see it in your eyes, the fear, the fight, you have it in your mind to run." He bent to bring their faces level.

Dark eyes blank, he watched her tiny pointed chin tremble, her eyes lowered because he spoke the truth. Kajic tucked a thick finger under her jaw and raised it, forcing her to look at him and see the deadly threat in his gaze.

His voice as harsh and darkly chilled as his eyes, he said, "You run, beautiful female, and loss of a lot of money or not, you will be punished. It will not be nice. I will have strips of your skin slashed from your body. Try a second time and you will not live to see the block. Am I clear?"

Angry blue fire blazed at him from her eyes, but his terrible words overrode the anger. She pressed her lips together to keep from retching in horror.

Black brows lancing down, he pinched her chin hard enough she gasped.

His accent thick through his cold voice, he told her, "Does not matter you are woman or not, there are full sanctions. You understand what I am saying?"

She regarded at him in silence.

His growl grated in irritation, "When I ask you a question, girl, you answer me. This is not a pain-free camp, there is blood spilled everywhere, my hands are drenched in it. Now, answer me, do you understand what I said?"

Blinking back the tears, Rebeka nodded.

His fingers tightened on her tiny chin, he demanded, "Out loud." Fingers pinching like steel clamps he ground out, "I will not say it again."

The tears made their getaway rolling down the apple cheeks that turned white as snow. Through quivering lips she whispered, "I understand."

He tilted her chin up so her neck was arched, and bored his fierce eyes into hers, piercing her with the truth of her dire situation.

"There is no escape little girl. You will be taken to an auction house, put on a block, and sold to the highest bidder. You will service men until your beauty, your youth, wears out. Wrap your mind around that until it sinks in. I want no more trouble out of you. Next time we are about to exterminate prisoners; you will keep your mouth shut and stay the fuck out of my business. You got that?"

He pinched her chin harder until her lips parted and her faint whisper came out, "Yes."

He stared with hostile threat for a minute, then released her.

She stepped back, her face now red with fright and tears.

"Go in," he ordered, and looked at the guard.

The soldier opened the door and she slipped inside.

When the guard closed the door, Kajic pivoted on his heel and strode away from the barracks.

Chapter Six

Rebeka didn't sleep a wink the entire night. The despair of her predicament roiled through her head.

The next morning she was woozy with fear and tiredness when the soldiers burst into the barracks sending squeals up and down the line of beds.

She sat up startled with a hand to her chest. She was on a tiny bunk in the middle of a row on one side of the barracks, identical to the row on the other side.

Like her, drowsy women squawked and complained as the soldiers strode up and down the center aisle.

"Get up, all of you." A soldier kicked one of the bunks making the woman in it cry out.

He said, "You will shower," nodding to the communal washroom at the back of the barracks. "Put on dress and line up outside of barracks."

On the end of each bunk was a bundle. No one moved.

The soldier marched to the nearest female, reached down and grabbed a handful of her hair and hauled her out of her bed to her feet.

He slapped her.

She cried out and cowered with her hand to her face.

He spat, "I said shower and dress, do it now, or I start shooting." He aimed his rifle at her head.

The woman's body shook from head to foot, she grabbed the bundle and ran to the washroom.

The other women hurried to follow her.

Satisfied, the soldier pivoted on his heel and exited the barracks, the other soldiers followed him.

Rebeka stood under a weak stream of very cold water and washed her body and hair.

When she'd dried off with a thin towel, she opened her bundle as did all the other shivering women. Inside was a toothbrush, toothpaste, deodorant, shavers and a comb. Along with a dress.

She pulled out the dress. It was identical to what each woman held. Beige with tiny flowers, it had buttons over the bodice, the skirt billowed to the ankles. Inside the bundle were under garments and serviceable ballet shoes.

Rebeka dressed. She brushed her teeth and combed her long wet ringlets, and followed the other women as they trooped out of the barracks.

Outside, the sun was rising, its heat warming the women that were freezing from the cold shower and wet hair. A brief breeze stirred the dust off the dirt, it rifled across the blades of grass and shook the leaves at the tops of trees.

Rebeka got in line with the other women.

The woman on the train who had spoken to her, Jackie, sidled in next to her. "Hey," Jackie gave her a quick grin. "How're you handling things?"

Too frightened to speak, Rebeka just looked at her.

"Yeah," Jackie's smile was friendly and understanding. "I know. You have green written all over you. I'm thinking somehow you were sent here by mistake. We were all talking last night about you when we were hustled into the barracks."

Rebeka's big blue eyes widened in confusion at her new friend, she had no idea what to say.

Jackie nodded. "Yeah. The way you refused to open your blouse or lift your skirt, then, shit girl, you got a death wish or what? Throwing yourself in front of those poor gays like you did?"

Shaking her head in disbelief, Jackie chastised her, "What the hell were you thinking? I don't get why the chief didn't take you down right then and there as punishment for failure to obey the soldier's order. I mean, we all figured it was because of your astonishing looks, but then," she shrugged and gave Rebeka a sly wink.

"He caught you when you fainted then picked you up in his arms and took you to his room. We figured you were, ya know," she nudged Rebeka with her elbow, "fuckin' your way to not being whipped or shot."

She waited, but Rebeka made no response. "I mean, you're worth too much for him to kill or maim, so it would have been either lashes to your back, or...you would be on your back, under him. So," she nudged her again with a smirk. "Is he big all over? The word is he is one rough violent fucker. Well? Tell me!"

Rebeka stared at her in horrid incredulity. "Jackie, no, when I came to," she blinked remembering the girl who had followed them into the cabin and propositioned the chief. "He didn't do anything to me." Then she recalled the red mark on her breast and the way he wolfishly gleamed at it while wiping his mouth.

A blush colored her face, she looked away in embarrassment at the memory. "Nothing happened. When I came to he brought me here. That's all."

Louise Furley

"Oh come on, girl, that lusty fucker? No way he had you alone and didn't fuck you. Please, every guy in the place was gawking at your tits. Hell, your blouse was wide open showing your wares. And honey," she nudged her again with her elbow, "you've got some goddamned outstanding wares, all right. No wonder he didn't kill you outright."

"Jackie, please-"

A male voice shouted, "All right, bitches," one of the soldiers strode in front of the women. Several more stood around them guarding.

The soldier told them, "You will come to breakfast, then further orders will follow. Move," he shoved one of the women. She stumbled clumsily then started walking, the others trod right behind her.

They were led across the grass to a long, large building. Inside, they could see the male prisoners were already there. Every eye rose to watch the females arrive.

The soldiers led them to tables to the far side of the room, away from the males.

The women sat down on folding wooden chairs at long, wooden tables. Pots of steaming porridge set in the middle of the tables, bowls and spoons were in front of each place with a glass of water.

"Tomorrow," the soldier announced, "you bitches will be cooking and cleaning. You ain't here for free. We will dictate in a moment your assigned duties. Now, fucking eat." He spun and strode to the side of the room to stand guard.

No one moved at first. Then one of the women reached for a bowl and picked up the ladle inside it. She scooped out some porridge and poured it out into her bowl and passed the large pot to the woman next to her.

Across the room, the men did the same.

After a few minutes, the room grew loud with conversation. Both men and women shot inquisitive glances across the room at each other.

Rebeka stared down at the lump of porridge in her bowl. Her stomach churned, she had no desire to eat. But, she planned to escape and she would need fuel to do that.

Reluctantly, she scooped up a spoonful of thick goo and forced herself to swallow it. Gagging as the thick gunk stuck in her throat, she reached for her water.

"It's funny," Jackie said, moving the heavy mush around in her mouth, "the head guy, Kajic, and the captains all have that unusual heavy accent, but most of the soldiers don't. And weirder, Kajic's accent is the same, yet thicker than the captains. His English is much more stunted."

Sliding another spoonful of goop in her mouth, Jackie made an mmm sound. Speaking through her porridge, she said, "I don't know, Kajic's screaming hot in a bloodthirsty dangerous, scary, tough kind of way. I bet he's crazy rough in bed."

Swallowing, she sighed, "I don't mind a few bruises, a bit of soreness. I'd take the chance, what about you? You were alone with him."

Sipping her water, Rebeka choked, almost spitting the liquid out. "Me? He's a vile monster. I hope I'm never alone with him, or within arm's reach of him again," a shudder rolled through her body.

Jackie laughed. "Hey honey, you haven't said your name, what is it?"

Without thinking, Rebeka replied, "Rebeka Benani, my friends at school called me Becky."

"Well, then, Becky, I-"

"All right, listen up," the soldier was at the front of the room commanding quiet.

Seeing the door open, Jackie whispered, "Speaking of the devil, and I truly mean devil," she nodded towards the doorway.

Kajic, Captain Ving Lankov, and three other men as big and brawny as the two came in to flank them.

Rebeka's eyes flashed by rote to the powerful men standing by the wall.

The chief was wearing black jeans and a black T that molded to his chest. Every time he moved, the muscles rippled under the cotton, his biceps bulged as they crossed over his chest. Tattoos revealed as his arms shifted. A visible tattoo scrolled up the side of his neck.

To Rebeka he looked very foreign. He would be better suited as an assassin, a hit-man maybe hired by the Mafia.

Her stomach cringed. As the leader of an illegal slave auction house, he might as well be the same as a hired killer. After all, he had ordered the coldblooded murders of the transvestites.

Thank goodness he hadn't carried through with it, she saw the men he had threatened. Not one of them moved or raised their heads from their plates. They appeared to hope if they drew no attention, they would be forgotten.

Rebeka's gaze rose from the neck tattoo to the chief's face. Her breath inhaled sharply, he was staring directly at her. Blanching, she quickly lowered her eyes, but she could feel his gaze burning through the crowded room at her.

"Becky," Jackie whispered. "God, girl, he's staring right at you. He has the hardest, most inscrutable face I've ever seen. He looks angry, but then," she shrugged, "he always does."

"Shh," Rebeka murmured.

"As I call your name, stand up," the soldier at the head of the room said loudly. He proceeded to call out male names.

When ten men were standing, the soldier said, "You are assigned to clean the mess and other main building. Mopping and such."

He nodded to another soldier and told them, "Lieutenant Moss will supervise you. I will read off the rest of the lists, when I'm done, everyone assigned to a soldier will follow that soldier. The rest of you will return to your barracks under guarded lockdown." He continued with a litany of names and their assigned tasks.

Suddenly, Jackie was poking Rebeka in the side. The soldier was repeating a name growing angrier as no one responded. Jackie whispered urgently, "Becky, he said Benani, isn't that your name?"

"Queenie Benani, stand up immediately or face severe punishment," the soldier snarled. His gaze strode over the table of females.

It was so quiet a dropped pin could be heard. Someone moved, accidentally knocking a spoon to the floor. Half the room jumped at the discordant sound.

At the same time, Rebeka climbed to her feet. Her legs shaking so badly she had to clutch the table to keep from collapsing.

All eyes turned from the red-face man who had dropped the spoon to her pale face.

"Ms. Benani," the soldier snapped, "next time you hesitate when your name is called you will receive ten lashes. Join the rest of your group." He motioned to a cluster of women standing by the kitchen door. "You women are assigned to the kitchen."

Jackie murmured as Rebeka hurried to do as she was told, "I thought you said your name was Becky?"

When the soldier finished his lists, he told the remaining people to return to their barracks under guard. The others with assigned tasks followed their supervising soldier.

Rebeka moved with the women in her group.

A beefy soldier with a crew cut and small round eyes directed them to enter the kitchen. "All right, ladies," he said, "you," he pointed to three women, "will do the prep work, cutting and peeling of vegetables and stuff like that. And you," he gestured to several other women, "will do the bulk of the cooking."

He motioned to Rebeka a several more women, "You will do the baking. Bread, and the chief likes desserts. So you will provide those. All of you," his arm swept towards all of the women, "will do the washing up and drying. Ah," he turned as two masculine looking women entered the kitchen.

He introduced them with a brief smile at the pair, "This is Fabrice," nodding to a stout muscular female with spiky dark hair and spiteful black eyes.

To the other he announced, "This is Annamarie."

The woman had a horse face and shaggy brown hair. Her expression was just as unpleasant as Fabrice's.

The soldier said to the group, "They are in charge of you. Guards will be in continuous patrol outside. Anyone not following these women's instructions will be instantly taken away and flogged. Now, get to work."

He snapped his heels, nodded to the two women in charge, and strode off with the other soldiers that had waited with him.

Rebeka spent the rest of the entire day until eight o'clock at night in the kitchen, baking, serving food to the tables out front for lunch, then dinner.

After serving, she and the other women washed and dried the dishes. She was so exhausted she was swaying on her feet. When they were done, the women were ushered back to their barracks.

The next three days went the same. By the end of the week, every bone in Rebeka's body ached.

Fabrice and Annamarie were not nice cooks. They took enjoyment in insulting the women, kicking them when they were annoyed, or swatting at them with anything that was in their hands at the time, be it a frying pan or a rolling pin. They got off on bashing heavy jugs into soft skulls.

The fifth day, between serving dinner and washing the heap of dishes, Rebeka imperceptibly inched towards a side door tucked around a short corner.

She had hours and hours every day to scope out every window, every door in the kitchen.

Through one window she could see the guards patrolling outside. She counted the minutes between each guard that passed by the window.

There was four minutes give or take between the times each guard moved by the window. She tried to judge if that was enough time for her to get out and get hidden in the dense forest.

It was dark outside, and inside the kitchen the lights weren't that bright. A ton of dishes were still piled waiting to be washed, food was still being put away in containers.

Clattering dishes, glasses clinking, women chattering as they worked surrounded Rebeka as she crept towards the side door. She planned when she would make her run for it.

If she left before preparing and serving dinner her absence might be noticed.

Every night she could feel the chief's fierce glare burning a hole into her while she maneuvered through the tables placing food on them.

Fingers of chilling nerves rippled up her spine as she felt his gaze on her. She knew he was waiting for her to screw up, cause more trouble so he could have her punished.

Two nights ago, while she dodged grasping hands from leering men, one of the male prisoners smacked her on the butt, then laughing with lewd nickering, grabbed her wrist trying to pull her onto his lap.

As she frantically fought him off, Chief Kajic narrowed his eyes at one of his captains.

The captain got up and trod over, curled his fingers around the man's neck, and bent to whisper something in his ear.

All the color drained from the man's face as he stood up and followed the captain outside.

Every eye wide with fright watched them leave, then flicked to the chief who sat calmly buttering a roll.

Captain Ving Lankov had made it clear the first day that no one was to molest the females on the penalty of death.

Rebeka never saw the man again. It urged her with even more exigency to get away from the deadly camp.

The first few nights, as the women left the kitchen, the guards counted them to ensure each one was present as they were marched back to their barracks. The soldiers grew lax as time went by and the men grew bored of their tedious guard duties.

The past two nights they hadn't bothered to count them. As far as the soldiers were concerned, the women were resigned to their fate. To run into the treacherous forest beyond the camp would be foolish. It would be certain death trying to reach civilization.

Between no food, no water, wild hungry animals, sand bogs waiting to suck down an unaware escapee, and hidden ravines would take their lives before they made it to the mountains. Then, if they got that far, sheer cliffs, illegal smugglers and trappers, and more danger lay concealed, poised to pounce and kill.

After the time that had passed, Rebeka realized that help was not likely coming for her. She was on her own. How crazy was she to believe Queenie would step up and tell their father what had happened to Rebeka.

And by now, Rebeka thought Queenie must have some awareness of why and who had taken her. Rebeka still though, held onto the belief that Queenie would eventually come through and she would be rescued. But she might not last long enough for that to happen.

Besides, Rebeka came to the realization that they were in fact in a foreign country, and the chances of the United States police finding them were zilch. No, help was not coming, she needed to take things into her own hands.

She waited until everyone was absorbed in their tasks. Glancing at the window she saw the guard approaching to pass by. She crept to the door behind the alcove and cast one more quick look to see if anyone noticed her.

When she saw no one was even looking in her direction, she slipped into the doorway. Holding her breath that the door wasn't locked, it hadn't been on previously checks, the soldiers believed the prisoners were fully cowed and would never dare try to flee.

She turned the knob. Letting out the breath with a prayer of thanks, she silently opened the door, and stepped outside.

Carefully closing the door, Rebeka didn't move for a second to see if anyone noticed her, see if anyone else was around.

Satisfied she was alone, it was dark, she saw the back of the guard as he marched around the building.

She had four minutes to get to the woods, and she ran.

Chapter Seven

Chief Jephunneh Kajic sat around a table with his captains in the makeshift office. One black jean-clad leg set casually over a knee, he pulled a lighter out of his pocket.

Captain Ving Lankov, the sandy-haired ox with gigantic hands deftly poured everyone three fingers of Russian bourbon then sat down in a cushioned chair at the round table.

Tipping his own drink to his rugged lips, in their own language, Ving said, "So everything is on time, and we're only down one male." His blue eyes slid to the chief, a smirk nicked the side of his mouth. "Thanks to your baby-eyed bitch, Jeph." He stretched out the f sound to his name.

The chief lit his cigar, puffed silently while perusing his friend through a cloud of blue smoke.

Sitting beside Ving, Captain Hubbard Shaw tapped the end of his cigar on an ashtray then stuffed it back in his mouth. He kept his dark blond hair shaved close on the sides and longer on top, and the chinstrap beard trimmed close.

Rolling a shoulder as big as goal post, he grunted, "Ving, the fucker knew the rules, hands off the female prisoners unless invited."

"Ha," Nero Madarov snorted, "how do you know the whore didn't invite him?"

Jeph's eyes narrowed behind the smoke, but he said nothing.

Hub Shaw laughed. "You got a load of her face, she was upset when that guy grabbed her, besides embarrassed the girl was jelly-boned scared."

"She's a whore, it's all practiced, it's called acting," Nero responded refilling his empty glass.

"Humph," Hub shrugged. "I read the report on her. Something doesn't add up. She's supposed to be King Martin's bitch that stole a couple kilos of smack from him. She's supposed to be 27 years old, red-haired not blonde, and green, not blue eyes. Plus, she's described as a seasoned whore.

"That girl out there is as fresh-faced as a teenager, the youth and innocence just pours out of those baby blues. Her legs," he lifted his glass to take a hefty drink, and shook his head. "You all saw her legs that first day. Really slender, but shapely, thin like a young girl's."

"Fuck cares?" Ving growled, sucking on his cigar. "We'll get top dollar for her hot little ass whether there's something up or not. She's not the law, not a setup. No way anyone could have known we would take her except King Martin, and he provided the address. She was snatched right out of her home. There's shit called hair dye and contacts you know. So, we sell her and move on."

As big and built as the others at the table, Tegan Turuk kept his brown hair neatly trimmed and short. Normally the quietest of the team, he ran a finger and a thumb down either side of his Fu Manchu moustache lining his handsome lips as he spoke, "I agree with Shaw."

Hub's brows arched at his friend.

Tegan said, "Yeah. She's almost painfully shy, avoids others, every time someone calls her name in roll call, Queenie, they have to say it several times before she blinks as if remembering something then says she's present. Sometimes she looks up and around like she's looking for someone else to answer. We've all been around con-artists our entire lives, that bitch is mighty terrified and as green as a new sprout, she ain't acting."

"Again," Ving grunted, "who the fuck cares as long as we get our bucks out of her?"

The door suddenly flung open, a soldier charged in shouting, "Zăffe!"

The five men looked over at the interruption.

"Soldier," Kajic warned with his brows low.

Catching his breath and gazing around in trepidation at each man at the table, the soldier took a deep breath before speaking. He was a veteran soldier but each man sitting there scared the beejesus out of him. "One of the women, sir, is missing. Gone, we-"

"Which one?" But Jeph Kajic already had a feeling as he got to his feet and stubbed his cigar in the ashtray.

"The pretty one, sir, the young blonde that tried to save the trannies, she-"

Starting for the door, Jeph spouted, "Where? When?"

The others rose and traipsed after him.

"Uh, uh, we think she got out of the kitchen. We, uh," he swallowed hard, "don't know when exactly. I guess Lieutenant Rikers miscounted when the women were returned to the barracks."

Gulping down his terror at having to tell the men this information, he rushed on, "She wasn't noticed missing until Lieutenant Missovitch was telling them lights out and he noticed the empty bunk. At first he wasn't that suspicious, but he waited and then told one of the women to go into the washroom and retrieve the girl. The woman came out and, uh, said she wasn't in there. We went back and checked the kitchen, but, hell, Zăf, sir, she just disappeared."

Jeph shoved past him muttering, "She did not just vanish you dumb fuck," he quickly strode across the lawn.

The soldier hurried after him. The captains stalked beside Kajic.

It was dark except for the gas lamps that were scattered around the camp, their boots shuffled through the cool dewy grass.

Jeph said to the unfortunate soldier, "She ran. Get a search party up. I want every inch of those woods searched until that broad is found." He snarled, "You do not find her and you will all lose your heads. You got that?"

The soldier scurried next to the chief, his lips quivering with fear, "Sir, yes sir, got it," and he tore off towards the guards' bunkhouse to get assistance.

"I'll get the dogs," Ving said in step with Jeph.

"Only to see the direction she went in," Jeph said to him, his long legs in a half-jog. "I do not want the canines tearing her up. She is young and small, she will not have gotten far. It has only been twenty minutes since the females were herded from the kitchen." He headed towards the kitchen.

Walking around the building, he searched for evidence of the girl. When he reached the back of the building, he saw small footprints in the dirt outside of a side door that was seldom used.

In the twilight darkness he followed the prints to the edge of the woods.

By the time he got there, flashlight beams swung everywhere, along the grass, up the tree trunks as a group of soldiers ran around the perimeter, several dashed into the shrouded forest.

Barking dogs growled and yipped as guards brought them to the edge of the murky woods.

Jeph spoke to the men handling the dogs, "Use the dogs only to locate her. Do not let them loose. I do not want her damaged, she's worth a lot of cake. *Bine*, go," he ordered. He followed the men with the dogs as they merged into the darkness beyond the first line of trees.

The soldiers scoured the woods, one of them with a dog on a leash met Jeph. "Chief, apparently the girl had scrambled up some boulders and it confused the dogs. They can't track her as well, and they couldn't get up the boulders."

Tersely, Jeph ordered, "Keep looking. Tis dark, she does not know the area, she will not be far."

The longer they were out there, flashlights streaming through the pitch black, the cool damp making it feel even chillier, the more aggravated and steamed the chief grew.

The girl was prized property, guaranteed to bring in the big bucks, they needed to find her before an animal chomped off a leg or she toppled off a cliff in the dark.

His phone buzzed, he pulled it out and read the text. One of the soldiers found her. He'd brought her to Jeph's room.

"*Bine*, everyone," Jeph called out, "we have her. End it, everyone go back." He sent a text to Ving instructing him to call off the search.

Jeph jogged carefully through the thicket of tall trees keeping his flashlight on the trail in front of him. His heavy boots thumping on the hard-packed dirt, his temper boiled, he was so pissed he could feel his ears turning red. He went straight to his room and threw the door open.

As he stood in the threshold he saw the soldier slap the girl. Her head flung to the side with the blow, she slammed into a wall then buckled to her knees, her wrists were tied behind her back.

It was difficult to tell where the scraping branches of shrubs and bruising from climbing the boulders ended, and the soldier's punishing fists began. Her legs, arms, face were scratched and bruised.

The soldier clenched his fist and raised it to swing at the girl.

"Lieutenant!" Jeph shouted. "You know better than to mark up my property."

The rustic cabin was small containing only a bed, a table, a few chairs, a dresser, desk and a tiny bathroom.

His round face huffing and red, the soldier glared at the girl cowering against the wall, but there was lust in his eyes.

"Sir, we need to use her as an example as to what happens if they try to run." He bent and wound his fingers across the front of her throat. "She needs training for the block, Zǎf, I can do that work for you. I'll show her what happens if she tries to run."

He crouched in front of her, tightening his hard fingers around her slim neck, grinning with lascivious glee at her terrified eyes bulging as she gasped for air.

Her hands bound, down on her knees, she was helpless to fight him. The long curls a messy yellow cloud around her face and bowed shoulders.

"Yeah, I'll ready her, sir. I'll flog her for ya, whip the shit out of her luscious hide, then fuck her raw, fist her deep, and yeah," his fat tongue rolled sloppily around his thick lips. "I wanna fucking stick my dick hard up her hot little ass. I bet her hole is the tightest-"

Jeph strode over to them, grasped the back of the soldier's collar and jerked him to his feet.

"Sir?" the soldier said in confusion, then quailed at the seething blackness in the chief's enraged eyes.

Then the red hazing rage in Jeph's eyes faded to total blankness, there was nothing but emptiness in the dark discs. The soldier knew what that meant. Gulping, he begged, "But- but, please don't, I found her, I wanted to help you-"

Jeph put a large hand across his jaw, and the other behind his head, and jerked hard with a twist.

The snap of his thick neck silenced the soldier's pleas.

Jeph dragged the body to the door and shoved it out then closed the door, and locked it. He took out his phone and mumbled non-English words into it then slipped it into his pocket, and turned to the girl.

She had managed to struggle to her feet and now hovered against the wall shivering with mindless fright. The blonde locks tangled around her head and down her front, her teeth chattered uncontrollably in her distress.

The big blues rolled up to him wide and terror-stricken. Seeing the chief so ruthlessly, callously kill the big soldier with his bare hands tinged her complexion green, her throat wobbled as if she was fighting to keep from puking up her terrible fear.

"You, woman," Jeph dropped his huge hard hands to curl the long fingers on his lean hips. He pierced her with furious eyes that glittered hideously under low lids. "Did I not tell you what would happen if you ran?" He jerked his head, flinging the hair off his hard-ridged brow.

Her hands bound behind her, Rebeka pressed her back against the wall to steady herself. Her eyes dashed around the room seeking an escape, but the huge enraged beast blocked her from moving in any direction. Blinking rapidly, she stared at the floor, she didn't answer him.

He stepped closer to her, guttural gravel in his angry, low voice, he demanded, "Queenie, answer me." Jeph studied her when he said her name. She didn't move.

"Queenie," he said, and watched her blink, twice hard, then raised her head to him. "Answer me," impatience trundled in his growl, he was at the end of his rope.

His body, a V of hard hewn rock, his chest cordoned with muscles heaved in his annoyance, the big shoulders twitched. He dug his fingers into his hips as if struggling to hold himself back from hitting her.

Her lips pinched closed, she kept her eyes on the floor, the long hair partially veiled her ashen face.

"*Motherfucker*," he cursed words in a different language and stomped to her, gripped her upper arms and shook her.

"I told you not to give me any more trouble. I warned you not to run, and I fucking told you that you will look at me and answer me when I speak to you."

He shook her so hard her teeth crunched together, the saffron curls flipped back and forth. Still, she kept her mouth shut.

"Goddamned obstinate bitch, I will open your fucking mouth," his accent so thick in his fury he was barely intelligible.

He put his hands on her delicate shoulders and shoved her to her knees. Sticking his hand in her hair he wrapped it around his fist and jerked her head back forcing her to look up at him.

"You tell me right now that you will not attempt to flee again, tell me right now, swear to me or I will beat the fuck out of you."

Jeph couldn't have her running about trying to escape, she would set a bad example for the others. If she did it again he would be forced to kill her, and lose a great deal of money for her ass.

He shook her head when she didn't respond. Just stared up at him with frightened wide eyes blurred with burgeoning tears.

"I have had it with you, you will open your mouth." He tugged the belt open to his holster around his hips with one hand and tossed the holster and gun on a table.

Then he ripped his belt open, unbuttoned his jeans and unzipped his fly. Spreading the fly open, he palmed his erection over the briefs, he had grown hard the second he'd stepped into his room and saw her there.

Gripping her hair, he rubbed her face against the hard-on straining against his briefs. Railing foreign curses down at her he shouted, "Tell me you will not try to escape again, woman, or I will pry your lips apart with my cock. You bite me and I will rip out every one of your teeth."

Pulling her back from his open fly, he reached in his black briefs and fisted his cock, about to pull it out and shove it down her throat. Huge tears spilled out, rolling over her red cheeks and splatted on the floor.

A frustrated groan ground from his throat, Jeph released her hair. He was damned if he'd let her tears dissuade him from punishing her. He commanded the entire camp, she would obey him, answer him.

If he allowed her to dis him, the other prisoners and soldiers would too. Furious at her stubbornness, he clutched her shoulders and pushed her, bending her forward so the side of her face was on the floor. Still on her knees, her wrists tied behind her, her small round butt was up in the air. Her body shook.

"The minute you start talking, woman, I will stop." He lifted her skirt to expose the white cotton panties all the women wore. As plain and unsexy as they were, Jeph's hard-on only thickened and throbbed at the sight of her ass.

Her little round bottom was begging him to hit it, spank her, fuck her from behind, stab into her so hard until she-fuck!

Lowering to one knee, he grabbed her legs and shoved them apart, scraping her knees on the plastic modular floor.

A panicked gasp burst from her, then Jeph slapped her sex with his big palm. She shrieked and struggled to get away.

Jeph had his hand splayed on her slender back holding her in place. He pushed a knee against one of her legs to keep them apart, and wacked her again on her sex.

She screamed with a jump, trying to wriggle from his hold.

"Woman," he breathed hard, the front of his hair flopping over his eyes. He snarled, "I do not know how to punish a whore, but I will slam you on your back, remove those panties, and strike your bare cunt until it bleeds. Now," he raked a shaking hand through his thick hair, pushing it back, and held his breath. "You have one second to-"

Gasping, "I- I, please," she was in a terribly awkward position. The side of her face rubbed on the floor, on her knees with her ass in the air, legs spread, skirt up, hands tied behind her back.

She cried helplessly. "Please, I- I-" sobs raced up her throat, constricting her breathing, she couldn't speak over the sobs overwhelming her. Her body shook like a leaf in a storm, chest heaving so hard with wracking sobs, she was choking.

Jeph moved his hand from her back, and she fell to her side. Her body curled tightly into the fetal position on the floor as she wept. The blonde hair webbed over her face growing wet with her tears. Her knees were pressed as hard as she could bring them into her chest with her arms bound behind her.

He stared at her in sheer consternation. In all the years he'd done the auction, he'd never had a woman fall apart so drastically at his feet. Or have one try to escape, offer her life for others, or be so goddamned stubborn.

Normally to avoid punishment for a violation, they would have offered to blow him, or offer him to fuck them to get out of a beating. Sure, some begged and cried when he refused. But this, this small female cried her heart out, and it hurt his ears. He had to make it stop.

Pulling his knife out of a pocket, on his knees he leaned over her.

Feeling the heat of his powerful bulk around her, gasping on tears, the girl looked up at him and saw the knife. Thinking he was going to stab her, she frantically tried to wriggle from him, the tears flowed harder. Her chest hitched as screams jumbled inside trying to get out.

He slit through the rope that bound her wrists and put the knife back in his pocket. Her arms immediately moved forward to tuck up against her sobbing body.

How was he to handle this new experience?

When she was hiccupping back the tears, calming slightly, he grasped her arms and pulled her to sit up and lean against the wall.

As he helped her lean back, she favored her left arm with a wince and a low whimper.

Jeph hadn't checked her for serious injuries because there hadn't been time. Now, he saw a huge bruise that went from her shoulder to her elbow.

He gripped her wrist to hold her arm out so he could see it, she cried out in pain, trying to pull it back to her body like a wounded bird.

He let go of her wrist but threaded his fingers around her forearm holding it so he could see the bruise. "What the fuck?" he grimaced. "Did you fall outside in the woods?"

Sniffing, her head lowered, she shook it.

"The soldier?" he asked, his tone angry. "The one I- the one who brought you here, did he do that?"

She shook her head again, when she tugged on her arm he released her.

"Please," her voice heavy with tears and despair, she turned her head and looked up at him. "Please, just let me go home. Please, I just want to go home," and her chest rippled with her helpless sobs.

His hard face stiffened. "You know I cannot let you go. You have a blood debt; you cannot get out of it. Now," he asked, mystified, "how? How did you get such a… such an extensive bruise?"

Keeping her eyes down, she didn't answer him.

Exhaling an aggravated breath, he snapped, "Dammit woman, tell me." In impatience he tucked a few fingers under her jaw and raised her head, forcing the blurred blues to connect with his dark angry orbs.

Her breath shuddered out through a throat raw with screaming from the soldier capturing her, dragging her back and knocking her around. Sobs of horror from watching the chief kill the man in front of her constricted her chest, making it hard for her to get the words out.

Her voice hoarse, she said softly, "It was from a...cast iron skillet."

He started. "A what?"

The blues flashed up at him then quickly away. "The...the cooks. They...can be...intolerant. If they think you're moving too slow or too clumsy, or, you try to stop them from striking someone else, they, uh, hurt you."

She pulled her knees up, wrapped her arms around them and hugged them to her chest.

Jeph stared at her first in confusion. "You mean the female cooks in the kitchen?"

At her nod he said, "Which one, Fabrice or Annamarie?"

She tried to shuffle away from him, but he reached out and grabbed her knee. His forearm like a rock, his strong grip held her immobile.

Realizing she wasn't going anywhere, she stopped. His hand slid down to grasp her thigh. They both looked down at his rough hand holding her thigh looking so incongruous on the feminine flowered dress.

"Tell me, which one is beating my fucking prisoners?" His harsh bark made her jump. He squeezed her leg at her closed lips.

"Please, sir," her wobbly voice filled with fear and tears, she pleaded. "Please don't make me tell, it'll only...be worse," she implored him lifting her face to his. Her eyes scrunched in weariness and fright, she bit her bottom lip to still the trembling.

His cold voice sterile of emotion, he insisted, "Answer me." His fingers were tight on her leg, but loose enough to not cause more bruising.

Taking a shaking breath, she let it stream out with a choke, her eyes on his hand on her thigh, she said quietly, "Both."

Black brows jumped, his skin darkened as he understood. The cooks were beating his prisoners.

Cursing in his language, he took out his cell and pushed a button.

When someone answered, he continued in the foreign language, his words clipped and cutting.

He'd brought in female cooks figuring that since they would be spending so much time with the female prisoners he didn't have to worry about one of them dragging a woman into a cooler and raping her or copping feels all day long. Hell, his watchdogs needed watchdogs.

Stuffing the phone in his pocket, he perused the girl. Her eyes had lowered again so he couldn't read her.

"Queenie," he said, and observed her.

At first she didn't react. Then her shoulders stiffened, she raised her eyes to him and murmured, "Yes, sir?"

His lashes flickered over his eyes that narrowed in suspicion at her. "Why do you not answer when someone first addresses you? Tis as if you do not recognize your own name."

At her lowered head he squeezed her leg and growled, "My patience is long gone for your silence, your resistance. Answer me."

"I...uh," her blues flit back and forth as she thought. "I go by my...uh, middle name, Rebeka. I'm not used to hearing, uh, Queenie."

Jeph sat silently for a moment regarding the beautiful female in front of him, her face damp with tears, puffy eyes shiny and reddened. She was lying, he could tell. Maybe not outright lying because she was terrible at it, but there was something up.

His hard breath expelled. The longer he stared at her, he noticed her eyes losing focus and drooping, as were her shoulders.

After working her ass off all day, she'd run hard and frantic into the night, his soldier had manhandled her, as had Jeph himself, even, he snorted, his cooks had hurt her.

The girl was exhausted. She was falling asleep leaning against the wall.

Tired himself, he shuffled to sit beside her with his back against the wall. A few minutes passed, and her head slipped to droop awkwardly to the side. The next thing he knew her head was on his shoulder.

He didn't move, just listened to her breathe. He wasn't done questioning her. "Queenie, uh, Rebeka,…"

She wiggled slightly, turning towards him so her face was on his shoulder and she set her little hand on his chest.

Jeph looked down at it. So dainty on his muscled chest. Her breathing slowed, she was asleep.

"Well, I be goddamned," he muttered, shaking his head. "Bitch falls asleep while I am in the middle of interrogating her."

He watched her chest rising and falling more gently than it was a few minutes ago in her terror. Long yellow lashes curled on her rounded cheeks, the prettiest lips he'd ever seen in his life closed as she went under.

His gaze fell to her bosom. He recalled how she had looked with her blouse ripped open- ah, don't need to go there, he was already semi-hard just sitting beside her. He slipped his arms under her and lifted her as he stood up.

Tromping the few steps to the bed, he placed her on it. Reaching for one of her ankles, he held it and pulled off her shoe, then did the same to the other one.

Then he stepped away to stick a key in the door ensuring it was locked both by the button and now with the key, and stuffed the key in his pocket. She wasn't leaving without his allowing it.

Jeph retrieved his holster and stuck it under the mattress then settled on the bed in his clothes to lie beside her.

He didn't draw the blanket up, just lay on his side and watched her sleep until he was pulled under too.

Chapter Eight

Rebeka was swimming, no, floating, it was if soft clouds cushioned her, but there was pressure on her mouth. It was, unfamiliar, yet, not unpleasant.

She felt a hand slip under her head, long fingers netting it, lifting it as lips, strong lips pushed her lips apart, strong yet soft they pressed against hers. She was being kissed. She was dreaming, and she was being kissed in her dream.

A smile curved her mouth as her dream lover licked her lips before thrusting inside to pursue her tongue. A passionate sigh left her lungs as her body softened to allow the fantasy lover to plunder her mouth, take every part of it captive.

Although it was a dream, she could smell the male, his utterly masculine scent sifted into her senses. His body, heavy on her was thick and hard, a muscular leg lay possessively over hers.

As his kiss intensified, she could hear his deep breaths growing faster, louder. Rebeka raised her hands in her sleep to comb her fingers into his thick hair that tickled the sides of her face. When he moved his mouth over hers, his whiskers rough against her skin only added to the heat building between her legs.

His hand still cradled the back of her head, another moved to nestle inside, under the collar of her dress. She felt a tingling of growing discomfort mixed with something else that was igniting heat at her core.

Something tugged at the buttons on her dress, then she felt a cool, rough hand slide over the swell of her warm breast, a husky moan growled against her mouth-

"Oh!" Suddenly realizing she wasn't dreaming, Rebeka tried to push the hand away and sit up.

Her confused gaze bounced all around the room, discombobulated, where was she? What was happening? She was lying on a bed; a strange bed in a strange room, and that man, that chief, that kidnapping murderer was next to her.

He had one hard thigh shoved between her legs holding her down, his hand clutched her head, and his other big hand was inside her bodice groping greedily at her breast. And he was trying to recapture her mouth. Looking like a marauding pirate, a lock of black hair hung over half-mast eyes that glinted at her with hungry desire.

"Stop!" Pushing at his huge, immovable shoulder, she squirmed to get out from under him. The sheets rustled under her, her skirt was pushed up and tangled around one of her legs.

Looming large and strong over Rebeka, with his heavy lids the chief looked as drowsy as she felt, but his fingers still curled over the swell of her breast, and he pressed the erection in his black jeans that was thick and huge, and hard as iron against her thigh.

His broad shoulders blocked out the rest of the room. Rubbing his erection on her thigh, he pushed her top open wider and gripped her breast, trying to squeeze his long fingers around the bare swell mounding over her bra, as his mouth hunted hers.

Rebeka turned her head and shoved at him. She rolled out from under him to the far side of the bed.

Climbing up on her knees, she yelled again, "Stop!" with her hands up as if she could really stop him.

Still lying on his back, ebony strands of hair fell over the heavy lids that lifted, displaying dark eyes sparkling with lust. They fell to her breasts half exposed in the top he'd unbuttoned and pushed off her shoulder.

His voice deeper and rougher with arousal and sleep, "*Na*, Queenie, Rebeka, whatever you call yourself, come here," he snaked his hand out to grab her wrist and pull her back to him.

Snatching her hand out of his reach, she wriggled further from the huge frightening marauder, to the edge of the bed. "No! What do you think you're doing? How did I get here?"

Jeph groaned, shoved his hair back with both hands and stacked pillows under his head to look up at her.

He told her, "You were brought here by my now deceased soldier after you tried to escape last night. You fell asleep leaning against the wall, I put you in my bed. It was easier than carrying you back across the grounds to the barracks."

His eyes devouring her rounded flesh, Rebeka yanked her top closed and quickly buttoned it. "Why didn't you just wake me? I could have walked back-"

"Come," he growled, a hint of anger shaded his deep voice as his eyes followed her trembling fingers closing the buttons. Holding his hand out to her, her said, "We were enjoying ourselves, it was just a kiss. Come back and finish what we started."

He had an unusual accent, it added to the danger he secreted, and it was so thick she had to work to understand his words. "Huh," she snorted. "What you started, not me."

His rough voice low, seductive, reaching his hand to her, he purred, "Come, *nishka*, you were intoxicatingly receptive to my mouth. Let me show you what else I can do to you with my mouth, my tongue, my hands. I want to fuck you, I have to fuck you, at least let me kiss you some more."

His other hand splayed over the huge erection in his black jeans. He squeezed it watching the look of horror race over her face.

"But- but, you said yourself," she uttered frantically, her eyes on the thick rod swelling even more at his stroking it. "You said there's to be no- no fraternizing between the females and the males, the soldiers included. Your rules, you said."

"Ah," his face flushed as he palmed his erection, his lids hooded over eyes boldly lusting over her. "You broke the rules when you ran. I broke the rules last night when I did not flog you for running. Besides, fucking is acceptable if both parties consent. After seeking my permission of course. And I give my permission for us to fuck."

She inched closed to the edge of the bed. "I do not consent, and, you, but you did, punish me, you…hit me," her cheeks flamed at the remembrance of what he'd done to her. Hit her in such an intimate…place.

His hand smacking her privates, touching her. She could feel that place burn and dampen as she thought about it, and his dark eyes lowered to her sex, as he recalled it too.

The vein at his temple beat, lifting the scar as it throbbed, hard salivating swallows bumped his Adam's apple.

The corner of his mouth quirked. "I am a lot bigger than you, and a hell of a lot stronger, if I had struck you with my full strength you would not be sitting right now. A couple of mild slaps on your sex certainly did not hurt you, and it was not the requisite ten lashes from a whip, sweetheart."

His gaze glued to between her legs, the onyx pupils flared. He sniffed like an animal, as if he could smell her arousal. "Actually, most women would have enjoyed those smacks on their cunts, while engaged in fucking."

A beet had nothing on the color that rode her face at his vulgar words. The image of what he described popped into her mind. She gasped, "I'm not- you can't-"

"Come here, small girl, I will show you what real fucking is," he lurched reaching for her, but with a squeal, Rebeka rolled off the bed to her feet and ran to the door.

She gripped the handle and tried to turn it, but it wouldn't turn. Frantically, she jerked at it, pulling, pushing, it would not budge.

From behind her, his voice laconic, rich and heavy with desire, he said, "Tis locked, little bird, you cannot fly away unless I let you. Besides, where are you going without your shoes? The ground is covered with sharp gravel. You were stupid enough to try to escape into the fucking perilous woods in the dark of night, are you so dumb as to traipse over sharp stones in your bare feet too?"

She swung around with her hands and back against the door. Clearing her throat to steady her voice, Rebeka said firmly, "Let me out. You don't own me, you can't keep me here."

His brows lifted in amusement. "Ah, but I do own you, and, as you can see," he looked around the room, "I can keep you here." The glittering eyes darkened further as his gaze traveled up Rebeka's body, until it reached her angry face.

"You," she said taking a step towards him then retreated back to the door. "You kidnap people, me, innocent people…"

Black brows drawing down in annoyance, he said coldly, "Not one of you is innocent, babygirl, remember that. Every one of you is here because you committed a criminal act."

Her arms crossed over her chest, she stated, "Well, you are wrong. Anyway, how could you just snatch people off the streets to sell them for- for slavery? What kind of person does that? How would you like it if someone enslaved you and forced you to work yourself to death?" Her lips thinned at the scary look hardening on his face.

He reached over his shoulder, gripped his shirt and yanked it over his head then dropped it on the bed. He pointed at the tattoo that wrapped around his wrist and another that crawled up the side of his neck.

He held up his arm, it had numbers and something in a foreign language written on it. "This is a slave tattoo, it denotes my slave number. These words," his hand swept over the tat on his neck, "say, 'Property of Centurión Složeným z 6.' "

"I…don't understand." Rebeka's stomach quailed at the ugly tattoos that twined him, seemed to strangle him. Her gaze flickered all over his massive chest, besides the tattoos, slabs of hard carved muscles covered his chest, over those was a matting of dark hair.

His body was an alarming work of color, words, pictures and potent strength. His powerful build terrified her and at the same time mesmerized her with his strapping physique.

He shrugged a huge shoulder. "I was sold by my family when I was a child for farmland labor. When I was 11, I escaped and thinking perhaps my family missed me, was maybe concerned for me, I found my way home."

His short laugh was ugly; the dark eyes glinted cruelly then emptied. "I was wrong. My father was using our home to distribute drugs. He got caught, but," Jeph's gaze shifted from Rebeka to his desk, he stared blankly at it.

"He, uh," again, Jeph's laugh wasn't pretty. "Somehow, when he was caught by the law, he convinced the authorities that the big bad dealer was me. I was fucking twelve years old by then. The worst of it was, he paid them off to believe him. They needed to show their superiors that they caught the guilty party, so they easily agreed."

Rebeka gaped at him, her horrified expression a mix of pity, and disbelief.

His reptilian gaze returned to her, cold, cruel. He said, "I was sent to prison. These are the tats they carve on an inmate in my country," he gestured to more ugly tattoos that crossed over his shoulders and down his biceps, a few littered his forearms.

"At fifteen, they took me from prison and sold me back to slavery, more labeling," he snorted with a casual shrug and turned so she could see the marks on his back. His wide back was a map of scars from bullets, knives, whippings, and more tattoos.

"So- so you should understand the horror of slavery, of captivity, torture, pity-"

An offensive snort with a remorseless sneer, voice devoid of emotion or compassion, he said, "I do. I told you so would understand what kind of man I am. How lethal I am, and why you cannot play games with me."

His lip hitched with a grunt at her wide-eyed dismay.

"I have never experienced kindness or nurturing or mercy so I am incapable of feeling those elements. Other than my captains whom I have known since our days in the prison, I have zero feelings for anyone. Nothing. I have *na* empathy, and I do not want your pity."

Nonetheless, Rebeka did feel pity for the wretched life he'd had. "You didn't deserve what happened to you, but then neither do the people here deserve such abhorrent treatment." She asked with curiosity, "How did you escape? I mean, you are no longer a slave, right?"

"Ah," he smiled, "my sneaky captive, you want to learn from me? Use my skills to attempt escape again?"

Surprised that he thought she was underhanded like that, she blinked at him, shook her head. "No. I am curious only. How does a man go from a slave in chains to being the one holding the chains?"

He regarded her silently. Her big blue eyes so innocent, radiating sincerity and naiveté. He wasn't even born that innocent.

Shrugging, he said with a sly smirk, "Does not matter, you are too delicate, you could never do what I did. At nineteen, after escaping, I killed my owner, and also the guy that was head of the organization, and I took over. Although I am not the owner of the auctions, I just run them. It takes an iron fist, little girl."

His eyes flit with mild amusement over the horrified shock on her white face.

The man's story confounded her. She said, "How could you turn so vile? You went from an innocent child to a beast that sells, harms, kills innocent people."

"Hell will do that to a soul, babygirl. There are no guiltless people here. Believe me, everyone here, R e b e k a," he sarcastically stretched her name, "is guilty of some corrupted act. There are pedophiles, thieves, murderers, prostitutes, traffickers, corrupt politicians, dirty cops, everyone is guilty of something."

"But, what about the innocent people you capture?" While she spoke she moved around the room, but he stayed with her like an intimidating shadow. Then, he sat down on the edge of the bed.

"Rebeka," his eyes narrowed across the room at her, "as I said, none of you are innocent."

"How can you be so sure?"

Glaring at her he stood up. "Because I do not make mistakes." When she backed away and held her hands up again, he frowned and moved towards her.

Before she could get away from him, he grasped her wrists holding her palms up. "What is this? From scrambling over the rocks?" He indicated the welting blisters on her hands.

She tried to tug her hands free, but he held them.

"Rebeka," he said softly, "unless you want a repeat of last night, a much harder, longer, repeat of punishment, minus the barrier of clothing, answer me. I will not ask again."

Feeling her cheeks heat at his threat of slapping her privates again, she said, "It's nothing. Just the kitchen work."

A brow arched then both drew down in a frown. "Kitchen work? How can that be? We have you work all day to keep you occupied and out of trouble," his lip twitched, "not that it worked with you, but," he sobered. "How can the work do this?" When she tugged again he let her go.

Inching away from him, she kept her hands behind her back. "It's 16 hours of labor, sir. Peeling, chopping, washing dishes, the floor, the counters, the walls, they keep us constantly moving. The only time we are allowed to stand still is to eat or when we're washing the dishes."

She casually moved away from him, back to the door. He watched her, the lids levering down again like a croc.

Crossing his huge arms over his chest he said, "I can change that for you. You stay with me, in my bed, until the auction, and you will not have to return to the kitchens."

Her eyes popped then shifted from him to his bed and back to him. "Are- are you saying if I- if we have…sex, that I would not have to work in the kitchens?"

He nodded, the long hair swinging. "*Da. Na* work, anywhere, except," he looked pointedly at his bed.

Flustered, her face reddening, she stammered, "But- but you have all those women, those groupies, why would you want homely me?"

His brows shot up. "Are you joking?" His hot gaze licked from her head, down her breasts, over her sex, even down her legs, and back up. "Homely is not the word I would use to describe you. Regardless," he shook his head. "Well?"

Blinking at him, the conversation beyond her, she parroted him, "Well, what?"

The full, harsh mouth pulled in. "Come on, Rebeka, my accent is thick, but, shit, how much clearer can I be? You fuck with me every night, sometimes I am going to want you days too," he thought about that.

Looking her over, at her face and down her body again, his pupils pulsed with heat, he nodded.

"*Da*, the days too when I am here at the camp. You will stay protected in my room, and you will share meals with me in the mess. When not in here, you will be with me. So, you fuck me willingly, and you will not have to do any labor, and you will be under my protection. *Na* one will harm you."

He waited but she just stared wide-eyed at him. "Rebeka," he growled in warning.

"What..." What an awkward conversation for such a green girl as her. "What about your...other women? Would I wait in the bathroom, or watch, or leave when you-"

He scowled. "Do not be ridiculous. I would have *na* other women. I would not need them with..." his pupils flared as he looked all over her body again, "you."

Her lashes flapped up and down as her face grew redder.

Then, she turned to face the door, put her hand on the handle and said quietly, "Take me to the kitchen."

Chapter Nine

*A*ghast that she would deny him, he just stood with his mouth hanging open. Snapping it shut, he stomped over to her, gripped her shoulder and spun her to face him.

In incredulity, he blustered, "Are you saying that you would rather work your fingers literally to the bone rather than spread your legs for me?"

Rebeka leveled her gaze steadily up at him. "Yes."

Jeph's lids flapped up and down, he didn't believe her. "I do not understand, why?"

She moved from his grasp. "You want to…have sex with me, for, however long, until the auction. Then you want to put me up on a block, where strange immoral men will stare at me, examine me, touch me, and then buy me so they can put me in a brothel where I will be raped day and night until I die from abuse or disease, drugs, or in attempts to escape. You are condemning me to a death sentence after torture."

He didn't move, his mouth tightened, her words rolled around in his head. Then he said, "What is the big deal? You are already a whore. Many women actually choose the life."

A sarcastic snort left her, "Huh. First of all I am not a whore. Secondly, those women that choose the life are also free to come and go, go to school, out to dinner, shop, go home. See their families, have children. I will be imprisoned.

"Jackie tells me they keep the women chained to a bed until they get them hooked on drugs. Then they are too incapable of fleeing, or they don't care, they just want their drugs. And, for you to think this is all okay, to reap money from others' torment? No thank you. I do not want your filthy blood-soaked hands on my body."

The bleakness of her description of her future, and her withering words about him, hung between them.

He was well aware of the life of a sex slave. Still, he was stunned that she would not eagerly spread her legs for him like any other woman would, even without the tradeoff of not having to do work.

Women were just as afraid of him, as were the toughest of men, but that didn't stop them from willingly fucking with him.

He's been told that the excitement of screwing the brutal chief of the dreaded auctions, the lethality and violence that swarmed around the stalwart man, the strength pulsing in his bulging biceps, his every ruthless, aggressive acts were helluva aphrodisiacs.

Power and cruelty were carved permanently into his hard face, and inked, shot, knifed all over his body. If half the women at the camp had seen him kill the soldier earlier they would have been creaming their pants to be with him.

However, this girl had turned white then green and had struggled to get away from him. She seemed horrified, repulsed, and terrified of his act.

Yet, her harsh words prickled somewhat. He said, "Regardless of the...outcome of the auction. I am offering you a soft way to live until that happens. Shit, girl, in my bed instead of working yourself to death. Why would you not-"

"Take me to the kitchen."

She's got to be kidding, Jeph stared at her. Her hand on the door, she turned and faced it, clearly, not joking.

He huffed a hard exhale of irritation then went to the bed and pulled his gun and holster out from under the mattress, and buckled it over his waist.

Reaching over the bed he picked up his shirt and shrugged it on. Turning slightly towards him at the sounds he made, Rebeka shrunk against the door, her eyes on the gun hanging low on his lean hip. Apparently she thought he was going to shoot her.

"Put your shoes on," he said nodding at them by the bed where he'd taken them off her. They were about a foot from where he stood.

She stared at her shoes, then at him, but didn't move. She wasn't going near him. He sighed and strode to the tiny bathroom.

While he was throwing water on his face, she put her shoes on and was back by the door by the time he came out.

Stunned that she had rejected him, he could not fucking believe it. Unlocking and opening the door, Jeph said gruffly, "You can change your mind, any time. You understand?"

When she didn't respond, he said, "Just tell a soldier you want to see me, I will come and get you."

Nothing. She stared mutely at the floor.

Annoyed with himself that he was *still* asking her to be his concubine when she'd turned him down, her silence infuriated him beyond belief. When had he turned into a whiny pussy?

She scurried past him and out the door.

He went to grab her arm to stop her, "Rebeka, you-"

Moving out of his reach she said quietly, "I am not going to change my mind." She walked quickly from the cabin.

Letting his arm drop in frustration, he closed the door and strode quickly to walk beside her.

Irritating him even more than declining to sleep with him, he noticed she strode quickly to the kitchen, as if eager to get away from him. He was not used to females running from him.

Even though they were afraid of him, he'd been told by the hesitant ones that he wasn't ugly, just brutal looking.

Keeping in step next to her, he fumed at her rebuff. Then the thought came that maybe she preferred another man there, one of the soldiers, the prisoners, maybe one of his captains.

His body burned with fury, well, too bad. He'd be damned if he would give his consent for her to fuck with another man.

Just the thought of the beautiful young blonde lying under another male, the man's mouth sucking on her plush lips, hands fondling her plump tits while he plunged between her willowy legs made Jeph's balls crimp, and his gut tighten so hard it hurt. Fuck, he had to try again.

She was almost to the mess hall, he said, "Rebeka, wait a-"

"Zăffe!" Patrisia clipped across the gravel and dirt in high wedges hurrying towards him. Out of breath, the blowsy brunette cried, "Chief Jeph," she slid her arm around his and clung tightly when he went to disengage her grasp.

He continued moving, to keep up with Rebeka's shorter but brisker stride, but Patrisia pulled at him, trying to hold him back.

"Jephy," she cooed, tugging at his big arm, "you look angry. Take me to your room, I will wipe that fierce look off your face."

"Patrisia, leave me a-" he watched as Rebeka flung open the door to the mess.

"Rebeka!" he shouted.

She paused, turned slightly back to him. At that moment, Patrisia was worming her hand down inside the front of his fly, her lewd grin smug at Rebeka.

Rebeka's face curdled in disgust at them, and she disappeared into the building.

"Motherfucker, Patrisia," Jeph cursed in exasperation grasping at her hand diving down his jeans.

"Chief," she wriggled her fingers over the tip of his cock. "I can take care of you, make you forget your lily-white infant." Squeezing the top of his shaft, she stood on tiptoe and stuck her tongue in his ear.

Even as he swatted her away she said to him, "I know you don't normally fuck the pussy here, that you get your rocks off in the city, but," she squeezed his cock, "I'm here right now, you look ready to explode. Let me take the pressure off, ease that pent-up raging testosterone."

Patrisia was one of those women, that if she'd seen him kill the soldier it would have made her horny and she would have clapped with sadistic glee and then tried to jump Kajic's bones.

Jeph stood, still staring at the kitchen in disbelief that the little cunt had rejected him. Her look of disgust pissed him off. Fuck her.

He hadn't invited Patrisia to fondle him out in the open like that. He didn't like it when she tried to the day he'd arrived either. But, damn, if his groin didn't snarl at Rebeka's turning her back on him. Bitch.

"*Yah, bine*, Patrisia," he growled, "come and take care
of me. And, Patrisia," he snarled darkly, "do not fucking call
me Jephy."

He jerked her hand out of his pants and stalked back to
his room so fast she had to run to keep up with him.

A few days later, Jeph met with his captains in a module.
The men were sprawled around the table, a few had beers,
the others hard liquor.

His arms crossed, Jeph stood at the plastic window
staring blankly out it.

At the table, Hubbard Shaw said, "They haven't called
you yet, J?"

Jeph didn't answer him.

"Jeph, bro, the liaison with the bidders hasn't contacted
you yet when they're arriving?"

The men looked at Jeph waiting for his response.

When he didn't comment, Hub joked, "Earth to Jeph,
come in, Jeph." The others laughed.

Slowly Jeph turned around, his expression mulish.
"Fuck you, Hub," he growled at the dark blond. Stuffing his
hands in his pockets he paced the room.

Pretending affront, Hub quipped, "Ooo, big bossman
angry at lowly captain." The other guys laughed again.

Ignoring him, Jeph strode over and set his hands on the
back of an empty chair at the table, his arms rigid, he
hunched his shoulders.

Hub said with a grin, "Tell 'em why you put guards in
the kitchens now, and why you have the women only
working two meals a day instead of three."

"Shut up, asshole," Jeph muttered at him.

"What the hell is eating your ass, Jeph?" Nero asked,
calloused fingers wrapped around his bottle.

"It's his girlfriend," Hub said with a snicker.

Jeph swung on him. "Fuck off, Hub, shut the fuck up."

Nero asked, "Which broad? The brunette with the big jugs?"

"*Na*, not that groupie slut," shaking his head, Hub brought the bottle to his handsome lips and swigged. Wiping his mouth, he ran the back of his hand across the chinstrap beard, set the bottle on the table and rounded his broad shoulders.

Curling his hands around the bottle, he smirked at Jeph who scowled back. Jeph had told him about Rebeka's turning him down. So Hub told the rest of them while Jeph stared blackly at him while he babbled.

"OMG," Nero pretended shock, his hands up, shoulders bunched. "A woman turned down the *Akbar*, the *Great* Zăffe Jephunneh Kajic. And a fucking prisoner for shit's sake, can you motherfuckers believe it?"

All snickering and pretending shock, the men laughed at him.

"Fuck all of you," Jeph cursed them.

Nero asked, "What about the rules, J? No screwing the prisoners? You've never gone that route before, even the ones that begged you, so why now?"

Hub choked, then grinned. "Have you seen that girl? A wet dream walking for fuck's sake."

"So, what the hell is the problem?" Nero shook his head with a frown.

Hub glanced at Jeph with a mocking grin. "Because he wants to fuck her bad, and she shut him down, said no to his big ugly mug."

"Hell, bro, who gives a shit what she wants, just fucking take her." Ving tipped his bottle letting the cold beer drizzle down his throat, the lump of his Adam's apple bobbing with each swallow.

"You're telling him to just rape her?" Nero grumbled.

With a shrug, Ving replied, "The kind of life she's led, it's likely she's been raped before, even the whores don't always like the fugly ones pushing on them. And, it's not like she's not gonna get raped the second the fucker who buys her drags her off the stage.

"That young broad is quite an act, with that sweet innocence she exudes mixed with her seeming unawareness of how damned sexy she is, he'll probably fuck her all the way to his brothel or massage parlor, strip club, or wherever he takes her."

As the other men nodded at his word, Ving went on, "The handler, her pimp that guards her will train her. He'll beat any resistance out of the bitch while he rapes her too. So, what's the difference if you have to hold her down while you stick it to her?"

Quiet for a moment, the men contemplated Ving's words.

Then Hub frowned at the blond ox, "Since when did you become a big proponent of rape?"

Snorting, with a smug smirk, Ving said, "I've never had to resort to that because the bitches always say yes to me."

Jeph groused, "Why the hell should I have to force pussy when tis thrown at me all day long?"

That brought a round of chuckles at the table.

His smirk mocking, lifting his bottle in salute to his friend, Ving told him, "Because that one is *not* throwing herself at you."

Tegan, sitting quietly in his chair toking on a cigar, took a puff and set the stogie on an ashtray. "Why don't you take it back to Patrisia after she heals from your round with her the other day? Use her hard again to fuck the blonde cunt right out of your brain."

"*Yah*, J, you pronged that bitch something vicious bro, she's still recovering," Hub told him.

Jeph shrugged. "She would not let up. I was boxed up, my balls were so blue I thought they were gonna drop off. I warned the bitch I was not in a good mood and it was gonna be fucking rough," he shrugged again. "She keeps texting me, as soon as she is on her feet she wants to have at again."

"Well," Nero offered, "there you go. Get your nads off with her and forget the blonde, screw her."

Hub laughed, "That's the point, Nero, he wants to screw the blonde."

"Fuck all of you." Jeph scowled and stalked out of the building, the men's laughter ringing in his ears. That was the problem, he didn't want Patrisia. Or any of the other whores at the camp. The entire time he'd been banging Patrisia he was thinking of the little blonde.

When Patrisia was on her knees blowing him, he pictured when he'd forced Rebeka to her knees and rubbed her face against his cock over his briefs, the frightened blues staring up at him through tousled yellow tresses.

He should have forced her right then and there to suck him off, shown her who the hell was boss. He should have thrown her on her pretty back and plowed into her.

Screw those tears, those terrified blues. Screw the bitch telling him no, *yah*, again the problem, that's what he wanted to do, screw her. Recalling being with Patrisia when he really wanted Rebeka made his stomach pitch with disgust. Disgust at himself for not pushing Patrisia away harder when she kept coming at him.

He'd been so mad at Rebeka he'd used Patrisia to work the blonde out of his craw. It was wrong, and he still felt sick about even touching the groupie. It wasn't going to happen again.

He slid his cell out of his pocket to check for a text or email on the status of the ETA for the bidders to arrive for the auction.

Hammering and sawing reverberated over the grounds. The men were almost done building the auction stage. They should probably make a permanent one they can dismantle and move, like the rest of the camp. He'll work on that for the next auction.

Striding over the grounds, he nodded to soldiers he passed. The prisoners were either working or in their barracks under guard.

Since seeing the blisters on Rebeka's hands he had slightly lightened everyone's workload. He couldn't put damaged stock up on the stage and expect to get good dollars for them. Of course, most of the prisoners there weren't as delicate or as fragile as Rebeka.

He remembered her small soft hands covered with angry blisters and a quiver wriggled in his stomach. She hadn't complained or sought treatment for them. He'd had to tell Fabrice himself to see to her medical care.

He thought about how Rebeka's dainty hand pressed on his chest as she slept on his shoulder. That memory led to the recollection of the make-out session in his bed.

Jeph had awakened with her lush body next to him. Half asleep himself, he watched her sleeping, so beautiful, sweetly feminine, sexy as shit. He couldn't help kissing her. And as soon as his lips hit hers he knew he was gone.

She was so fucking receptive. Those tiny plush lips pressing against his, they parted as he thrust his tongue through them. Her body was ripe as hell and he could tell she'd been aroused by her little moans and squirming.

That weird innocence he kept detecting flowered around her with her every move, whimper, even the tentative way her fingers curled in his hair. She just didn't feel, seem, experienced like she should.

God, her odd, apparent greenness in the way her body moved sensuously against his was so fucking hot, his rod hardened at the palpable memory.

Except, she thought she was dreaming. She wasn't even aware it was him caressing her, kissing her. That stuck in his gut. He had an unbearable hunger for her, and she had fucking zip interest in him. He was nothing but the big bad slave trader, not good enough for her ladyship.

She'd been imagining some other man kissing her. Fuck her. His strides hard and angry, he made his way to check on the progress of the stage.

After that he would go review the paperwork on the human merchandise. See how much each prisoner could be expected to bring. What their value was.

Yeah, he would check on the stage, and then the paperwork, but before he knew it, his boots were tromping into the mess hall.

A few stragglers were there from lunch, some of the women were cleaning the tables.

Jeph nodded at the guard posted near the door, the guard acknowledged him. He didn't look Jeph in the eye, most of the soldiers knew Jeph's fierce reputation and feared pissing him off.

Jeph paused when he neared the soldier. "How is it going, Soldier? Any troubles?"

Shaking his head, the guard kept his eyes straight ahead. "No, sir. The cooks took your warning seriously, they have not abused the prisoners in any way."

Jeph nodded then headed for the kitchen.

Outside the entrance, he paused. What the hell was wrong with him, chasing after some skirt? Some prisoner skirt no less. He stood still thinking of the past few days.

He'd seen Rebeka each time he came to eat. Part of her duties was to serve the food. Normally he would have taken some of his meals in his room or in the office with his team. But, he hated to admit it to himself, he wanted to see her.

He wanted to be there to see if any of the men, soldiers or prisoners put any moves on her. And they did. Nonstop. But none she seemed to have any more interest in than she did him.

Yesterday, after seeing one more smack her on her shapely ass as she tried to serve, Jeph saw red. He'd gotten up, slammed his fist into the man's face, then beat him into the ground until he breathed no more.

Everyone in the room watched as if it was a show. When the slaughter stopped, they all went back to what they were doing as if nothing had happened.

Jeph had grabbed a freaked-out, shocked and horrified Rebeka's arm and dragged her into the kitchen where he gave the cooks orders she was not to do any more serving.

Told Fabrice she was to stay in the kitchen at all times, he didn't want a brawl over her on his hands. And he told himself that was why he was here now, to ensure there were no disturbances at the camp. Right. That was the only reason.

He stepped over the threshold and into the kitchen.

It was a big area, most everything ran on gas fuel and enormous batteries, but they also had generators. Every woman looked over at him when he entered, except of course, Rebeka.

She was bent over a bowl peeling potatoes.

Jeph trod over to where Fabrice and Annamarie were directing the women in their tasks.

As he approached, concern etched on both the females' faces. Concern and fear. He'd threatened them with their own demise if he heard of any hitting, kicking, any kind of abuse to the prisoners.

He so very seldom came to the kitchen that they assumed something was wrong. He was terrifying, dressed in all black. Long hair combed back off his harsh face, eyes dark and cold and forbidding, his huge presence loomed pure threat.

"Chief?" Fabrice's voice cracked with nerves.

Both cooks were wringing their hands as he neared. Fabrice said nervously, "Is everything all right? You may inspect the women, no cuts, no bruises, we-"

"*Yah*, fine. I came to check that you are preparing for tomorrow."

Nodding vigorously, Annamarie never said a word.

Her voice tight with anxiety, Fabrice said, "Of course. The sort of party we always have prior to the auction to help relax everyone, before the buyers arrive."

She was speaking to Jeph, but his eyes weren't on her. Jeph hated that they flicked relentlessly over to that fucking blonde bitch, no matter how he tried to stop, it was as if he were made of steel and she was a magnet. Perhaps cliché, but true nonetheless.

"Yes, sir, we are preparing food and the men will move the tables to allow visiting between the people. They have music prepared for dancing." Fabrice rambled on until Jeph gave her his attention.

As they talked, the boldest prisoners slowly, unnoticeably worked their way across the kitchen to crowd around Jeph.

Jackie was one of them. She brazenly put her hand on his shoulder. Fluffing a side of her fraying blonde hair curling on her shoulder, she said, "Sir, it's nice to see you for a change, we never see much of you except at meals."

She bent her head and whispered, "And I would love to see more of you," her eyes flit down his body clearly indicating she wanted to see more of him, as in naked.

Jeph stiffened at her nerve in touching him. He normally wouldn't have tolerated it, but, behind Jackie he could see Rebeka watching them.

He smiled at Jackie, making sure he spoke loud enough for the blonde bitch to hear, he said, "Sure honey, maybe that can be arranged."

His gaze skewed to Rebeka. Her lips pursed out, but he couldn't tell her thoughts on that beautiful heart-shaped face of hers.

Unfortunately, the older woman hanging on him was making his skin crawl. She wasn't the blonde he wanted under him. He was extremely tall, but Jackie maneuvered so his view of Rebeka was blocked.

He was both pissed and glad. Great. Besides twisting his balls in a bunch, the little girl was bolloxing his brain too.

"*Yah*, so, good to hear, Fabrice that you have everything in hand." His abrupt turn knocked Jackie's hand off his shoulder, he started for the door.

When he reached it, he slowed and glanced over his shoulder, and scowled. Rebeka was not looking at him, her full attention was on the fucking potato in her hand.

He needed to go grab some pussy and get her out of his head, out of his dick's head. Except, he found no other female appealing.

As it was, he thought again how disgusted he was with himself for agreeing to fuck Patrisia. She grossed the shit out of him, but he'd been so goddamned horny for Rebeka and furious at her for spurning his offer he couldn't think straight.

He stalked out the door and made his way across the grass to check on the stage like he had originally planned to do.

The stage that very soon Rebeka would be displayed on wearing practically nothing or even fully naked while the basest of men bid on her.

Some would have the right to touch her.

Chapter Ten

The party was no big shindig or anything, just a night to allow everyone to blow off steam.

Rebeka had begged the guard to let her stay in the barracks, but he told her everyone was to be in the mess so the guards could enjoy a bit of fun and relaxation too.

The room grew louder as people became more boisterous, drinking, talking over the music, laughing, pairing up.

Tomorrow, Jeph would be getting hit with a shitload of requests to allow hookups. That was nothing new, there was always a steady stream of them as the prisoners eyed each other, and the soldiers, and the camp groupies.

Rebeka was blissfully unaware of the dozens of requests from soldiers and other prisoners to be allowed to be intimate with her had landed on Jeph's desk. And they weren't all from men. None of course had her acquiescence on them. They would not have been approved anyway.

Rebeka wanted nothing to do with the party or the people. She was at the dreadful camp in the first place under mistaken identity, and, it didn't appear Queenie was doing anything to rescue her.

Of course now that Rebeka became totally aware of what she'd gotten herself into, there was no way Queenie would ever tell anyone that it was she who ripped off King Martin.

No, Queenie's self-preservation would never let her take Rebeka's place. Queenie didn't do cops, and she wasn't going to endanger her freedom either by telling their father what was a foot.

Rebeka knew she was in deep, grave trouble, and there didn't seem any way out.

At this point no one would believe her if she told them the truth, and they probably wouldn't care anyway as long as they got someone's pound of flesh.

It was horribly likely that she was going to spend the rest of her life chained to a bed while being raped, beaten, and plied with drugs. Her only hope was to escape.

Since she wasn't chained here, her best chance to escape was before the buyers came. But, because of her last attempt, she was watched like a hawk while in the kitchen working, and the barracks were heavily guarded at night.

She kept herself plastered against a wall behind a troop of women to keep the hound dogs off her. The men were relentless in their pursuit of the standoffish blonde beauty.

At least that's what they said to her. It was so strange that they told her she was beautiful. It made no sense because it had been so ingrained in Rebeka from a young age how plain she was. Her stepmother and Queenie always made comments about her looks.

"Not quite ugly," Queenie would frown as she regarded Rebeka's reflection in the mirror. "But you'll never be cream of the crop like me. Pity. I'm lucky *my* mother was beautiful, right?"

Glancing around, Rebeka saw that the beast, the chief, wasn't there. If she was going to go, now would be her best opportunity because whenever the chief was around, she could feel his eyes burning a hole in her.

Women swarmed him, but he was always staring at her. Whenever she looked at him, he would instantly put his arm around the nearest woman and act interested in her.

To Rebeka's young eyes, putting his hands on the other women told her Kajic was deliberately showing her he was no longer interested in having sex with her. He was mocking her, throwing her denying him in her face.

The odd thing though, Rebeka pondered, was that so far Kajic had not put another woman in his cabin like he had offered her. The other women talk, and there was much complaining that the big chief had not taken a woman to his bed. It appeared he did them somewhere else.

He must really regret his offer to Rebeka because now it seems he was just playing the field. Getting his rocks off with a myriad of women, not just putting one egg in his bed basket.

However, often one of the captains would take her aside and ask if she'd changed her mind about spending the rest of her time at the camp in the chief's room, of course she said no.

It made no sense that they asked because he was obviously no longer interested in her. Which was fine with Rebeka.

Unfortunately, that didn't stop the wild and crazy dreams she was having of her and the chief in his bed, kissing, his hands all over her body, him rolling on top of her-

"Hey, Becky," Jackie's friendly voice slurred to the side of her.

Rebeka turned to greet her only friend in the place. For once they were allowed to wear the clothes they came in instead of the floor-length gowns.

Jackie wore her short-shorts and tight blouse. A man was practically slung over her, his lips sucking on her neck. She giggled and sipped at her drink.

"Hi Jackie," Rebeka greeted her but kept her eyes averted. It was embarrassing, the man was trying to feel Jackie up, and Jackie just giggled and batted at his hands.

Her eyes blood red, Jackie said, "No handsome guy got your attention, hon? There is quite a selection here."

Shaking her head, Rebeka smiled and answered, "No." She was wearing the flowery dress the women wore on a daily basis.

"Huh," Jackie slurred and giggled, pushing at the man's hand that was creeping up her blouse. "The way the head honcho is always staring at you I thought you two might hook up?"

"Uh, no. No way." Rebeka's chest rose with a deep sigh at the reminder again of his offer of sex instead of work.

Jackie told her, "You might as well pick someone else anyway, 'cause I heard tonight him and a few of his friends hit the truck to go into town. He's not coming to the party. He and his buds are probably planning on getting laid in the city."

Rebeka felt a confliction of relief and...she didn't know what the other feeling was. He was probably screwing every woman in the city.

Biting back the queasy feeling it gave her, this was her opportunity to get away. "Oh, that's good. Anyway, I'll see you around, I need to go to the restroom. Nice to meet you, uh-" she broke off at speaking to the man wrapped around Jackie.

He was blatantly grinding his erection into Jackie's butt while his hands were now all the way up inside her shirt.

Jackie's drunken giggles in her ear, Rebeka started moving surreptitiously towards the bathrooms. They were more like port-o-potties that the male prisoners got to clean, but they did the job.

If anyone saw her headed that way they would assume she was just going to the bathroom. It took a long time to get through the rowdy crowd. People bumped into her, men still hit on her, she kept going.

Passing a dark corner, she saw several people making out. One couple was literally screwing up against the wall!

She was in a den of iniquity, how on earth did she get here? It's undoubtedly a good thing she'll never see Queenie again because she'd want to kill her for getting her in this dire mess.

Hurrying now, she moved closer to the bathrooms, there was a side door she might be able to slip out unnoticed.

When she reached the door, the bathrooms added more tiny alcoves of privacy, and every space on all sides and even along the wall, there were people tucked away hooking up.

Rebeka wondered if they had all gotten permission from Mr. High and Mighty. Probably, since no one was objecting and the soldiers weren't interfering. She didn't care.

There was a couple starting to hunker down in front of the door. This was her chance; no one would see her slide out. She hurried over and slipped behind them almost to the door.

Suddenly, someone shoved her into the door, and out it.

With a squeak, Rebeka went flying out the door and tumbled to the ground. A soldier leapt out after her and threw himself down on her.

Too surprised to scream, Rebeka tried to get up but the soldier pushed her back down.

"Hey pretty baby, finally, I got you alone, damn I've been waiting for this!" He wrestled her, grabbing at her wrists, twisting them, trying to hold her down and push her dress up at the same time.

"Let go of me!" she shrieked punching at him. Rebeka recognized him as one of the men who relentlessly pinched her bottom and tried to grope her until the chief had ordered her to stay in kitchen all the time.

"Fuck no, babe, I caught you, you're mine now. Come on, gimmie that pretty pussy," he shoved at her dress while unzipping his pants.

With a scream and a furious shove, Rebeka managed to roll out from under him. When he reached for her she kneed him in the balls, climbed to her feet, with his curses bellowing behind her, she ran.

She only made it a few yards and he caught her. Hurling obscenities at her, he slammed her up against a building.

"You little whore, who the fuck do you think you are? You're gonna give it to me or I'll beat the shit out of you and take it anyway," he slapped her and brutally slammed her back at the wall when she tried to run again.

He pushed her hard against the wall, roughly shoving her along it as he moved her around to the back where they would be less apt to be seen.

He didn't care that he was hurting her, banging her against the metal wall. When he got her to the rear of the building, he shoved her to the ground and jumped on top of her again.

While he struggled to get his pants open and her dress up, Rebeka screamed, he clamped a hand over her mouth.

Her arms flailing out in both directions, she felt all over the grass for something, anything to hit him with, a rock, a stick, anything.

The man crawled between her legs and gripped her panties- and Rebeka's hand landed on a rock. She grabbed it up and swung it as hard as she could at his head.

A big clunk, and he stopped moving, a dazed look passed over his face, his eyes closed, and he slumped to the ground.

Rebeka wriggled out from under him. Panting, she peeked quickly to see if he was going to come after her again, but he was out cold. "Good," she uttered breathlessly and climbed quickly to her feet.

Huffing and panting, she started to run across the grounds to the woods, when, suddenly, two soldiers loomed in front of her. She surprised them as much as they surprised her. She came to a screeching halt.

"Miss!" one of the soldiers exclaimed. "What are you doing out here? Everyone is to be at the party!" He appeared worried that something was wrong with her. Her hair was a mess, dress torn, she had a cut on the side of her face, and she was obviously distraught.

"I- I-" she didn't know what to say. Surely they wouldn't believe her about the soldier attacking her, he was probably awake and gone by now.

"Yes, I wasn't feeling well, I didn't want to get others…sick…too," she gulped for breath, trying to still her frantically beating heart. "I was going to the barracks to- to lie down."

The second solider eyed her with suspicion, but the first soldier stepped back so as not to catch whatever she had. "Oh," he said. "We will escort you to the barracks, come."

She had no choice.

The soldiers flanking her, marched her to the barracks.

When they got there, the second soldier said, "I am on patrol tonight, I will stay guard until the regular ones are done at the party and return. You," he frowned at Rebeka, "go inside and do not attempt to leave."

Her hand on her chest, afraid her voice would be no more than a croak, Rebeka nodded and went inside the barracks.

She hurried to the bathroom to clean up.

Chapter Eleven

$\mathcal{J}$eph had business to conduct in the nearby city of Hólq, which was still over a four-hour drive through partial savannah type terrain and periodic groves of forest.

The roads were mostly dirt. When they reached the outskirts of the city, the roads became a blend of gravel and tar.

After completing his business, Jeph and his team hit a local bar.

Hólq was a city but it was a tiny, rural place inhabited mostly by farmers, cowboys, and drug smugglers.

The bar was just as rustic as the city. Grungy white paint peeled from the one-story saloon. A grocer was on one side of it and another bar on the other side, which indicated the type of town it was.

They made their way inside the pub, dim lighting and sawdust greeted them. Men hunched over mugs at the bar, only a few of the scummy tables had people hunkered at them.

A couple of tough looking women hung around a group of seedy men at a jukebox that played 80's music. All heads turned when the five men trod into the bar, hesitating inside they searched for seats.

103

Glancing back over their shoulders, the male occupants viewed Jeph and his captains with distrust and antagonism, the women lit up with interest.

Nero and Hub went to the bar to get them drinks, the rest found a table and sat down.

They got their beer pretty quickly, thirsty as hell from the long dusty drive and the seemingly endless meeting; the men guzzled their drinks and retrieved more.

"I don't fucking believe they didn't have those RV's ready for when the buyers arrive," Nero said shaking his head in disgust. "I mean," he burped, "they know the longer it takes to get this auction up and running the more costly it is, feeding those prisoners and the soldiers, paying them for extra days, it's bullshit."

Draining his mug he went to get up and get another when Jeph said, "Take it slow, Nero. We are in a strange town with our back-up 400+ miles away. We do not know these people and we need to keep our wits about us."

"*Yah*, bro," Ving squinted one eye at Nero, "you know better."

"Fuck you," Nero muttered but stayed put.

"We are having just a couple then hitting the hotel, we leave before dawn," Jeph reminded them. He did not like being away from the camp.

"Hey boys," a sultry voice hummed near Jeph's ear, a hand slipped onto his shoulder. A woman stood between Jeph and Hub with a hand on each of their shoulders.

"You guys look like cool guys, ya wanna have some fun?" She leaned into Jeph, whispered in husky invitation, "You wanna dance a few, Mr. Big and Dark and Brooding, or just go to your hotel room and make friends?"

Across the table, Ving's voice cold, he muttered rudely, "We ain't innerested, honey, take off."

Her painted slashes of brows arched with a crooked heavily red, lip-glossed smile, her gaze roved over his massive musculature. "My, you are a big one, you don't need to be jealous sweetie, I can handle all of you. Or, if you'd rather," she winked at him and nodded to the jukebox.

"My girlfriends are bored out of their minds. I'm sure we can all have some fun. Whaddya say?" She bent over Jeph, her hand stroked down his chest, her lips nipped his ear.

The coldness in his voice abrasive, Jeph uttered brusquely, "You heard the man, we are not interested. Get lost." His friends grinning at him only pissed him off further.

Ever since that blonde bitch came to the camp he'd been cranky and short-tempered. He couldn't wait for the goddamned auction to get over so she would go and he could have peace again. Feel fine to fuck whomever, whenever he felt like it.

Right now, even with this whore running her palm down his chest, to his abs, starting for his jeans, his nuts felt like lead. But he knew if a pair of baby blue eyes were there batting at him, his cock would be fighting to get out of his pants. Motherfucker.

He'd never been like this before, it must be because she'd refused him and it was a unique experience for him.

"Aw, come on, hunky. You are the meanest toughest looking man I've seen in forever, with the most hellacious scary accent, but, I bet you are a wicked wild ride."

The woman's hand continued her journey over his fly. She murmured in appreciation, "You aren't even hard and you are big, honey, let me get you-"

Jeph abruptly stood up, so fast the woman toppled backwards almost losing her balance. "I said *na*, we gotta go. Brothers," he jerked his head and all the men got up.

Hub gave the woman a cheeky two-finger salute off his forehead and grinned. "Maybe next time, toots," and they left the bar.

They crashed at the hotel and left the next day before the sun was even thinking about rising.

The five men piled into the Humvee custom built to hold a lot of people, even men as huge as the captains were, and travel easily over the rugged terrain.

It was still morning, a little after 10 when they rolled in. Everyone hopped out and went in different directions.

Jeph paused by the truck, half-turned towards the mess. No, he told himself, not going there. He needed to get over the mindboggling obsessive lust he was feeling for that girl. He spun and strode off to his office.

Letting his held breath grumble out, he entered the office. Instead of going to his desk where the paperwork from past auctions, the current one, and a future one gathered for him to review, he wandered to the window. Outside, the activity at the camp was at a lull.

Soldiers patrolled, the prisoners were all inside working at different tasks except for the men that were still building the stage and the stalls that would be attached behind it.

He saw several groupie whores sneaking into some of the soldiers' barracks. One of them had his permission, the two others didn't. He'd deal with them later.

Forcing himself to not look towards the mess, he turned away from the window. Pulling out the leather chair that came with all the other furniture and modules, he plunked down in it and glared at the paperwork on his desk.

Powering up the laptop, most of the information was on there, but he liked to compare and make sure nothing had been missed, left out.

The stage had to be completed, and modules to be put up for the buyers to hang in while they waited for the auction to begin, and after the bidding, to pay up.

They needed a comfortable space to see to their acquisitions, and to retire to while refreshing and waiting for everything to get set. All funds paid, and transfers of the prisoners completed, they would get back on the RV's that would take them to their private planes.

The remote airport was three days travel north of Hólq. The buyers also needed space for their own guards, security that would keep their new property from fleeing.

Jeph pondered the security. There hadn't been a lot of trouble in the past with the prisoners attempting escape. Jeph had too many men guarding, and most of the captives knew the severe punishment when, not if, they were caught.

Plus, they were situated so far out in the middle of nowhere with no food, water, or shelter, and wild hungry animals roaming the perimeter, they wouldn't likely make it to a town alive.

They were not foolhardy enough, or they were too cowardly to try. Except for one petite delicate blonde. Damn. Standing up for the trannies and attempting to escape, he shook his head with a wry twist of his lips, the girl had chops.

Each prisoner had been carefully investigated and assessed. They couldn't take the chance of abducting an undercover cop, or someone deathly ill, or someone who really was innocent of the charges.

He picked up the report on Rebeka. Queenie that is. The girl hardly resembled the person depicted in the review. It had said she was a street-wise, tough, foul-mouthed, whoring thief.

King Martin wasn't the only one who talked about her when Jeph's recruits went out interviewing when Martin put her up for sale.

Only those living underground were aware of the secret auctions. Where, if they wanted someone punished for wronging them, or getting money for their sale as recompense, they could sell them to Jeph and he would make his money back selling them at the auctions.

The paper in his hand described Queenie Benani as a solidly built, 27 year old woman of approximately 5'8, give or take.

Dragging his fingers though his hair, scraping the tips hard along his scalp, Jeph read the report again. Rebeka, a fine-boned tiny thing, probably not even 5'2, would hardly be described as solidly built. And, she barely looked older than 18.

But, the people that conducted the report were clear that they had the right address, they'd watched her go in and out of the house, and when asked if she was Queenie Benani, the girl had admitted she was. There could be no mistake.

He set the report aside and picked up the stack of paperwork to review.

Less than an hour passed, and he took out his walkie-talkie. They could text easily, but satellites were few and far between out there in the vast, uninhabited land.

They chose that type of location for security reasons. They had scouts planted way out in the perimeter and could see the law coming well in advance and prepare for them, if that happened.

His cell buzzed. He pulled it out, glanced at the text with a puzzled frown, then slid it back into his pocket. Unhooking the walkie-talkie, he set his dial for Tegan's access number.

When he answered with a bit of static, "Tegan," Jeph said. "Tell that soldier I put guard duty on the girl to come to my office." He released the button.

The instrument crackled and Tegan said, "Roger. Out."

That was it. Jeph was feeling like a fucking fool, his friends knew he had it bad for the bitch. Tegan hadn't even asked 'what girl?' Of course, he'd only put a guard on one woman, and he'd never done that before.

He rifled through some more papers while he waited. It seemed to be taking the soldier a long time to get to him. Finally, the door opened and the soldier stepped inside.

The man's voice had a funny wobble to it, there was no strength in his words, "Sir? You asked to see me?" His olive green and red uniform appeared slightly rumpled, his eyes red.

Jeph raised his eyes from the paper in his hand, and narrowed them at the nervous soldier.

The soldier's complexion paled, his gaze was on the floor, not up and at Jeph in respect.

"Medville," Jeph growled, "what the fuck is up with you?"

Medville's eyes hopped up and instantly dropped. "Uh, I, uh, nothing Chief."

Staring at him for a few beats, Jeph shrugged then said, "Give me a report on your activities last night."

Medville blinked. "Sir?"

Jeph's frown deepened, he perused the soldier under low lids. "Last night. You were to guard the girl, Queenie Benani. Tell me how it went. Was there any trouble?"

The soldier's eyes shifted back and forth before looking straight at Jeph, then they dropped. "Uh," he cleared his throat, swallowed hard, then cleared his throat again.

Jeph calmly, slowly, pushed his chair back and got to his feet. He noticed the soldier pale further and almost imperceptibly cringe.

Setting a hip on the edge of his desk, Jeph pushed his hair back off his forehead with one hand. Threading his fingers together, he set them on his thigh and said, "Let me help you. I received a text from one of my captains that the word is that last night, you had to go to see the medic for a head wound."

"Uh," Medville's mouth hung open but he didn't speak.

"I am rapidly losing my patience, soldier. You know what happens when I do. So," Jeph folded his arms over his big chest, his jaw firmed. "Spit it out, or lose the ability to speak forever."

Medville's chin chopped up and down for a second, then he gulped and said, "The, girl, you know, the one you wanted me to watch."

When he didn't continued, Jeph grunted a warning, "Go on."

"Uh, yes, sir. Well," his eyes shifted back and forth again. "You see, the little chit was, I mean she got out. I saw her run out the side door at the back of the hall. Of course I went after her." He dragged the sleeve of his jacket across his sweating brow and peeked at Jeph.

The darker the chief's face grew, the more slit his eyes became.

"Uh, so, somehow she got the drop on me, sir. I guess when I went around the corner of a building she blindsided me. Clocked me with a rock I think. I was knocked out cold. Came to in the infirmary."

Jeph remained silent, but the vein at his temple pulsated like a snare-drum, the scar over it fluttered with the beats. He could feel red rolling up his neck.

"The girl? She is still here?" He was sure he would have been told immediately if she had escaped, but still... "Speak up!" he barked and slid to his feet.

Medville took a hop backwards; his hands went behind him to grab a chair to steady himself. He stammered, "Sh-she is still here, sir. I heard two soldiers caught her and- and took her to the women's barracks."

Mouth clenched, Jeph growled between grit teeth, "How do you know she is still at the camp?"

"Uh, sir, I saw her go into the mess with the group of females this morning." His face was so white there wasn't a drop of blood left in his skin. The hand gripping the chair back shook like an old man with palsy.

Pulling out his cell, Jeph said to Medville, "Go to your station." When he looked up the soldier was gone. Jeph texted Hub to bring the girl to him.

Scrubbing a hand down his face, he leaned back against his desk and tried to picture the slightly built Rebeka, catching the big soldier by surprise and whacking him in his thick skull enough to knock him out cold.

He went to sit at his desk. His stomach had time to crimp as he waited.

Chapter Twelve

*J*eph's head was down when the door opened.

Hub stepped in with puzzlement on his good-looking, fair-skinned face. His dark blond hair was as always neatly shaved on the sides with the top long. The chinstrap beard neatly trimmed. His quizzical dark blue eyes leveled on Jeph. His fingers twined around Rebeka's slim arm, he gently pulled her into the room.

Jeph raised his head, he only gave Hub his attention. "That will be all, Captain," he clipped.

Another quizzical arch to his brow, Hub nodded, released Rebeka, and closed the door on his way out.

Rebeka stood silently in her long flowered gown with buttons up the bodice. He didn't tell her to have a seat, or even glance up at her.

Neither moved.

Finally, Jeph sat back in his chair, his dark eyes blankly focused on her.

He said, "Tell me, Rebeka, what happened last night."

Her head jumped up, eyes blinked in guilt. She had no poker face, that was for sure.

Jeph pushed back and stood up, she moved a hair towards the door.

Coming around the desk, he said, "We are not playing this game, Rebeka. You tell me precisely step-by-step or I swear to God I will strip you and beat you within an inch of your young life. Your broken bones will not be healed until the next bloody auction." His voice deepened, hardened as he spoke and moved slowly to her.

When he was a few feet away, she visibly swallowed.

"O- okay. I was at the party. I needed to go to the restroom. So I went to the back where they were. As I passed by the side door," her fingers clutched the sides of her skirt, "just as I was in front of the door, this man, soldier, suddenly shoved me out it. I tumbled out and fell to the ground. He landed on top of me. We- struggled, I- kicked him, you know where," her cheeks pinked.

His mouth twitched at her pretending to be shy, avoiding saying balls. He nodded for her to keep going.

Breath hitching in nervousness, she went on, "Yes, ahem, then I scrambled up and ran. But he grabbed me, shoved me at the wall and dragged me against it to the other side so no one could see us. He pushed me to the ground, then tried to- to-"

One brow lifted. "To what, Rebeka?" he asked drily.

"Uh, to assault me. He- he tore my dress, and he- I grabbed a rock and hit him in the head. I ran, right into two soldiers who escorted me to the women's barracks."

She took a deep breath, exhaled, peered anxiously up at him. Fingers tugging at each other, she said, "That was it."

"You fucking bitch," Jeph snarled stomping to her. He snatched up her arms and shook her so hard her head snapped back and forth.

"You lying bitch. You tried to escape, you sucker-punched my soldier with a rock or brick or some-shit," he shook her harder. "I have had it with you, I told you what would-"

Rebeka wrenched from his grip, stumbled back and lifted her skirt.

A stunned gasp choked in Jeph's throat.

Rebeka's thighs were bruised, cut, clawing fingerprints gouged into smudges on her fair skin. She didn't move when he came to her and set his hand above her white panties on her belly.

"*Nishka*," the air left his lungs.

It was only then that he really looked at her. There was a cut on the side of her cheek, scratches on her neck and arms. She dropped her skirt, and he reached to her and unbuttoned several buttons on the top of the dress, she didn't move. He laid back the bodice, and his stomach roiled. There were bruises on her neck and chest.

"My God, Rebeka," his mouth fell open, dark eyes wide with disbelief.

Her voice icy, she said, "I have the torn dress, do you wish to see it?"

Ignoring her question, he asked, "Rebeka, did you go to the medic?"

She looked at him like he had two heads.

He moved closer to her, gently grasped her shoulders. His voice coarse yet gentle, he said, "I will take you to the infirmary on my way to see my soldier," he started nudging her towards the door, she dug her heels in.

"No. I don't need to see a doctor, they are only cuts and bruises. Chief," her anger dissipated, "are you, what are you going to say...to uh, the soldier?"

Jeph slid his rough fingers through the hair at the side of her head, smoothing it back with a caress. "It is not talking I am planning. Now, come, I want the medic to look at you."

He was tremendously relieved that she had been honest with him, that she hadn't willfully attacked the soldier while trying to escape, and therefore he would not have to institute whatever discipline he would have had to come up with for her misdeeds.

Jeph knew he would never be able to truly harm her, and that would cause problems with his leadership. In his job, he could never show an iota of weakness. On the other hand, he was burning with rage at his soldier. He wasn't going to have the same issue with handing out Medville's punishment.

She tried to move away from him but he rolled an arm around her to set on her lower back, and cradled the side of her face.

Rebeka said softly, "Mr., um, Chief Kajic, please, he was, I think he was drunk, please don't hurt him."

His ridged brow rose, he moved both hands to hold her shoulders. Thumbs brushing her arms, he said, "There is no excuse in the world, *nishka*, for my soldiers to manhandle, sexually assault, *my* property. They are all well aware of the consequences. And you, especially you. He hurt you, the bastard will die, simple. I will take you to-"

She swung from his grasp. "No, please. Please," she gripped the sleeves at his biceps, pleading, "I beg you, don't put the death of another human being on my conscience. I cannot live with that."

"Ah, my little *nishka*, tis not on your conscience, tis on mine. It will join the…many others already there. Now, come on." He realized he shouldn't have told her the man would be executed for what he did, it desperately upset her.

The fucking man who assaulted her getting punished upset her more than her own threat of discipline did. Not that he would make good on his threats, he could never hurt her.

It was bad enough he'd believed the story the soldier told him over her, and he had cursed and threatened her.

At first she'd looked so distraught, terrified, and betrayed. Then, her expression turned to anger as she lifted her skirt.

Injured, assaulted, and now accused of assault herself yet, so tenderhearted she couldn't bear that someone was harmed. Make that executed.

"No!" she insisted, "it would be because of me. Please, don't do this, don't have yet another murder on your hands. Please, for both of us, he probably has family," her fingers clenched his shirt, she clung to him. "He's someone's son, maybe brother, father, please."

He stroked a hand around her neck, set it on her nape under her hair. His thumb brushing her soft skin, he murmured, "I do not see where such a compassionate heart comes from a-" he was going to say whore, but shut his mouth.

Containing his fury and compelling need to destroy the person who put those ugly bruises on her fair skin while trying to brutalize her, rape her, frighten her to death. The man had been ordered to fucking protect her, not attack her himself.

Jeph's gaze lowered to her lips. Pink and lush, she was chewing her bottom lip in anxiety.

"Rebeka," he said quietly, his hand rising to cup the back of her head, tilt her head to look up at him. His other hand stroked around her to splay against her back.

"Have you thought anymore about, my…offer? To sleep with me. Stay here, with me. You will be under my full protection and not have to do any work."

Eyes heavily hooded, he watched her lips, waiting to see them move when she spoke. So full, heartbreakingly pretty, he wanted to sink his teeth into them.

She stiffened. Only just realizing she was in his arms, her hands clutching his shirtsleeves. He had a burly arm around the back of her, his hand pressed hot against her back, the other hand lifting her head, bringing her mouth closer to his.

Their eyes connected, electricity sparked between them. Rebeka licked her lips, and watched his eyes lower and gleam at her wet her mouth.

Rebeka pulled away, as much as she could, and said, "I thought you withdrew your offer. You seemed to be occupied with others…"

She saw the smirk that lifted a corner of his mouth. He had shown interest in other women only in her presence, hoping she might be jealous and be more malleable to his offer.

The heat in his crocodile eyes burned brilliantly at her. "*Nay*, my little, *nishka*, the only woman I want in my bed is you." His fingers pressed harder on her back, tightening around her head, lowering his head he pulled her to him.

He turned his head slightly to whisper at her lips, "Say yes, my beautiful girl, say yes," his mouth covered hers, encompassing it before she could respond.

He was pretty sure he didn't want to hear what she was going to say. But, as he ground his mouth on hers, and pushed her lips open for his ransacking tongue to explore and capture everything that was Rebeka, she didn't struggle in his arms. She still clutched his sleeves, her hands too small to go around his huge biceps.

Jeph was instantly lost in the voracious kiss. He attacked her mouth, his mind, body, urgent to engulf her with all that he was. Wanting to taste every inch of her, his tongue swept over her teeth, chased her tongue, he sucked on it hard, until she surrendered.

Her whimper against his mouth stirred his blood to boiling. He spread his hand wider on her back to hold her, then reached out with his arm and swept everything off his desk; it all fell to the floor with a clatter.

Ignoring the papers flying, laptop crashing to the plastic floor, his hand under her back, he slid the other under her legs and lifted her to lie on his desk with her knees bent off the edge, and quickly leaned over her to thwart any decision on her part to object and try to get up.

He dropped to his elbows on either side of her and went at her mouth again like he could never get enough of tasting her.

Moans rolled from Jeph's chest as he devoured Rebeka. She kissed him back, but still with that odd inexperienced way, it confused him, but still turned him on like crazy.

He pushed his hips between her legs, bent over her and kept kissing her even though his cock was screaming to be let out and drive into her lush little body.

His chest brushed against those plump tits he loved, he licked her mouth, the side of her face; her panting breaths huffed against his skin.

Jeph kissed down her cheek to her jaw, then to her neck, he licked her fragrant skin and grabbed a handful of her curls. Crushing them in his fist, he brought them to his nose and inhaled deeply of her cock-pulsing scent.

Damn, he had to look at her. Jeph leaned back slightly and gazed down.

Rebeka lay on her back, she had moved her hands to spread open on his chest, her cheeks were vivid with scarlet passion, eyes half-closed, the blue shimmering unfocused with the desire he was building in her. Hell, she was seducible after all.

Her lips were damp and swollen pink with his rugged kisses. He'd shaved, but his shadowed jaw still roughed up the soft skin of her face. He was too strong for her, he knew it, but couldn't stop himself, he had to have her. He'd have to be extra cognizant of his moves, extra careful not to hurt her.

He shouldn't have stopped to look at her. Her eyes were gaining focus, brows drew down, "Sir, Chief, I don't think we-"

"*Na*," he murmured, "do not think." His lips opened on her neck, he licked her flesh then sucked, hard, deliberately hard like the day he'd marked her breast.

He couldn't help it, a caveman kind of thing to do, mark her as his. Stroking his mouth over her neck, her throat, he stopped everywhere to lick and suck. Tiny moans slipped from her full lips, *ah*, he smiled against her skin, she was coming around. A bit more skilled seduction and she would give to him freely.

He shifted her half-open bodice so his mouth could trail down with kisses over her collarbone and down to the swells of her breasts. He caught the top of the blouse pulling it open and down so he could see both breasts, sink his face into their fullness.

A deep satisfying groan rumbled from his chest, a growl of pleasure at her sweet plump flesh mounding over the bra. He wanted like mad to see them bare. But, he needed first to get her so fired up she wouldn't stop him from doing anything and everything to her.

Slowly, he palmed over the swell of a creamy breast giving it the barest squeeze then kept moving down her body as she squirmed under him. He didn't know if it was a good squirm, or she wanted him to stop squirm.

When his hand reached her hip, she said something he couldn't hear through the lusting buzzing in his ears. She brought her legs up, but she was trapped by his body. Jeph pushed one of her thighs back down, then pushed her dress up. The squirming increased.

"Chief," she inhaled fretfully, "please, don't." She shifted her body but was still trapped under his body; she couldn't move her legs because his hips were between them.

"Hush, baby," his purr a rugged sound. He stroked his hard palm over her warm stomach, and to the side of her hip. His long fingers curled around the slenderness of her, his thumb on her pelvis, inching inside the top of her panties. She felt like heaven, but he could feel nervousness railing through her.

Her legs stiffened, she kept trying to shift from his hand. How can she be so shy and unwilling when she was a known whore? A grimace scrunched his face, last thing he wanted to think about now was Rebeka being with other men.

Rebeka tried to turn her body on the desk, but she was wholly trapped by him. "Chief-"

"Honey, call me Jeph, please," the rare word 'please' sounded anomalous in his head. He moved back up and sunk his tongue into her mouth. God, he loved kissing her lips, so soft, juicy, fiery.

Their breathing increased, her bosom rose to brush against his billowing chest, he wanted to feel those naked nipples piercing his bare skin. Feeling her relax again, he slid his hand inside her panties and cupped her sex. She froze then tore her mouth from his.

"No, stop, I want you to stop," she gushed breathy with fright.

He put his hand on her shoulder to keep her still and pushed his face at her trying to seize her mouth. Rasping against her lips, he murmured, "Let me, Rebeka, relax, you are so fucking wet, I can feel you through the material. I am insane with need of you."

His chest tight with the strain of holding back from just taking her. Every bit of her was so damned juicy.

He hissed, "*I have to fucking have you.*" His palm squeezed her mound before he stroked his fingers into her soft folds picking up some of her silk on his fingertips, making everything slick.

"No," she struggled under his body that held her down with his weight, and the hand at her shoulder pressing her onto the desk.

Her legs were spread with his hips between them. When he dipped the tip of one thick finger inside her tiny channel, she cried out, "No! Stop! Please!" The agitation clear in her voice, her struggles, her words plainly telling him no.

Jeph hesitated. She was so wet, heavily aroused. He could see it in the blurry misted blue eyes, the way her tongue circled her lips, her panting breaths, the way she kissed him.

Murmuring, "Rebeka," he stroked her sex, rubbed her tiny nub, and she jumped with a cry, her hips shimmied.

"Please, no," she whispered.

When he didn't stop she hit at his arms with her small fists shouting, "Stop!"

He looked down at her, saw the panic clouding out the passion in her pretty eyes. Her blouse open, swells of her beasts rising in her panic, so sumptuous he wanted to bite them, chew the fuck out of them, the same as her sweet pussy that he was trying to slip his fingers into.

But she was wriggling all over the place now to get away from his hand.

Pressing her down harder with his palm at her shoulder, he entreated with a burning growl, "Rebeka, I can make you feel so good, just give me a chance. Just let me-"

"No, let me up," she tried to shout a demand but her voice came out weak, strained, scared.

"Rebeka-"

"No, let me up."

He dropped his head with a harsh exhale, his long hair swept over her chest. He removed his hand from her panties and pulled the skirt down over her legs.

Reluctantly, and with all the will power he could muster, he leaned back from her.

Her eyes were wide and frightened; she clutched her blouse together with shaking hands.

He didn't fucking get it. She acted like she was a goddamned virgin. Hell, maybe she was so scared because someone had hurt her bad, maybe King Martin.

"Rebeka, listen, *nishka*, I will not hurt you. I will go slow, gentle, I swear," but she was shuffling to the edge of the desk.

"Ah, *bine*, all right," he sighed. Grasping her waist with both hands, he lifted her off the desk and set her on her feet.

She quickly fixed her skirt and buttoned the bodice.

Staring down at the top of her head, Jeph tried to ignore the iron bulge in his pants raging at him to shove her back down on the desk, or bend her over the desk, or- "Rebeka, come on, you were hot. I know I got you turned on, why are you denying us?"

She pushed past him and hurried to the door.

"Where the fuck do you think you are going?" he barked at her back.

Grabbing the handle, Rebeka flung the door open. As she stepped out, she said, "To the barracks," and didn't look back.

Cursing, Jeph strode to the door and watched her practically running across the grass.

"Goddamned women," he muttered in frustration, raking his angry fingers through his hair. "Who the hell can understand the bitches-" he broke off.

Patrisia was scurrying across the grounds heading straight to Rebeka, and she wasn't looking friendly.

Jeph rushed out the door, but Patrisia already reached Rebeka.

"You bitch!" Patrisia shrieked and shoved an unaware Rebeka as hard as she could.

Rebeka went flying with a small squeal landing hard on the ground with an '*oomph*!' Patrisia dropped down next to the stunned blonde, and moved to her knees.

"What are you-" Rebeka only got those words out and Patrisia started wailing on her. She threw punches at her head, her back, when Rebeka raised her arms to protect her head; Patrisia slammed her fist in Rebeka's stomach.

While she pummeled her, Patrisia cursed, screamed, "My man! Jeph is my man! You stay away from him you bitch or I'll fucking kill you!" And she smashed her fist into Rebeka's jaw snapping her head hard to the side.

Jeph reached them- while still moving, he bent, grabbed a fistful of Patrisia's hair and jerked her to her feet.

"You fucking whore, what the hell is the matter with you?" he barked in her face, then gave her a hard shove. He crouched beside Rebeka who was writhing on the ground.

"Baby," he uttered, rolling his arm around her back, "are you all right?"

"Me!" Patrisia screeched. "You want me! Not that scrawny bitch! You're mine, Jeph, mine!"

Jeph helped Rebeka to her feet, keeping his arm wrapped around her to hold her steady. Scowling at Patrisia, he snapped, "I do not want you, Patrisia, I have told you that."

"Oh yeah?" she squawked. "What about the other night? You rode me fucking hard, Jeph, you were so rough, so violent, I was in bed for days recovering." She gleefully observed a green hue staining Rebeka's face at her words.

"Yeah, bitch," Patrisia snarled at Rebeka, "he was with me. For hours. He fucked me good, honey, so, there, he fucking wants me." She jabbed her thumb into her chest. Then smiled broadly up at Jeph. "Right, Jephy?"

Jeph slid his hand under Rebeka's jaw to lift her head to see her wounds. His eyes on Rebeka, he ground furiously through his teeth at Patrisia, "No, I fucking do not want you, you crazy cunt. And it was only minutes, not damned hours you-"

He regretted his words at the quailed expression on Rebeka's face.

Tears streamed down her cheeks to her trembling mouth, she pushed at him to release her. When he did, she turned and headed for the women's barracks.

"Rebeka, wait," Jeph called. But she kept going, not looking back, her hand pressed against her side.

Infuriated, Jeph turned his livid face to Patrisia who saw the danger she was in.

He leaned into her and bellowed an inch from her face, his spittle hit her on the cheek he yelled so hard. "You ever, fucking *ever*, touch her again, I will fucking tear your head off your shoulders and toss it to the lions. You hear me? I should expel your ass right now but I cannot afford to waste the manpower to take you to the city. Now, get the fuck out of my face."

She was cowering. He spun around so fast and left her she almost fell over.

Jeph stalked through the tall grass, his boots stomping the blades, crushing them in his fury. Fucking Rebeka turned him down again, and then than bitch Patrisia goes crazy on her ass.

If he hadn't been there to pull her off, he was pretty sure she would have killed the smaller woman.

Patrisia carried a knife, and Jeph had seen her putting her hand on it while she punched Rebeka. Rebeka apparently couldn't fight, again, at odds with the street-wise thug the report had indicated.

He needed a goddamned drink. His fucking balls ached; his boner was chafing at his briefs making his jeans painfully tight. This was it. He was done with her.

As of now he would no longer be thinking of, or seeing that girl until she was up on that goddamned block. He would enjoy the day Rebeka became someone else's problem. In someone else's bed. Motherfucker.

He headed for the building he and his captains used for meets and camaraderie, drinking, and forgetting.

Chapter Thirteen

A week passed and she was still upset. What the heck had she been thinking?

Rebeka chastised herself as she scrubbed a pan. Letting that…beast, criminal, *killer*, kiss her, touch her so intimately? He marketed in human slaves for heaven's sake!

The tingling and burning that she had felt when he had her on his desk eddied between her legs. Horrors, she cringed, she felt her underwear growing damp at the memory.

The thought that he planned on putting her on the block rushed through her like ice water chilling the sensations that prickled her sex. Why would she allow herself to succumb to a monster like him?

She would never be with a man like him. She had a refined, sedate upraising in the all-girl boarding school. If she ever had the blessing to have a boyfriend he would be a gentleman, calm, gentle, kind.

Not a violent, misogynist, murdering, sex-trading man-whore. And he was so big, terribly strong, mean and tough looking, just walking past the prisoners stuck fear in every one of their hearts.

Except the women who wanted to have sex with him. Rough sex. A shiver rippled through her body. Was it a shiver of fear, or, worse, a frisson of desire?

No, she scrubbed harder, he was too hard. His eyes too empty and cold, pitiless, except, her body quivered again, a rush of dampness pooled between her legs, when he looked at her. Those dark eyes smoldered, then flamed with wicked heat.

But, she reminded herself, he was a pig, the second she ran from him the other day he went right off and had sex with Patrisia. Not that she cared, at all, no she did not.

"Becky?"

Jackie's voice broke Rebeka out of her reverie.

"Uh, yeah, hi Jackie." She handed the clean pot to the older woman to rinse then to the next to dry. Like an assembly line.

"You thinking about the auction? The sawing has stopped. I think they're done with the stage. But that damned relentless hammering and drilling, now they're putting together the modules for the buyers. You, uh, getting nervous?"

Seeing tears blurring Rebeka's soft blue eyes, Jackie set the pan down she was rinsing and turned to her.

Gripping her arms, she rushed to say, "Becky, you shouldn't worry, you're so young and beautiful, it's more likely a rich man will want you for himself rather than put you in a brothel. You might have a wonderful life of wealth and luxury."

Rebeka moved from Jackie and picked up another pot setting it in the dishwater. Her skin ashen, she brushed at the tears with the back of her wet hand.

"You don't really believe that, Jackie. I've spoken to the other women. The best I can hope for is to not have a too terribly violent pimp. Or hope for one who gives me drugs to survive the hell."

"Becky, listen, it might not be-"

Rebeka snorted, "Huh." Her voice sardonic, she sighed resigned, "Look at that, I have already accepted my fate. I'm actually praying for a pimp who gives me drugs so I can deal with the...life. If you want to call it that."

Rebeka absently scrubbed the pot while her stomach roiled in turmoil. Thankfully she hadn't been able to eat because of her anxiety, otherwise she would be puking up her lunch.

The woman next to Jackie, using her damp pinky to push red curly hair out of her eyes, said hopefully, "The captains, they have money, and hell, they are as hot as they come, maybe one of them will buy you?"

"No," Jackie replied, shaking her head. Taking the soapy pot from Rebeka she rinsed it under the running water. The chief had the men dig wells so water could be pumped for drinking and bathing and washing.

Jackie told them, "It is against the rules. The laws of the organization. No one involved in the auction can purchase a prisoner for themselves, upon punishment of death. It's to deter cheating." She handed the pot to the redhead.

Freckles covered most of her exposed skin, the redhead took the pot to dry. Shrugging, she said, "So what about the big man himself? Kajic?" A shudder rolled across her shoulders at the thought of being at the mercy of the ruthless chief.

"Him neither," Jackie replied.

"Yeah, well, I would prefer my chances with the brothels than have that hulking creature fucking me." The redhead shivered again.

"Hey, look," another woman said, pointing out the window.

The sound of rumbling of engines flooded the outside.

The females rushed to look out.

A stream of RV's was rolling into the camp. They parked in a long line semi-circling the camp.

Soldiers scurried about assisting buyers, male and female, emerging from the RV's. People stretched from the long ride, they chatted with each other as the soldiers led them to the modules to start paperwork and discussion for the oncoming event.

Clapping her hands, Annamarie ordered, "All right, ladies. Let's go, your duties for today are done. The guards will take you back to the barracks."

The prisoners gathered into a line. The guards left their posts inside the kitchen and ushered the women back to their quarters.

Rebeka gaped at the people exiting the RV's with enthralling, angry, curiosity.

At first they appeared to be just like normal, everyday people. Then, as the women paraded closer to them, Rebeka saw the cunning, garish dissipation in their shifty eyes, the way they walked, laughs more sneers than true mirth.

The women appeared hard, tough, coarse. The men, worse. Rebeka tried to blend into the line of prisoners so their creepy lascivious gazes couldn't reach her.

The soldiers quickly urged the women into the barracks. Kajic normally wanted the buyers to catch only a glimpse of the women before going up on the block. Give them a taste so the bidding would begin eagerly.

Another entire day went by.

Rebeka's skin crawled, her lungs so tight with nerves, stomach wracked with fear. Inside the barracks, she could hear the buyers wandering about the camp chattering and laughing.

There were constant bawdy raunchy jokes about the female prisoners. How they would get their taste before the woman were put to work on the street or in the brothels.

Some of the older or plainer women would be purchased as field help, others as free housecleaning.

Rebeka had been told again and again by person after person that she would be chained on her back while men after men came in and took her. She slumped on her bunk, head in her hands, and sobbed.

She had prayed and prayed and prayed for rescue, but, clearly, there would be no last minute liberation for her.

Jackie sat down beside her and draped her arm around Rebeka's shoulders. "It'll be okay, hon, it won't be as bad as you think," her words were as weak in her own ears as Rebeka's.

A soldier opened the door and stepped in, a few others were behind him holding sacks.

All of the women stopped what they were doing.

The soldier announced, "All right, ladies. Tomorrow morning the auction will begin. You will prepare yourselves, bathing, grooming, there is attire for each of you." He nodded to the sacks the other men held.

"These sacks have your names on them. When we come for you in the morning, you will be wearing what is in the sacks. Fail to do so, and we will be forced to rip your dresses off your back and dress you ourselves. Any questions?"

It was quiet for a second, then a woman asked, "How is it to go? The auction I mean? Are we all put out there at once?"

Hands clasped behind his back, his boots akimbo, he shook his head. "No. You have a number, you will wait behind the curtain and be brought out one at a time in order. Monsieur Eyáhdi, the auctioneer, will, uh, point out your...assets, and then start the bidding.

"He is quite experienced. Some of you," his eye wandered around at the women, hesitating on several attractive ones, including Rebeka. "Will be," his face reddened, "bound to a scalboard."

At their quizzical looks he explained, "It is a thin vertical beam with a rod across the top like a T. The vertical rod is very thin, so thin so your body will not be blocked by it. Your wrists will be secured to the horizontal bar at the top. The T is used to display the most...attractive females' bodies. It's also used to secure the recalcitrant, uncooperative prisoners."

"How- how soon will we be...taken once purchased?" A woman asked nervously.

"As soon as the funds are in our system, the guards will handcuff you and you will be taken to the respective buyers' RV's. Several buyers came on the big busses. A few days drive and you will be brought to where they will board you on their private jets and flown to whatever country they are from."

He shrugged, then continued, "From there, you will be sent to wherever your owner purchased you for. For housekeeping, the fields, hooking on the streets, or the brothels."

Dead silence followed his words.

"Any other questions?"

When no one said anything, he nodded, then had the soldiers distribute the sacks then they left.

Jackie dumped her sack on her bunk. "Huh, check this out, not too shabby."

She lifted a skimpy mini-skirt and halter with spiked stilettoes. "Looks like they plan on my being bought to hook, thank God. I was afraid I was destined for the fields. What did you get?" she asked Rebeka.

Rebeka picked up what appeared to be an almost sheer scarf, and pretty much a thong. No shoes. "I…don't understand," she mumbled.

Jackie glanced over. "Oh, honey, they think you have a body to really show. They're looking for the big bucks for you."

"But," Rebeka looked down through blurry tears at the pieces of cloth. "I…I mean they can't expect me to go out on a- a stage wearing only, I mean, my underwear covers more than this!"

Jackie got up and came over to sit next to her. "You have no choice sweetie. You heard the soldier, you put it on or they'll do it for you."

A woman stood up holding a pair of overalls. Her mouth twisted in distaste. "Ah, it's the fields for me. I hope it's an easy one with modern equipment." She smiled harshly at Rebeka.

"Count yourself lucky, girl, half the time the women are displayed totally naked at these auctions. Not this one, usually, but a lot of the others run by a different chief."

Rebeka dropped the swaths of cloths and stared in deep despair at them. She would never survive a brothel. She'd kill herself first.

Maybe, if the stage was high enough, she could break free, run and hurl herself off the edge, and die before it even started.

Chapter Fourteen

"Well, J?" Ving said to the chief. "You regretting not poking the bitch? At least this part of the shit is almost over. The hell of it is," he smirked at Hub, "it's a good thing 'cause that little girl was rubbing off all Jeph's violent jagged angles, making him an ol' softie. He fucking let Medville live."

Hub said, "Can you believe it? First time ever letting a guy live after the transgression he committed. But the broad pled for his life, and just like the trannies, fucking hard-ass Jephunneh Kajic balked and let him live."

"Fucked him up goddamned good first though, bro, he ain't gonna be walking again no time soon," Nero put in.

"If ever again," Hub added.

"Will you girls shut the fuck up," Jeph muttered, and they laughed.

The captains and Kajic hung near the stage to ensure everything was kept above board. No cheating, no fighting. Of course the grounds were littered with soldiers.

The open front of stage, auction block as it were, stood about eight feet high and was about fifteen feet wide and fifteen feet long. Steps led up to the stage on both sides.

Behind the open front of the stage, on the left, the women were sequestered in wooden stalls that were built onto the back of the stage.

The stalls were enclosed on three sides and opened facing the back of the dark purple curtain. The curtain hung the entire length veiling the prisoners from sight of the audience.

The soldiers and male prisoners had built the stalls as part of the entire staging area.

On the right housed the waiting males. They would be brought out first.

Once they were bid on and paid for, they would be returned to the stalls until the buyers were ready to leave, then they would be brought to the RV's ready for travel. All of the prisoners were handcuffed.

The buyers were conversing, greeting familiar faces and introducing themselves to others as they took their time taking their seats. A hundred or more chairs were grouped in front of the stage where they would be sitting.

Without responding to his friends, Jeph left them, hit the steps to the stage and wandered around to the back.

It was almost as noisy as out front with the prisoners yakking back and forth from the open sections of stalls.

Jeph strode by the stalls glancing in each one. Half the women greeted him with offers of sex, right then and there if he wanted. Ignoring them, he kept going until he came to the stall Rebeka was housed in.

He stepped in front of it, and frowned.

Each stall had a wooden seat built into the side. Rebeka wasn't alone. She was sitting on the seat, a soldier stood beside her with his hand clutching the hair at the back of her head, yanking her head back arching her neck.

Jeph barked, "What the fuck is going on here, soldier?"

The soldier jumped and stepped aside from Rebeka letting go of her hair. He stammered, "N- nothing, sir. She was very...uncooperative. Fighting, screaming, Monsieur Eyáhdi said to give her a mild sedative so she would be docile on the block. I just gave it to her. She uh, refused, so I had to...force her, sir."

"Get the fuck out," Jeph commanded.

When the soldier slid warily past him, Jeph moved inside the tiny stall.

Rebeka got to her feet. Swaying as the sedative was hitting her bloodstream, she had to put a hand on the wall to brace herself.

Jeph said nothing, just stared at her.

She was wearing a blush colored piece of gauze like an almost transparent scarf that swathed the front of her, tying in the back. It very, barely covered her breasts. Most of the velvety mounds were exposed. He looked down.

A tinier swath the same blush color only just covered her sex, and less in the back. The hot, round little cheeks he'd always wanted to grab, and squeeze, and stick his face in to rub and bite, were half bare. He had wood in an instant.

"Mr. Chief." Her beautiful eyes were slightly unfocused and filled with tears. She tried to move to him but was jerked back by her wrist chained to a metal bar.

"Please, please don't let them do this to me. Please. I swear I'm innocent, please help me," her shaking, plaintive voice was almost slurring from the drug.

Standing out of her reach, he saw her bruises from Patrisia had faded. His face impassive, eyes blank, he said coldly, "I cannot, Rebeka. There is nothing I can do for you. It is out of my hands. You need to make your last confession."

Her brows rose shakily. "Confession? The worst thing I remember ever doing in my life was borrowing Katie's blouse at the convent without asking and spilling sauce on it."

At his bewilderment she blinked hard, heavy, then said, "Have you come here to gloat at me? Because I wouldn't...sleep with you?"

At his silent regard, she said, "Go on then, tell me you're happy to see me about to be sent off with someone so I can be beaten and drugged, abused and broken. Tell me you're glad I'll be hurt," sobs wrenched up her chest.

Hysteria rose, constricting the air in her throat. She clutched the wrist chained to the rod with her other hand and cried, "I'll kill myself if I can't escape. Not that you care, but I will. I won't live like that. I wouldn't survive anyway, so I'll cheat the torture."

He remained as still as a granite statue except for the vein hammering at his temple.

When he spoke, zero emotion reflected on his hard face. "Rebeka, if anyone can survive tis you. You are frail and petite but with a spine of steel. You will find a way to survive," his husky voice trailed off to silence, dark eyes blank black discs.

She begged, "Please, Chief, please, I will do anything you ask. Anything. I- I promise, anything you want, any time you want, please help me, I'm so afraid." The sobs choked out of her as the tears fell.

He gave her one more long look, his hooded dark gaze taking her in from head to toe and back. "There is nothing I can do," his voice flat, devoid of any sentiment. He suddenly turned on his heel and abruptly left her.

As he strode off, he could hear her soft, tortured voice crying, "Please, Chief, please help me. Please..." He didn't even glance at the other prisoners as he made his way back around to the front.

When he silently rejoined his team, Hub's gaze stroked over his wan face. "Hey, bro, you don't look so great. You saw her, didn't you?" A hardened mercenary, yet, Hub sounded distraught at Rebeka's fate.

He'd spent time, albeit brief as it was with Rebeka, and found nothing but sweet, soft, kindness and compassion in her. Her bravery, as timid and trembling as she'd been, had actually impressed the captains.

"Ah," even Ving's rough timber sounded sad. "Jeph, is there is nothing we, you, can do to help her?"

Jeph stood staring grimly at the stage. But his eyes were blank to the mild activity up on the wooden block.

Soldiers' boots clomped on the thick wood as they checked the microphone the auctioneer would use. They fussed with the dark purple curtain ensuring it was closed but would open easily when needed, and some soldiers were posted sentinels.

No one would get off the stage, and no one would get on without authorization.

Watching the soldiers moving about, Ving grumbled, "We should have helped her escape when we had the chance."

Tegan glanced at him in surprise. The austere captain said, "This from the man who said rape the bitch?"

Ving shot him an angry look. "I said, if he was going to dwell on her and be a grouchy douche all the time that he might as well just fuck her whether she wanted to or not and clear his shit. I didn't mean her any real harm. She's not a bad kid, you can tell."

The other men murmured their agreement. Jeph stood silently, his eyes on the stage.

The auctioneer grandly swept the purple curtain aside and strode confidently to the front of the stage.

A boisterous sound of cheering and clapping broke out through the audience. A soldier handed him the microphone.

His fleshy face was all aglow with self-importance and a big smile. "All righty then, folks," he blared into the microphone. "Everyone grab a seat and let's get this party started!" The crowd cheered. There was a noisy bustle as people took their seats.

Grinning ear-to-ear, the auctioneer was a hefty man with a thick face and small black moustache. He had a subtle accent and round greedy eyes.

He wore a suit coat over a white, button down shirt with a large turquoise stone hanging from a leather tie around his neck, and black slacks and black tasseled loafers.

His voice bold and arrogant, he introduced himself. "Welcome folks to today's Nikolai Łizhiní's semi-annual auction. I, as most of you know, am Monsieur Ivod Eyáhdi." He bowed pompously to the audience's clapping.

When everyone was settled, Monsieur Eyáhdi held the mic to his thick lips. "Okay now, let's all quiet down so we can get the bidding started."

Grinned a leer, he said, "We have a special treat for you. I know you've heard about our angel we will be bringing out."

The crowd roared with excitement. The buyers had been deliberately titillated with stories about Rebeka. She was likely the youngest, and most beautiful slave they'd auctioned to date.

They never sold minors, that would catch the attention of the law. Only adult criminals, if missed at all, would be presumed locked away in prison somewhere, gone hiding underground, or dead.

Rebeka's breathtaking beauty had been greatly extolled. Stories of how the chief had to keep her sequestered in the kitchen or the barracks to keep the horndogs off her had reached the secret website that only the buyers and the auction personnel were aware of.

When everyone calmed down again, the auctioneer started with the men.

Each male was brought out in cuffs. Prisoners had been known to suddenly hit out at people, including Monsieur Eyáhdi, and try to make a run for it now that the realism of their situation was right in their faces.

As each man stood on the stage, Eyáhdi described him, his age, weight, musculature. Every part of the male would determine what kind of work he would be bought to do.

Their criminal background was also outlined as some buyers may bid on the experienced felons to continue in criminal enterprises for their own riches.

The smallest, weakest males were left until the end. They would be bought up in bulk at a cheap price to pick fruit with the migrants, or do tedious labor such as scraping paint off houses or working mines all over the world.

When the last of the males was sold, Eyáhdi started with the females. He began with the ones deemed to do field work, they would be the roughest, the most sturdy.

Then the next group for housekeeping, they would be the older ones too frail to work the painstaking fields.

After all the rougher and weaker prisoners had been sold, the auctioneer had one woman brought out for the streets.

She was gaunt, her face pinched, she'd obviously had long years of drug use and prostitution behind her. Bids were poor and slow for her.

She was finally bought to hook on the streets. The hardest of the life in prostitution. Especially depending on what country she was taken to. She merely shrugged, it was scarcely different from her normal life.

The auctioneer had one of the better looking females brought out.

She fought her guards. "No!" she shouted, "I refuse to work for anyone!" Grunting and twisting in the guards' clutches, she yelled, "Get your fucking paws off me you bastard half-breeds!"

"Ah," Monsieur Eyáhdi grinned, the moustache twitched in glee. A little drama kept bidding hot and heavy. "We have a reluctant one."

He loved this part. "Put her on the scalboard, fellas."

The crowd grew jittery with delight as the guards dragged the struggling, screaming, cursing woman to the front of the stage.

She wore something akin to Rebeka's outfit. A wide scarf scantily covered her large breasts, but she wore a tiny miniskirt of the same gauzy material.

The scalboard was attached to a twelve-inch by twelve-inch platform on wheels, with a handle attached to easily turn it.

The guards lifted her up on the platform then forced her hands up and bound her wrists to the upper horizontal bar. Small leather binds attached to the platform were tied over her feet keeping her legs apart and immobile, basically displaying her standing spread eagle.

Eyáhdi was pleased. She was relatively attractive with big fake tits. Perfect for his first demonstration. It was time to whip up the heat in the crowd before he brought out his special merchandise. He's the one that chose each outfit for each prisoner.

"Now then," he sauntered around the woman bound to the scalboard, amused at her enraged struggles. She jerked her hands at the cuffs, tried to pull her feet free from the leather bands. Her middle jolted violently back and forth as she worked to get free, to no avail.

"This, my friends," the auctioneer announced gaily, "is Lily Johnson. Lily is 28-years-old, she stands 5'7" tall and weighs 155 pounds. Her hair is obviously blonde, at the moment," he winked, "and she has hazel eyes."

While he spoke, he kept strolling around her while describing her body parts. "Look at those long legs, see her strong hands. Our Lily is one of the best pick-pockets you'll ever meet, aren't you my sweet?" Eyáhdi goaded. Lily cursed at him.

Then he gripped the stick that came out the side of the platform and pushed it, making the scalboard turn so the audience could get a 360 view of the woman.

Her back was now to the audience, they exclaimed their pleasure at that with catcalls and whistles.

"What am I bid for this lovely hunk of female flesh?" the auctioneer called out to the audience. Bids were quickly shouted out. Staff with iPads off to the side kept tally and track of everything.

"She has quite a broad ass, gentlemen, means she can take on as many tricks as you send her. Do you like it?" Eyáhdi reached up and lifted the tiny gauzy miniskirt to expose her ass.

Grabbing a handful of a very big, naked cheek, he squeezed, grinning at the shrieks of a very angry Lily.

"Oh yes, large but firm, gentlemen, and ladies." Bids poured from the audience. He swung the platform around so Lily faced the front of the stage.

"She looks good in clothes, folks, does anyone want to see the full package?"

"YES!" The crowd roared their approval like gamblers at the horse races.

"Okay, you asked for it, you got it!" Eyáhdi grinned. He untied the back of the scarf and let it fall exposing Lily's bare breasts. The crowd cheered.

The auctioneer gripped a big breast, lifting it as if weighing it, he said, "Ah, fake, but still looks and feels good."

Lily cursed him and jerked her body but she was too strapped in to move much.

Dropping his hand, Eyáhdi stuck his fingers in the top of the miniskirt and yanked, it came off in his hand. Lily was spread eagle and totally nude, struggling like mad and screaming curses.

The crowd went wild, and the bids kept coming.

Jeph stood near the stage with his arms folded over his chest. His teammates clustered with him. None of them were smiling. None of them really cared for the actual auction. It was pretty degrading.

Nero muttered, "Most of the prisoners really don't seem to care, it's here or prison, likely in a poor, third world country. But still, it's sick watching people bid on human flesh."

When the bidding concluded for Lily, several soldiers wheeled the scalboard to the back behind the curtain where they would release her from the contraption but bind her and hold her until her new owner paid his fee and came to collect her.

Monsieur Eyáhdi brought out two more attractive women to wet the buyers' appetites. None of them were put on the scalboard because, they didn't fight, and frankly, they weren't as interesting for Eyáhdi to display.

He only had to tell them to remove their clothes and they did without missing a beat. The bidding wasn't as raucous as for Lily, and it was over quickly.

Several of the groupie whores wandered up and down the aisles with refreshments and food, as if they were at a ballgame. The girls laughed and played with the buyers.

Sometimes a dimwitted groupie would think she was being offered a great job opportunity in a strip club or the like, and would eagerly, willingly, go with the buyer, and he or she would get someone for free.

Even so, Jeph usually demanded a commission for the female. After all, she wouldn't be there if the auction wasn't.

Jeph's attention waned. Normally he didn't hang around for the auction. He was usually in his office finishing up business and planning for the next one. Or for other employers he did per diem jobs for.

Then, Monsieur Eyáhdi beamed at the crowd.

"All right, folks, I'm going to bring out the treat I promised." He had presented a fleabag female first, then Lily to get the blood heated, then the next two females as a foil to show how much more extraordinary his special treat was. He expected the bidding to skyrocket.

"Okay, ladies and gentlemen," he nodded to some soldiers on the stage. The men dashed to the back behind the curtain. The audience rustled about, murmuring, discussing who he could be putting on the stage, wondering how many females were left.

The soldiers came out from behind the curtain with Rebeka bound to the Scalboard.

Chapter Fifteen

Jeph straightened, his eyes pinned to the girl.

Rebeka was more naked than not, her slender body stretched, spread and tied to the adjustable T-bar. The tiny gauze across her breasts left little to the imagination.

Instead of a skirt like Lily wore, Rebeka was wearing that swath of cloth that hardly covered her privates.

Her hair tumbled in glorious bright curls down her back. But her eyes were half-closed, her head tipped slightly forward. It was from the drug. She would have fallen if not for the scalboard.

The crowd screamed their approval. People were already shouting out bids.

Eyáhdi was exhilarated. He couldn't ever remember a time they'd had someone as luscious as this lush girl.

She was young and fresh. Vitality radiated from her creamy complexion and round pink cheeks. Her skin glowed like lustrous pearls under the makeshift stage lights.

Monsieur Eyáhdi said into the mic he clutched in his hand, "Unfortunately, this little girl had to be given a mild sedative. She was even less cooperative than Lily."

The crowd booed.

Eyáhdi held his palms up. "Calm down, you can see it makes no difference. Her stunning beauty shines like a rainbow in the aftermath of a black storm. And, it proves she has energy, fire, eh?"

The crowd cheered, and Eyáhdi beamed.

The auctioneer moved to Rebeka. He grasped the back of her hair and tugged, forcing her head up. Her eyes half-mast, the small plush lips parted.

The crowd ooed and ahhed.

"See? Quite intoxicatingly lovely, isn't my extravagant treat?"

The crowd clapped and yelled, the bids grew larger by the second.

Releasing her hair, he stroked his palm over her flat abs. Her stomach quivered at his obtrusive touch.

"Ah, she is soft as hell, but toned, people, in excellent shape. Supple, eh?" He set the curve of his hand under a breast, just barely touching it. But he was teasing the people.

He turned the scalboard so her back was to the audience, a collective gasp rolled over the area. Her perfect ass was covered by a slip of cloth.

Monsieur Eyáhdi cupped under the bottom of one cheek and the crowd screamed for more, the bids flew fast and furious.

Eyáhdi practically rubbed his palms together in greed, and lust. After all, the little blonde was hot as shit. He'd never seen another broad comparable to her.

He only wished he could have her for himself. But the rules say he can't. So, next best thing is to cop as many feels of her luscious body as he could get.

When he maneuvered the scalboard so she was turned back to face the audience, her full breasts swayed slightly.

Eyáhdi slid his beefy palm to cradle her breast, about to grope her, he teased the audience, "Well? Who wants more?"

People jumped to their feet screaming bids. The audience went insane. "Rip it off!" they yelled, "show us her tits! Crush 'em, pinch them, slap them! Let's see if they're real!"

Others shouted, "Her pussy, show us the goods, Eyáhdi!"

His grin taking up most of his sneering face, Eyáhdi kept one hand under Rebeka's breast so he could fondle her soft bare tit as soon as he removed her top. His other hand went to her back to untie the material.

"I bid one million dollars," Jeph said loudly, but calmly.

His friends gawked at him.

"Bro, you know you can't bid on her," Hub whispered.

On the stage, Eyáhdi paused. Frowning, he didn't move either hand, he wanted a feel of the girl, and he wanted to see her naked.

But, the Zăffe looked about ready to commit murder. No one in their right mind would not do as Chief Kajic commanded.

With a small, itchy, apologetic squeak, and a fake weedy smile, Eyáhdi said quietly, "Zăffe, sir, you know you cannot bid on her for yourself." *Otherwise I would have.*

Kajic stared blankly at him.

Eyáhdi went on quickly, "The rules clearly state no participants involved in the auction can. You can be put to death just for the-"

His voice icy, without inflection, Jeph said, "I buy her for another of my employers, comrade Rumân Brașov."

"Fuck, bro, you can't-"

Jeph cut Ving off. He said calmly, "He told me to keep an eye out for a comely broad. He wants to get married, have heirs. A new wife. This is his way of shopping for her. He wants a hot bitch that isn't afraid of the more unlawful, salacious aspects of life."

The audience was astounded.

First there was silence, then excited murmurings, then it grew silent again as the people's rapt attention went from Jeph to the auctioneer, to the girl's half naked body strapped to the T board, stretched to full display.

Hub tried, "Jeph you can't-" The chief was already hitting the steps up to the stage.

Totally unsure, his hands still on Rebeka who was barely conscious, Eyáhdi stood with his lips flapping open and closed. He couldn't wait to feel a chubby tit and then he'd go for her privates.

If he planned it right, turned her just so, he could get his fingers up inside her without anyone seeing, if he-

Kajic approached him quickly.

The auctioneer spouted, "But- but, I don't think you can-"

"Get your bloody hands off her. I can buy her for another. Braşov is my employer in a totally separate capacity than the auctions. I am his representative just like many in the audience are sent to purchase for someone else."

His boots stomping on the hard wood, Jeph strode arrogantly across the stage to Rebeka. He said to Eyáhdi, "I will have the funds transferred to the auction account as soon as my bid is concluded and the contract for the sale of Queenie Benani is signed."

Eyáhdi stammered, "But- but-" he stopped at the determined intent in Jeph's dangerous eyes, and relented. "Uh, well, all right then."

He turned to the audience and asked feebly, "Can, will anyone raise the million dollar bid?"

There were murmurings in the crowd, some angry, some amused, some objecting, but no one offered a higher bid.

Dropping the disappointed hand at Rebeka's back, Eyáhdi said sourly, "Sold, to Zǎffe Jephunneh Kajic for one million dollars."

Jeph snatched the auctioneer's hand, deliberately, discreetly snapping several fingers as he removed it from the front of Rebeka's body.

The chief's low levered reptilian eyes dared Eyáhdi to cry out or complain. Under his breath Jeph said, "That is for touching her, and," pretending to turn, he slammed his fist into the auctioneer's nuts.

"That is for drugging her. Now, get the fuck out of my way," he gave Eyáhdi a rough shove.

Staggering backwards, the man doubled over, trying to hold back retching from the pain in his groin. His broken fingers burning in agony, he shuffled quickly out of the chief's path.

Jeph pulled a huge knife from a sheath at his hip and slashed at the leather cuffs holding Rebeka's feet to the platform, then he lanced at the binds on her wrists.

He managed to slip the knife back in its sheath before she crumpled into his arms.

Carrying her down the steps, her head draped over his burly arm, long curls flowing, Jeph moved through the hushed crowd, his friends hurried after him.

"Jeph, dude, what are you thinking?" Hub said, worry furrowing his brow.

"You can't buy her, bro," Ving told him as they all circled Jeph, forcing him to stop walking. "It's a death sentence."

"Get the fuck out of my way," Jeph ordered.

"Come on man, think," Hub said, "you can't have her. You can't buy her."

In their language, Jeph replied, "I did not buy her for myself. As I said, I bought a wife for Braşov. It is totally legal, I checked the contract for the auction."

He told them calmly, "As a participant, I cannot purchase her for myself, but I can buy her for another as long as they are not connected to the auction, and he is not. So, get out of my way. I have some things to do before we leave tomorrow."

Hub's blond brows arched. "Tomorrow? You're leaving tomorrow? You're not going to wait until the place is dismantled and on the trucks and everyone leaves?"

"Correct. There are bound to be issues regarding her," he glanced down at the completely unconscious woman draped in his arms.

"And I want to be halfway to Braşov before the shit starts hitting the fan. My actions are wholly legal, but there still could be possible trouble. Especially from those I outbid. You guys will stay and make sure all the break-down, and transfers of the prisoners are completed. I will meet you in Montenegro. I will be in contact."

He muscled his way past them and stalked across the smushed grass heading for his room.

When he got inside, he laid Rebeka on his bed.

She stirred as she felt the stiffness of the bed under her. Her lashes fluttered over blinking fuzzy eyes. Still woozy from the drug, trying to clear the fog from her sight, she looked around in confusion.

Kajic stood over her. Blearily she peered up at him. Her words slow and thickly slurred, "Chief? I...don't understand, why am I in your room?"

Louise Furley

Last thing she remembered was being in abject humiliation as she was bound spread-eagle on a contraption wearing only a few wisps of cloths.

A horrid fleshy man was greedily squeezing her half-naked bottom, and his other fat hand gripped the under-swell of her breast while people cheered and called out for him to strip her, molest her more. The mortification of it all stole her mind, and her breath.

Everything had grown hazy as the drug took full effect.

She remembered pandemonium of crazy people screaming out dollar amounts, some were jumping up and down shouting. Behind her prisoners wept or grumbled.

Right now, her head ached, she raised a shaky hand to it and recalled the chief suddenly on the stage with her and slashing a big knife above her head.

She had thought he meant to kill her. That he regretted the horrendous life she was going to have to endure and decided she was better off dead. He was going to kill her out of compassion.

Then, her ties cut loose, and she tumbled, she thought, into the chief's arms.

Shaking her head, it must have been a fantasy of her delirium. Lying on her back, she felt at her clothes. She still wore the gauzy scarfs.

Her words barely audible through the drug-induced malaise, licking her dry lips, her tongue thick, she mumbled hoarsely, "What happened?"

Observing her wobbling eyes trying to focus, her small tongue circling pink lips, as usual, he replied coldly, "I bought you for my employer who resides in Montenegro. We will start for there tomorrow."

Confusion rippled across her face. It was a struggle to understand him, his accent was even heavier than normal.

Her lashes fluttered as she tried to focus up at the dark brooding chief hulking over her.

"But, why, why would you do that?"

He crossed his arms over his chest, gazing down at her. "Because he wanted a wife, and you did not want to go to the brothels. He is not," he was going to say Brașov wasn't a bad man, or a violent one, that he would not harm her, but he would be lying.

His employer was on the same line as a cold-blooded murdering mobster. A cartel boss of sorts. He was as ruthless and violent as they come.

At her bewildered expression, his chilled command brooking no dispute, he said, "I will have no discussion of any of this. It is done. Tomorrow we leave for Montenegro. You will not resist, or attempt escape, you will do what I say, when I say without arguing, and answer me when I question you." His voice was as frigid as his eyes were grim. There was no hint of compassion or leniency in them.

He bent and caught one of her thin wrists, pulled it up and cuffed it, the long chain was attached to a rod to the bed.

"And," he said just as coldly, eyes empty, "you will give me what you promised. You said anything and everything I wanted."

Her lips parted, eyes widened. "But-"

"No buts, Rebeka. You asked, begged me to save you, and I did. You promised me you would do anything I asked. I expect you to do so willingly, without fighting or tears. I will take my due before I hand you over to my employer. He will not presume you to be a virgin, he will not care that I fucked you."

His dark eyes narrowed at her. "Do you have a comment to make?"

She blinked, swallowed hard, but said nothing.

"Good," he said tersely, then left the room closing and locking the door behind him.

Chapter Sixteen

𝒯he drug had taken Rebeka over, dragging her down a dark, frightening tunnel. The darkness, the closed-in walls smothering, she struggled to fight her way out of it.

Her eyes popped open.

They flit back and forth. She was still in the chief's room. Dim twilight haloed around the small plastic window told her it was almost morning. A blanket covered her.

She moved, and realized her wrist was manacled to a rod on the bed.

It all came barreling back at her. The auction, the auctioneer's filthy hands grabbing at her, the chief slashing at her with a machete, her falling into his arms.

She must have passed out, and he'd put her in his bed?

He had been as cold and mean as always, glowering down at her with his blank eyes scarcely visible under the hooded lids. He had told her...what?

She rubbed her eyes, then remembered. He had told her he'd bought her to give to his employer as a...wife. A bride. A shiver ran up her body and ricocheted back down to her core.

He had told her he was going to...have sex with her before turning her over to the man, and that she couldn't refuse, she had promised to do anything he wanted if he saved her.

Had he really saved her? He was giving her to a man, a gangster that she understood was as cruel and vicious as Kajic himself. She would still be a prisoner, still a slave. What would the man expect of her? Would he hurt her?

Undoubtedly. Maybe pass her around to other rapacious men like him. She vaguely remembered hearing men talking in the room while she was floated in and out of consciousness.

The chief had been quietly talking about the gangster he was taking her to. Because of his lawless and savage ways the man couldn't go about normal routes in choosing a wife. Any normal, sane woman would run like the wind from the likes of him.

Has she jumped, or more like, was she thrown from the frying pan to the fire? No, a glimmer of hope flickered; her new life would offer better opportunities for escape. He couldn't keep her locked up in a dungeon, or, anything 24/7. Could he?

Her mouth twisted bleakly, of course he could. Yet, he wanted her as a wife. What did that mean? What did that entail?

He would want children. She was still going to be raped no matter how it happened or by whom. What kind of man buys a kidnapped female, and doesn't care if her procurer has sex with her first?

Rebeka wriggled to push her pillow against the wall and lean into it.

The door opened and one of the captains, Hubbard Shaw came in with a friendly smile.

"Hey Rebeka, how are you feeling?" He kept his dark blue eyes trained on her face and not dip to her mostly exposed bosom.

Rebeka squirmed harder against the wall and brought the blanket up past her nose. Big blues blinked trepidation and fear over the blanket at Hub.

He entered slowly to show her he wasn't there to attack her. "Hey, Rebeka, I won't hurt you, I swear."

Inching into the room, he held his hand up and stayed several feet away from the bed keeping a personal safety bubble around her.

"I have some clothes for you." He held out a small suitcase. "Jeph borrowed some stuff from a few of the whorer, girls here, and he had one of them collect the toiletries that were yours from your barracks."

Stuffing his grin at the thought that Jeph wouldn't have asked Patrisia for help, she would have snuck a viper into the case.

Following his movements with her wary eyes, Rebeka held the blanket up as if it were a wall of protection from the captain, and just blinked at him.

"Uh, so," Hub cleared his throat and set the case on a table. "Jeph is finishing up some business and getting the SUV ready for you guys to start travel so he asked me to bring you this stuff so you can get ready."

Her brows inverted indicating her puzzlement.

He explained, "Jeph and you will be traveling alone across this land to your destination."

The team had argued with Jeph about traveling alone without them, or at least have some soldiers for security, but Jeph wanted to be as invisible as possible on the journey and a retinue of soldiers would garner attention.

Speaking for the first time, her voice was a little hoarse, raw from the terror of the auction, and her screams as they dragged her to the stalls, she sounded breathy and tiny. "He said he's taking me to…a…man that will marry me."

No way was Hub going to discuss her and Jeph's personal business; Jeph would kill him.

Forking fingers through the longer top of his dark blond hair he took a deep breath. "That is all between you and him. I was just sent here to get you out of that," he nodded to the manacle around her thin wrist. "And stay here as protection until Jeph is ready to come and get you."

Yellow brows arched in slight sarcasm, Rebeka lowered the blanket to her chin and raised her cuffed hand. She rasped, "I've been left here all night, totally vulnerable, why do I need protection now?"

Hub's mouth twitched. "Jeph was with you until just an hour ago, and then Captain Ving has been outside the door."

His voice lowered, he said softly, "Listen, Rebeka," he unlocked and removed the cuff then sat down on a chair.

"Believe it or not, we captains are relieved the way things turned out. Jeph has taken a huge chance in buying you for his employer. It's never been done before, and he may take some big hits for it."

Hub didn't elaborate on who might actually go gunning for Jeph for swiping Rebeka out from under some of the biggest buyers. A few of them were beyond livid at what he had done.

"Captain Shaw," her raw throat made her voice quiet and raspy. "He is giving me to a…from what I understand, a mobster kind of guy. To marry!"

Her pretty face scrunched in anger. "He has no right. He had no right to have me abducted in the first place. He has no right to buy me, sell me. I am a human being and I won't stand for it!"

Hub stayed quiet during her tirade. She had every right to be furious, and alarmed, but it wasn't his place to agree or disagree with her. He was there simply as protection.

She could cry all she wanted, but she had no choice, she was now considered merchandise. Jeph's property until he turned her over to Rumân Braşov.

Hub was aware of the man's sinister reputation as a sadistic brutal man who has been known to have hospitalized women he's been with, some just disappeared.

Damn, he hoped Jeph had a plan, another plan. At least he got her off that fucking stage and kept her out of a miserable squalid brothel with a hopeless future.

"Um, I feel you, honey. So, you can change in the bathroom and I'll wait here, *bine*?"

The air whooshed out of Rebeka leaving her sagging like an empty balloon. This wasn't the time to fight, she would save her energy and wait for her opportunity to run.

She pushed the blanket aside and swung her legs off the side of the bed and then slid to her feet, took several quick steps then almost passed out. The sedative was still in her system, her knees buckled, light-headed she was going down.

"Shit-" Hub raced to her to catch her before she broke her head on the floor. He got there in time to wrap his big arms around her and support her.

Holding her against his chest to give her a chance to gain her balance, Hub moved them back closer to the bed.

An arm around Rebeka's back supporting her, he lifted her legs and lowered her gently to the bed.

Helping her to lie down, he put a knee up on the mattress to brace himself. It looked like he was climbing on top of her.

Suddenly a burst of belligerent fury bellowed from the door in non-English, it translated to, "What the fuck is going on here, Hub!"

Hub glanced up and grinned at his infuriated friend.

Jeph stomped into the room, his face black with wrath, eyes flashing retribution. In their language, Jeph snarled with murder written all over his face, "Why the fuck are you fucking on top of her?"

Rolling onto his side next to the prone Rebeka, Hub laughed at his friend's anger. He was now lying next to Rebeka like they had been sleeping together.

It looked bad, she was wearing practically nothing, every curve out there to be ogled and groped.

"Explain yourself, brother, while you get the fuck off her before I come and get you off her," Jeph threatened the laughing blond.

Hub sat up and moved to sit on the side of the bed. Looking down at Rebeka, her face was pale, eyes almost closed, he said, "Hey honey, you all right?"

He smoothed her hair back off her face and laughed at the growl behind him.

Hub grinned at Jeph. "Chill, bro, the drug that fucker gave her is still affecting her. She got up too fast and about passed out. I just helped her back to the bed to lie down."

"Huh," Jeph grunted, "you were here as protection, not to fucking feel her up."

That irritated Hub. "You want to stop talking now, bro, she would have knocked her noggin on the floor if I hadn't grabbed her."

Rebeka struggled to sit up. Hub wound his arm around her back to help her. The growl rumbled again.

"Rebeka." Harsh with his rage still boiling, Jeph moved near the bed to look at her and said in English, "Are you *bine*, ah, all right? Should I get the medic? He is still here."

At the sight of her pale face, his voice softened. "Shall I get him, Rebeka?"

She covered her eyes with her hands and rubbed them. Lifting her curls she set them off the back of her shoulders and said quietly, "No. I will be fine."

The two men shared a look and Hub stood up.

Speaking more gently, Jeph asked her, "Can you get dressed? Do you want to sleep some more?"

Shaking her head, she shuffled to the edge of the bed. "No. I'm okay. I'll get dressed." Hub helped her to her feet.

Ignoring the lowering of Jeph's brows at the arm around her, Hub steadied her while walking her to the bathroom.

Jeph said, "Do you need help getting dressed, Rebeka?" His mouth bunched over clenched teeth seeing Hub holding her half-naked body against his, and his shit-eating grin.

Rebeka replied softly, "No, I'll be fine."

Hub walked her into the bathroom, when he came out, Jeph was standing almost in the doorway.

Pushing past him with a grin, Hub said, "She needs her clothes, bro, quit breathing down my neck." He trod to the suitcase, picked it up and took it into the bathroom, then came out and closed the door.

Folding his arms across his chest he chastised his friend, and leader, "You need to back up the bus, bro, stop acting like a jealous boyfriend. You bought her to give to another man. Get used to seeing males other than you with their hands on her."

Jeph's lips pursed with his frown. "Listen, Hub-"

There was a disturbance at the door. Three men were piling over the threshold.

"What the fuck-" Jeph said crossly as he and Hub turned to see what was up.

One of the men stepped forward. He was a huge muscled brute. He said, "Kajic, our bosses are pissed at your underhanded behavior. You cheated them out of bidding for the bitch."

The other two men stood behind him, just as big and threatening.

The first man continued, "Yeah, they say you can't legally bid on her. You can't have her, you foreign bastard. We were sent here to get her and bring her to them. They will decide between them, legally, who will buy her."

The only thing that moved on Jeph was one brow arching.

Beside him, Hub stayed quiet, but grinned.

Jeph said coolly, "Who are your bosses?"

The man said, "Mine is Art Reacher, and his," he nodded to one of the other men, is "Tai Ming, and his," nodding to the third man, "Bruno Maratelli. So, just hand her over and we'll be on our way. Trust me, you don't want to fight us on this."

One of the other men said, "We have orders to forcefully take her if we have to."

Crossing his arms, Jeph stood with his boots planted on the floor even with his shoulders. As he started to say something, the bathroom door opened and Rebeka stepped out.

She was wearing snug jeans and a frilly blouse that revealed the very upper curves of her breasts. She was still barefoot, and combing her hair. When she saw the intruders, she stopped abruptly, blue eyes big and round with uncertainty.

All the men stared at her.

Jeph turned from her to face the intruders, but he said quietly to Rebeka, "Go back into the bathroom, Rebeka, and close the door." He didn't look to see if she obeyed him.

When he heard the door to the bathroom close, and the lock click, his face impassive he said to the men, "Come and get her." Neither he nor Hub moved a muscle, but Hub still grinned.

"Come on, Chief," the man who had first spoken cajoled, "make it easy on yourselves. Don't make us have to fuck you up over a broad. She's just a whore with a goldmine of a pussy. They will give you your money back, go find yourself another one."

Jeph and Hub didn't move.

"All right, champs," the man said over his shoulder, "he's refusing. Get them!"

All three of them bolted into the room with their fists swinging.

The first one that reached Jeph, swung at him, Jeph ducked and bashed his fist into the man's stomach. He doubled over, and Jeph smashed the guy behind him in the nose. Blood spurted with the man's scream.

Hub waited for the third man to come at him. When he did, Hub chopped him in the throat with his fist crushing his windpipe. Gagging, choking, the man dropped to his feet.

Together, Jeph and Hub wiped the floor with the thugs, ensuring that all three with broken necks would never be able to attack anyone ever again, and would not be able to come after Jeph and Rebeka.

Louise Furley

A second to catch their breaths, they shoved the bodies out the door, and Hub took out his walkie-talkie and called Ving to get the others to dispose of them.

Hub said to Jeph, "I'll help them, you take care of her," he winked at him before going outside.

Last thing Jeph needed was for Rebeka to see the dead thugs. She'll think it was her fault, their deaths on her head, she would probably freak out on him seeing the slaughtered fucks right in front of her.

Thank God the fight was quick and done before she was able to plead for their useless lives. He'd already spared the lives of people for her that he normally would have easily exterminated.

The guys were right, he was getting soft. Well, he was done with her shit. She would not be telling him what to do, batting those tear-filled big blue eyes at him making him do things that weren't normal for him.

He didn't have a heart, he never claimed to be a nice guy or have compassion, and the sooner she realized it, the better for them both.

Jeph grabbed a towel to wipe the blood off his knuckles and the floor. He tugged the black long-sleeved shirt off, examined it for blood, secured the holster and gun at his hip and put the shirt back on.

Not that they'd needed them, but he and Hub hadn't used their weapons on the thugs, gunfire would have drawn unwanted attention.

Combing his fingers through his hair, he shoved it back off his forehead, his breathing calmed. Buttoning the shirt, he trod to the bathroom door and rapped lightly on it.

"Rebeka, tis safe to come out now." He stepped back as he heard the lock disengage and the handle turn.

162

The door opened slowly. Standing behind it, her wide eyes anxiously scanned the room.

Her throat still sore from screaming, Rebeka rasped, "Where did they go?" She stayed a few inches inside the bathroom, warily eying Jeph. He was tucking his shirt into the black jeans.

Her fear of him palpable, Jeph moved back to give her space. He walked to the small plastic window and peered out to see if his men had gotten rid of the bodies.

Seeing it was almost clear, not looking directly at her, he said to her, "They are gone. Are you ready to go? I have food in the car, we can eat on the road."

He was eager to get going, now so much more so after what just happened.

Letting out a heavy breath, she murmured, "I, uh, guess." Why did he bother asking her, she had no choice. He wouldn't let her stay, and clearly, if she didn't do it on her own, he would just pick her up and toss her in the car.

At least at the moment he didn't have handcuffs on her wrists. But she had noticed the cuff that she had been attached to last night was gone.

She tried anyway, "Chief Kajic, please, can you just please leave me here and let me find my way home?"

Turning his dark blank discs on her, he pointed to the shoes she carried in her hand and said, "Put your shoes on. Do not ask stupid questions."

They glared at each other. Then, with a beleaguered sigh, Rebeka went and sat on the bed to put them on.

Jeph had packed up his stuff and already put it in the car while she was still sleeping. He had lain next to her last night, listening to her soft breathing.

She'd barely stirred all night from effects of the sedative. He wanted to wring the guy's neck that gave it to her, especially forcing it down her throat, but, actually, he had done both of them a favor.

She would have been lying there all night, unable to sleep, terrified of what had happened, what was going to happen, and of him.

She might fight him at every step, yet had been so damned receptive to his kisses. But she was afraid of him, and she'd made it clear she didn't want him. Didn't want his hands on her.

Well, she had promised him she would do as he says, and he would be holding her to it.

"*Bine*," he said and headed for the bathroom.

He came out with her small suitcase of borrowed clothes and tried to ignore the way she shrunk from him when he neared her.

"Those- those men," shudders and goose bumps in a wave of apprehension furled over her body. She folded her arms in an X over her body as if protecting herself. "Where did they go?"

He started for the door. "Ah, we persuaded them to move on. You ready?" At her slight nod, he opened the door and peered out, then holding it open he motioned for her to go out.

He bit back a growl of annoyance as she slid past him being very careful not to let their bodies touch.

She needed to get over that shit, he thought. It took everything he had in him to keep his hands off her, and she strode past him with her little nose up in the air like he was nothing but horny gangster trash. Which, technically, he was. Still...

Outside, she stood a few feet away unsure of what to do.

When he reached her, he held her case in one hand, and set his other hand around her waist. He felt her start under his sudden touch.

She tried to move from his grasp, but he held her. He was done screwing around, she would learn right now he was the boss. She would do as he ordered, without argument, and she would get used to him touching her. Because he was going to be doing a lot of it. He was done treating her with kid gloves in the hopes she would accept him, come to him, desire him.

The grounds were emptied of the RV's. The soldiers were dismantling and loading the pieces of the modules they'd lived in for the past few weeks into waiting trucks.

Drills and hammers reverberated throughout, men called out to one another as they worked. They were all careful to keep their eyes off Jeph and Rebeka.

Jeph had warned them all to mind their own business when he brought her out. He walked her to the waiting SUV.

Big, black, with dark tinted windows, the doors were open. Jeph set her case in the back with his things then helped her up the high step of the vehicle.

The step was pretty high and awkwardly wide, and Rebeka was petite. Jeph twined his hard fingers around her upper arm and practically lifted her into the seat. Closing her door, he trod around the front of the vehicle to the driver's side.

Before he got in, he glanced over to one of the structures still standing and saw his team gathered there. He nodded to them, a couple gave him a brief wave.

Hub smiled faintly.

They all looked worried.

Chapter Seventeen

*J*eph wasted no time hitting the bit of gravel road that only extended a quarter mile from the end of the camp.

After that the road was dirt. It was rutted and packed down much more than when they had arrived from the trucks and the RV's going back and forth.

He glanced over at Rebeka.

Her fingers twined together in her lap so tightly she was squeezing the color right out of them. He could see it wasn't doing much to still the anxious shaking.

Her head was turned to the passenger window. As she stared out the window, the side of her face moved. She was biting the inside of her cheek. He'd seen her do that a few times now and knew it was a nervous habit.

His gaze dropped to the frilly blouse, her breasts bounced gently under it, he forced his eyes away from them and noticed she hadn't clamped her seatbelt on.

"Rebeka, we may be out in the middle of nowhere, but an animal can run in front of us or we could hit a hidden hole or rock, put your seatbelt on."

As he expected, she ignored him. Suddenly he whipped the wheel and jerked the car to the side of the dirt trail and shoved it in park.

Rebeka gasped and threw her hands out to grab the dashboard as the car jerked to a hard stop.

Jeph had the Lincoln SSX SUV custom made like the Hummer. It had no divider in the seat. He didn't want to be boxed into a car seat, he wanted the space. His fingers clenched the wheel as he struggled with his temper.

"Rebeka," he grunted.

She sat back in her seat and crossed her arms over her front, her hands on her shoulders.

"I am not going to repeat myself, Rebeka," he waited, she didn't move, didn't even look at him. He was about to lose it.

Turning to fully face her, he suddenly snagged her arms and pulled her across the seat, right to him, up in his face. He could feel the heat of her fear, her breathy puffs against his face.

He could see the mix of shades of blue in her wide eyes, and he could see the terror clouding them. His fingers squeezed her soft flesh, her hair curled over the black sleeves on his forearms.

"Please," she gulped. "I- I couldn't understand what you said. Please-"

"No." Grim, ominous, he said, "We are done with please. I am done with your disobedience. This is your warning, your last goddamned warning. You will look at me when I speak to you, you will answer me when I ask you a question, you will do what the fuck I tell you at once with no argument. And you will not cringe when I fucking touch you." Like she was doing now.

Her shoulders hunched up to her ears. Of course she was a slight small woman, and he was huge, cobbled with muscles, heaving with anger and roughly handling her.

He scowled in her face. "Rebeka, we have a deal. We made it in that crummy little stall when you begged me to save your life. Know right now, that I will be touching you, a lot. We will be spending a great deal of time together for a bit. You will not draw away from me, or avoid me. And I will be kissing you.

"Per our deal, you will not only allow me to kiss you whenever, wherever I want, you will reciprocate, willingly kiss me back regardless of where we are or who is present."

She started to speak, he gave her a rough shake to cut her off.

Without a lick of warmth or emotion, cold and hard as granite, he said, "And, my little ice princess, you will give me more, much more. Whatever I want from you, whenever I want it. When I say spread your legs for me, I expect you to comply without hesitation."

"It'll be against my will-"

"*Nishka*, it is not against your will. You begged me, anything I want, you said. I bought and paid for you, your body is mine. You are mine until I turn you over to my employer." He spoke very slowly, as clearly as possible so she couldn't claim she couldn't understand him due to his accent.

"I am tired of fighting, arguing with you. I have never allowed a female to give me this much trouble. I have been soft on you because you are young and scared, but you are gonna be more scared if you keep resisting me. Now, tell me, yes, you will do as I say, look at me and tell me right now."

Her eyes closed, she was holding back the tears. Her plump bottom lip quivered, her arms trembled in his hands.

He said coldly, "Right now, Rebeka, open your eyes, look at me. Last warning. I do not want visible bruises on you, but every time you disregard me and what I tell you, I will rip those jeans off and drop you over my lap and blister your bare ass until you cannot sit for a month of Sundays." She blinked wordlessly at him, angering him all the more.

"If there are people around, I do not give a shit, I will strip you naked in front of them and wail on your ass. You want that pain and mortification," he shrugged, "go ahead and not do what I say."

She still didn't move. Keeping her gaze down, she murmured, "You can't do that, you would be arrested."

"Rebeka," he sighed, "do not test me. We are not in your lawful USA, no one in this land will stop me from correcting my woman. Look. At. Me. Right now."

When she made no response, he groaned. Gripping her arms he turned her back to him and reached around her for her belt.

"No!" she shrieked and punched at his hands.

Moving like an unstoppable bull, he ripped her belt open, popped the button on her jeans, and shoved the zipper down then grasped her under her arms to turn her back around, and forced her to lie on her belly over his lap.

The SUV was big enough that he shifted over on the seat, and her stomach was on his thighs.

Screaming as loud as her hoarse throat would let her, she flailed her arms and kicked with all her might.

Her struggles were futile, he had ten times the strength she had. His hand spread on her back holding her down, he jerked at her jeans, yanking them over her butt.

Rebeka shrieked, "No! Stop!"

He paused, bent over her and said quietly, "See, you *can* talk to me. If I let you up, will you agree to abide by our deal? Do as I say?"

One hand splayed on her back, he felt her warmth through her blouse on his palm as well as the trembles that rolled up and down her body. Her breasts hitched against his legs with her frantic panting.

He gripped the top of her jeans with his fingers ready to drag them off of her. Not only did they have a deal, but they were possibly heading for danger, he needed her to promptly do as he said without question or hesitation, for their safety. Besides, her disrespect and resistance pissed him the fuck off.

The fight flowed out of her, she knew he would do what he threatened, she nodded.

Pressing her slender back down with his big hand, "Say it," he commanded tugging on her jeans.

A sob choked out with her fraught rusty voice, "Yes, I will do what you say."

Still bending over her, he stroked her hair off her face and said near her ear, "No more chances, Rebeka, I will not go through this shit again. Do as I say, when I say or your ass is fucked. Got it? And I want to hear it out loud."

Swallowing a sob, she murmured wearily, "I…got it. I will do what you say. Sir."

His mouth nicked in at her sarcastic Sir, but he let it go. For now. She may be timid and shy, but she had a backbone. Unfortunately, it tended to show at the wrong times.

Grasping her shoulders, he lifted her to sit up, and without another word, he shifted back behind the wheel. His big hand over the drive shaft, he took the car out of park and they were back on the road.

Rebeka sat frozen, until he grunted, "Put your seatbelt on."

She hesitated, his fingers gripped the wheel, the vein at his temple pounded. Rebeka bitterly did not want to do anything he told her to, even buckle her darn seatbelt. But, she had pushed him too far, and she knew it. Her resistance would earn her nothing but a sore butt and embarrassment.

She slid back to her seat, fixed her pants and her belt then buckled the seatbelt.

His eyes hard on the road, Jeph scanned the area as he drove. He didn't know if they were out of danger, and they could always come across illegal trappers or smugglers.

Huddling against the door, Rebeka sniffed back frustrated tears and stared out the passenger window.

He was surprised when she spoke.

"You are a bully, a big mean bully who pushes and smacks people around that are weaker than you."

His lips quirked. "Because I can. Do not forget that." The edges of his mouth tugged up in a short grin at the huffing sounds she made while crossing her arms.

Jeph reached over to the back seat and brought out a small cooler. He set it on the seat between them and said, "Here, take the stuff out, be careful, there is hot coffee inside."

For once she didn't hesitate, she opened the cooler, took out a wrapped sandwich. Unwrapping it, she handed it to him. He grunted his thanks. She took out a sandwich for herself, and two coffees. There was sugar and cream inside.

Without looking at him, she stiffly asked, "Do you want cream or sugar?"

"*Na*," he accepted the coffee she handed him and put it in a cup holder. Stifling his amusement, he watched her pour in several packs of sugar and a bunch of creamers before stirring and then tasted it.

Wrinkling her nose, she added more sugar and set the coffee in the cup holder nearest to her. Taking napkins out of the bag, she opened one and laid it on his knee, then started nibbling on her sandwich.

His gaze went to the napkin on his knee, his mouth twitched up at the corner.

After eating, Rebeka stuffed all the wrappers and debris into the cooler and deposited it in the back seat. They were both quiet for a few hours, each deep in their own thoughts.

Then, Rebeka, said, "Mr. Kajic, do you know what happened to Jackie? She was in the same train car as me. A blonde woman, in her mid-thirties, I think."

Jeph nodded. "I know who every single prisoner was."

"Do you know what happened to her?" she prodded when he didn't elaborate. But he said nothing.

Yellow brows down in a frown she asked, "Please, can you please tell me what happened to her?" She worriedly wrung her fingers in her lap at his nonresponse.

They rode in silence for a mile before he said, "See how frustrating it tis when you ask someone a question and they do not answer you?"

Her mouth dropped, she gave him an angry look. "There's a big difference between ordering people around for your own ego, and concern for a fellow human being."

"Hmm," his thumbs tapped on the wheel, he glanced briefly at her then back to the road.

They were following a road that traversed around a forest, he wanted to get as far as possible before stopping for the night. There could be a million dangers out in the rugged terrain; he had to keep his eyes peeled.

The car jounced over the rough uneven dirt road, passing scrubby rocky grass pegged thinly with scrappy trees.

He said coolly, "Should I pull over again so we can discuss how you will speak respectfully to me?"

"Oh!" she gasped.

Turning her body towards him she said, "Respectful? I don't owe you any respect, Mister. You kidnapped me, displayed me half-naked on a stage, let some horrid pig fondle me in front of dozens of people, then you BOUGHT me to GIVE to your vicious criminal employer. And, you just pulled my pants down threatening to spank me. What part of that earned you any respect?"

His lips pushed out. One brawny arm now rested on the door handle, the other hung relaxed around the wheel.

Without looking at her, he replied, "I broke the auctioneer's fingers for touching you the way he did, and punched him in the balls for drugging you. Does that make you feel better?"

Stunned, she blinked at him, her hand went to her throat with a croaking sound. "You- you what? You hurt him? But- that's so barbaric!"

He shot her a quick glance, his gaze slid down the front of her and back up to her angry eyes before looking back out the window. "He is fucking lucky that is all I did. Trust me, if he had stuck around long enough, I had other plans for him."

When he glanced over at her again, her face was white, she covered her mouth with her hand.

"Rebeka," he said softly, "you are in my world, tis very different from the way you were raised. Tis violent and merciless, and people get paid back brutally for the bad things they do. And," he reached out suddenly and cupped her chin forcing her to face him.

"Any man touches you, I will tell you right now, whether you want him to, or not, I will destroy him." His fingers squeezed her jaw when he said, "Do not test me with other men. As you have seen, I mean what I say."

Trying to free her chin, she said, "You bought me to give to another man, what gives you the right to tell me that I can't allow another man to touch me if I want? You are so-so dictatorial, hypocritical, so arrogant."

He released her as suddenly as he'd grabbed her, then muttered, "Regardless of how you feel about me, I will not allow you to be disrespectful to me, Rebeka. As you said," he looked over at her. "I am a bully, and you will be punished if you are insolent to me. I said no males but me touch you, and I fucking mean it."

She glared at the tough man. She only just noticed he had cut his hair. It was short and wavy around his head, he had shaved but as usual there was a dark shadow on his strong jaw.

Scars carved the skin around his face making him look as dangerous as he was. He was big and mean and strong, she didn't have a chance fighting him. With a sniff, she shuffled her butt over as close to the door as she could get, away from him.

They rode in silence again.

After a few minutes, he said, "Your friend Jackie was bought by an elderly woman. She had a representative there bidding for her."

He looked over at Rebeka with a rare kind smile. "Mrs. Wildersmith is really a nice old lady. She treats her servants kindly, does not beat them or punish them. Your friend will be fine with her. Probably the best thing that could have ever happened to her."

"But the woman used an illegal activity to gain Jackie! She can't be honest and good."

One of his shoulders bumped up. "She is a widow. Her husband was the one originally who worked with the auctions for his mines in Africa. Since his death, the people she hired lawfully cheated her, robbed her, one almost beat her to death. In truth, she is safer going through us. Our product knows what will happen to them if they harm or rob one of our buyers."

"Product. Nice," she mumbled.

"Anyway, your friend is safe and probably for the first time in her life she will reside in luxury and comfort while dusting and cleaning a little. Mrs. Wildersmith will let Jackie have friends, boyfriends if she desires.

"And at some point, the old lady always sets her servants free. Most stay with her because it's a good cushy job while living in stable comfort."

Glancing at Rebeka, he waited for her response, but she stared straight ahead. When he looked again, a single tear rolled down her cheek, she didn't stop it.

"You *bine*, ah, okay Rebeka?" He'd given up hope she'd answer him when she said faintly, "Yes, thank you for telling me that." They fell quiet again.

Jeph stopped the vehicle every few hours and handed Rebeka a roll of biodegradable toilet paper.

After wrinkling her nose, she accepted the roll.

He came around her side to help her down the high step. "Stay near, keep an eye out for animals. You see or hear anything, run to me and yell."

They drove for another hour on an asphalt road that wound through a darkening forest as the sun was setting. Hazy light still streaked through the thinner foliage.

Exiting the woods they came upon a tiny rural town.

Jeph had scouted ahead, he knew where there was a small hotel used mostly for traveling big-game hunters to flop in.

Parking the car in front, he shut it off and went around to open her door.

Her voice small, she asked, "We're staying here?"

The building, the entire town was rustic, decrepit, but the Bate's-looking hotel appeared clean. The waning light made the strange area surrounded by looming forests appear dark and spooky. She stifled a shiver.

"*Yah*," he said, then, "wait a sec," and he ran around to the back of the SUV. He came back with a jacket.

"Tis chilly. I did not think to get you a jacket, put this on." Before handing it to her, he wrapped his big hands around her tiny waist and lifted her out of the truck setting her on her feet, then helped her put the jacket on.

Before he closed up the truck, he grabbed a duffle bag and her case. "Come on." He nudged her to towards the front of the gritty hotel.

Carrying both the duffle and case in one hand, he opened the door for her and followed her inside.

The murky building was almost dark from the lowering sun. One lamp hanging over a stuffed chair by a fireplace gave little light. Two couches and another chair with two tables sat on the worn carpet.

Jeph went to the front desk and hit the bell that was there.

It didn't take long before an elderly man wearing overalls came trudging from a door behind the desk. He had white hair and white whiskers.

His eyes darted back and forth from one to the other. He gave Jeph a perusing look, then tentatively choosing English, he said, "Hello folks, what can I do ya for?"

Jeph said, "We want one night." Glancing at a board that indicated the rates, he pushed some bills across to the old man.

Picking them up, he nodded to Jeph then looked to Rebeka. "On your honeymoon?" he inquired, his gaze flowing up and down Rebeka. Even in the oversized jacket she was stunning.

The old man felt Jeph's glare at him and shifted his eyes back to Jeph. He reached under the desk and pulled out a key setting it on the counter, then pushed a ledger in front of him.

"Okay Mister..." he waited, but Jeph didn't fill in his name.

The old guy sighed, then said, "Room 3, down that hall then to the left. It's got a king-sized bed. You being a big bruiser, I'm sure you and the missus will enjoy the big mattress it's a-"

Jeph's face dark and dour, he snatched up the key and gave Rebeka a nod to go.

"Miz Munster will put a basket of pastries in front of your door in the morning. Don't want to interrupt you and the wife right in the middle of things, right bloke?" The innkeeper winked at Jeph.

His face like a rock, Jeph said nothing as he bent and picked up their bags then nudged Rebeka, muttering, "That way."

"Ya'll have a good night, sleep in as late as you want. No one will bother you lovebirds-" his voice cut off as Jeph and Rebeka went around the corner.

Sticking the key in the door, Jeph held out a hand stopping Rebeka from entering the room. "You wait here until I say to come in."

Strange town, Jeph was taking no chances. He searched the room then told her she could go in.

Chapter Eighteen

Stepping gingerly into the room, Rebeka stood just inside the doorway.

Jeph moved next to her to lock the door bringing them into very close proximity.

The taut inhale sucked in sharply, she stepped away from him so quickly, her back bumped up against a wall.

His black scowl squeezed even more air out of her lungs.

Stomping past her, he set her suitcase on a table and his duffle bag on a chair. Pissed that she had moved away so their bodies wouldn't come in contact, he squelched the urge to lash out at her. She had every right to be afraid of him, and she should be.

Doesn't mean he liked it or was going to tolerate her flinching from him. Clearing the anger from his face back to the impassive stony harshness, he said, "Go clean up, get ready for bed."

Standing still with her back against the wall she looked around the room.

It wasn't too bad. The pale yellow paint on the walls was fairly new. The comforter and curtains matched, green with yellow flowers, the shag carpet green and worn.

There was a desk and chair, a dresser, a small round table with two chairs and two nightstands filled out the room.

Her eyes hopped to the bed. Then to Jeph who was quietly watching her. Dark pink suffused her face before she quickly lowered her eyes.

Prodding, "Rebeka," he nodded towards the small bathroom.

Clearing her throat, she pushed her hair back off her shoulders and went to her suitcase. Taking out her toiletries she started for the bathroom without once looking at him.

"Rebeka," his voice stopped her, but she didn't turn around. "Are you going to sleep in your clothes?"

She wheeled around slowly. "Yes. There is nothing of…night attire in the case."

Pursing his lips, he went to his duffle bag, opened it, rummaged around and pulled out a white, long sleeved shirt.

He held it out. "Here, wear this."

She didn't move. Neither did he.

Quietly he said, "Come here and take it."

When she didn't budge, he sighed, looking down at his open palm. "I guess we are back to your bare ass meeting my hand, eh?" A brow rose at her.

She walked slowly over to him, stopping a couple feet away and held out her hand.

"Closer," he said. "The longer you take, the more violent my temper becomes."

Rebeka suddenly snatched at the shirt, but he caught her wrist, jerked her to him and pulled her up on her toes. The big blues rounded with fright.

Jeph dug his fingers into the back of her head and held her in his hard grip while he roughly enslaved her mouth. His kiss aggressive and rough, slanting his head he tore at her mouth until they both were out of breath and then he abruptly broke off the kiss.

She stumbled back a foot, he still held her wrist. Stunned lips parted, fear mixed with heat darkened the blue irises as her pupils expanded in them, her head tipped up in a foggy stupor, her breath lodged in her throat.

He shoved the shirt in her hand, and released her.

When she turned in a daze and trod to the bathroom, watching her, Jeph let out his held breath and set the back of his hand against his damp mouth.

The bathroom door closed, and he strode quickly to the front door and went out into the chilly night.

Completing a quick, stealthy scope of the surroundings, he returned with the cooler and set it on the small table.

Checking that the door was locked, he peered out the curtain before pulling it tight to the side of the window making sure it was closed and no one could see inside.

Rebeka emerged warily from the bathroom with her jeans and blouse in her hands.

"Come and eat." Jeph motioned for her to go to the table where he had taken out more sandwiches, a bag of chips and two sodas.

He waited while she set her clothes down then walked slowly across the shag carpet to where he pulled out a chair indicating for her to sit.

Both starving, they made fast work of the roast beef and swiss sandwiches and chips. When they finished their sodas, Rebeka left briefly to brush her teeth.

When she returned, Jeph got up, took out the handcuff and chain from his duffle bag, went over to the right side of the bed, and clamped one end to the bed. When he turned to her, he saw her plush lips push out in a pout.

"You're going to chain me? Really, Mr. Kajic, where would I go? We're in the middle of nowhere."

"Hmm." He unbuckled his belt and slid it out of the loops, tossed it on a chair. Unbuttoning the top buttons on his shirt he said, "So, would you promise not to run if I did not bind you?"

Her lips opened to say something, then, she shut them.

"Ah, I did not think so. You would run, Rebeka, knowing you are in a rural, foreign, hunting town surrounded by vast miles of forest and mountains.

"Anyone you tried to seek help from would probably do worse than what you would experience in the brothels, and if you made for the woods, you would surely perish in them. The nights are downright frigid and the animals ravenous. Yet you would attempt escape regardless, right?"

At her silence, he said with a sigh, "Get on the bed."

He wasn't surprised she hadn't lied and told him she wouldn't run. So far, everything she did and said had been with integrity. Even to escape, she hadn't broken her moral code and lie to him.

She appeared to be about to argue, then she slowly came to where he stood, and sat on the bed.

He clamped the cuff on her wrist. Ignoring her angry moue, he went to his duffle bag, took out a pair of boxers and a toilet kit and went into the bathroom.

A few minutes passed. The door opened and he came out wearing the boxers and no shirt. Jeph dumped his clothes by the duffle and made his way to the left side of the bed.

Rebeka sat with her back against stacked pillows, knees drawn up and arms wrapped around them.

Jeph didn't say a word as he flicked the lamp off by his side of the bed. He had kept his holster in the duffle bag, and the gun in his back waistband while they checked in. Now had he stuffed both under the mattress and settled in the bed.

Clutching her knees, Rebeka stayed on guard waiting for him to pounce on her.

She waited a long time until she heard him snoring softly and realized he was asleep.

"Huh," she mumbled, thought to herself, the lust he had conveyed for her had apparently fizzled out. Good. He would not make good on his threats to take her whenever he felt like it.

Letting out a long breath, she wiggled down under the sheets and was soon fast asleep.

Slits of early morning sun etched around the curtain leaving tiny traces of light across the bed.

It felt like that day, when Rebeka had thought she was dreaming, a weight of hard muscles and masculine scent curled over her.

Whiskers roughed up the side of her face while he pushed her lips apart. His tongue lapped over her lips, he sucked the bottom one then the top, licking his way around her mouth before invading it.

She could feel him, licking, sucking, kissing the side of her jaw down her neck to suck hard on her tender flesh before returning to grind against her mouth. Rebeka was in such a deep haze of sleep, it was like fighting through quicksand to wake up.

Little mews muffled against his mouth as he took it again and again until his groans rifled down her throat.

Rebeka worked to awaken, push her heavy lids up. While his mouth controlled her, tongue plunging, she felt his big fingers at her shirt, opening each button, his knuckles brushing over her breasts. His hand, large, hard, pushed inside her shirt to cuddle a bare breast- he was groping her!

Her eyes flew open, she shoved at him, her one hand fairly useless chained to the bed.

"Mr. Kajic, stop!" Her small hand pressed against the hair on his bare chest, she pushed as hard as she could.

Jeph moved his hand from inside her shirt to cup her face, holding her immobile. One leg flung over hers holding her in place, his engorged erection shoved into her hip. Black locks fell over his lust-saturated, hooded eyes

He rolled over her, pushing his legs between hers and shoved his erection against her sex. The hard ridge of it pressed into her cleft protected only by his boxers and her thin swatch of silk panties.

His fingers webbing her jaw, making sure their eyes connected, he said, "Anything, remember Rebeka, anytime I want." Nudging her thighs wide he rubbed his hard shaft over her sex.

His eyes drifted down to her open blouse, arrowed in on the pink budded nipple of one exposed breast. He lowered his head to take the nipple in his mouth, and she wrenched her body away.

One wrist manacled, she spread her other hand on his chest, pushed and turned her face to the side, avoiding his mouth when he brought it back up to pillage her lips. He stopped moving.

She peered at him, a smirk twisted up one side of his hard face. He rolled off her and off the bed to his feet.

At his sudden action she sat up and huddled back against the pillows. Jeph grabbed his clothes and went into the bathroom

Listening to the shower running, Rebeka sat holding her knees to her chest, her body shaking, wondering why he had stopped. He could have easily forced her, he was as strong as a bull, and, she'd felt his rod thrusting on her, he'd been hard enough to stab through a manhole cover.

The tension eased from her shoulders, he was only playing with her, deliberately screwing with her, making her nervous on purpose. Jerk. She could do nothing until he uncuffed her, so she settled back against the pillows and closed her eyes.

She must have dozed off, a sound wakened her.

Jeph was dressed in a black shirt and black jeans, he was setting a bag on the table. She could smell coffee.

Hearing her rustling, Jeph looked over at her. He said, "I got breakfast, coffee. I grabbed a ton of sugars and creams," his mouth turned up at her surprised rounded brows.

"You go ahead and take a shower, then we can eat and hit the road." That's when she noticed the cuff was gone. There was no reason not to, so Rebeka hustled into the bathroom.

When she came out, she was combing her long wet curls. Jeph sat casually at the table staring out the window, coffee cup in his hand. She quietly pulled out a chair and sat down.

"Oh, you are done? *Na* hair dryer, huh?" He had waited for her before he started eating. With a smile, he reached out and lifted a damp curl then let it drop when she stiffened. He pushed a take-out container at her.

"I hope you like eggs and bacon, hash browns. I put the pastries they left at the door in the cooler for a snack later. I need more substantial fuel for breakfast than sugar."

Her gaze rolled quickly over his huge muscled body. She nodded and grabbed some packets of sugar. Jeph was halfway done eating before she had finished doctoring her coffee.

After breakfast they cleaned up and were soon on the road. The land was mostly brush, brown grass, and extended forests cluttered with colorful autumn leaves. They passed rolling fields of wheat and cabbages, occasionally driving by sporadic homesteads that were mostly farms with lazy cattle dotting the pastures.

Jeph felt more secure as time went by that no one was following them, he relaxed his vigilant scanning the land for trouble.

Rebeka sat quietly watching the few farms and fat cows roll by. The road they traveled was still mostly dirt and rocks.

Breaking the silence, she asked, "Can I drive?"

"Huh?" He glanced at her.

"Can I drive?"

"Why do you want to drive?"

Shrugging, she said, "I just would like to, that's all." Her critical gaze settled on him taking in the rough face, strong jaw covered with dark shadow, big hand draping leisurely over the wheel that he commanded with ease and confidence.

"'Tis a big car and you are a little girl, I do not think you could handle it," he shot her a mocking grin.

Rebeka glowered at him. "Oh really? Hello, welcome to the 21st Century where women drive big rigs and bulldozers. You're a sexist pig. Humph," she grunted in disgust.

"Hmm," he pondered, glancing over at her. "Do you even have a license?" A shot in the dark but it hit home when he saw her cheeks redden. "Ah, what kind of modern day woman does not have a driver's license?"

Turning back to look out her side window, she said glumly, "They didn't teach driving in the boarding school, and even if they did, there was nowhere to go even if we could have a car."

His brow lifted. "Boarding school?"

"Yes." She nodded. "When my father married my stepmother, she didn't want me around, didn't want any competition she said for her daughter. So," Rebeka shrugged again. "She shipped me off to school in another country, far enough away it was seldom I was brought home even for holidays."

"But, you were home, when…ah," he stared at the road, eyes tapering in contemplation.

"When I was abducted?" Nodding again, she told him, "Yes. I'd been home about six months, and," she clasped her hands, tipped her head back and closed her eyes with a smile. "It had been heaven. Until…"

Jeph looked at her, watched the smile fade. "Your da did not teach you to drive?"

Shaking her head, she turned to stare sadly out the passenger window. "No. My stepmom begrudged any time he spent with me. Besides," her shrug nonchalant as if it didn't matter, "I was gone so long that we hardly knew each other."

"Would he go to the police? Tell them you are missing?"

Her shrug was casual but her eyes were bleak. "I don't know. Probably. Then again, they might be happy I was out of their hair again and just hoping I was staying with friends. Of course," she let out a little wry laugh, "I haven't been home long enough to make any." She turned her face away and wiped at an eye.

Jeph pulled the SUV off the road and put it in park. He opened his door, got out and shut it.

She assumed he had to go to the bathroom, but he came around and opened her door.

"Come, I will show you how to drive, little one."

At her surprised breath, he swooped in, unlatched her seatbelt and said, "Go on, slide over." Giving her a small push, he moved into her seat and shut the door.

Seeing her so small behind the wheel, the seat was too far back for her.

"Ah, wait a minute," he got out, got his duffle bag, came to the driver's side, opened the door and said, "Lean forward."

When she did, he stuffed the bag behind her back and got back in the car. Smiling at her he told her, "My legs are too long for you to pull the seat forward, they would be up my chin. Can you reach the pedals and the wheel all right?"

A huge grin brightening her soft face, she nodded happily. "Yeah. Wow, this is great! What do I do first?"

Shaking his head, he might regret this, he inched over to her and told her how to disengage the drive shaft, how to work the brakes, the gas, they wouldn't worry about signal lights right now, it had been hours since they'd seen another vehicle.

When he felt she was ready, he set his arm behind her on the seat, and put his hand to the side of hers that were clutching the wheel, and turned it as she pushed on the gas.

The car lurched several times as she pressed the gas anxiously with her toe, Rebeka squealed then giggled.

"You will get the hang of it, *nishka*, go slow. When in doubt, slow down, tis easier to correct a mistake when you go slower."

She maneuvered the vehicle back onto the road. His arm around the back of her seat, he was curled around her with his hand on the wheel still slightly controlling it.

When she had things going more smoothly, he let go of the wheel, but stayed close, keeping his arm around her shoulders.

Her fingers wrapped tightly around the wheel, she didn't dare look at him, she said, "I think you should put your seatbelt on, Mr. Kajic, I don't want to be responsible for your head smashing into the windshield."

"Ah, you are planning to knock me out so you can make a run for it?" he chuckled, then scooted back to his seat and buckled in.

"Hmm, now that you mention it, there's an idea." The tip of her tongue slipped through the corner of her mouth as she carefully maneuvered around a fallen tree.

"There you go, *nishka*, you have it, you are doing great. You are a fast learner, little pet." He leaned back more comfortably so he could keep his eyes on the span of land around them.

She drove steadily at a moderate speed but the speedometer started inching up the more confident she became.

When the speedometer moved past 50, he said, "*Bine*, Rebeka, you are doing perfect, but you are a novice, I think you should moderate the speed."

Giggling gleefully, she chirped, "I love this, Mr. Kajic, the freedom, the speed, it's so wonderful. No wonder kids run right out at 15 to get their licenses!"

Her hands clutching the wheel, she leaned forward intently, pushing down on the gas, the car rocked and jostled over the rugged earth.

"Uh huh, but, slow down a speck, *bine*?" Her enthusiasm was infectious, Jeph found himself smiling.

He smiled genuinely so seldom sometimes he thought he was incapable of it. And now, driving in the rural land of a foreign country in a car with a first time driver grinning and giggling, Jeph found it impossible to keep his mouth in a straight line.

"Mr. Kajic, I love going fast, I love it!"

"Hmm, *níshka*, I will take you for a ride on my Hog, hell, you would be out in the stratosphere of delight. The speed, winding along curving roads, hurtling down mountains, the wind in your hair, ah, you would revel in it."

Keeping her eyes on the road, her brows knit, she said, "You ride pigs? You do come from a land different than mine."

Jeph's head fell back with his laugh. Wiping an eye, he said grinning, "*Na*, tis a motorcycle. I think you would enjoy it."

Her lips pulled in, she sat back slightly. "That's not likely to happen is it? I'm thinking it will be a short time before I'm either pregnant…or dead." Her tone a death knoll sucked the happiness out of her, stole the light from her eyes. She was smart enough to realize any children she had would be owned by the gangster, not her.

If- when she escaped, she'd have to do it fast, before she got pregnant. Her chances of fleeing with a baby would be nil.

Picturing her with Rumân Braşov's seed growing in her tiny belly turned Jeph's stomach. "Rebeka," he didn't really know what to say, he was saved by the rabbit that bolted out in front of the car.

Rebeka screamed and covered her eyes.

189

Jeph lunged over and grabbed the wheel with one hand. Jerking it, they missed the rabbit and he held the car steady.

"*Bine*, Rebeka, let off on the gas, all right? Just tap the brake gently like I taught you." He controlled the wheel while she slowed the car down.

When it was slow enough, he guided it to the side of the road and put it in park.

Rebeka turned to him her face aglow again. "That was dynamite! It was the best thing that I've ever experienced in my life! Thank you so much, I don't know if I'll ever get to do it again," the big smile lessened, "but I'm glad I got to do it at least once. Thank you."

He just sat and looked at her. Her biggest thrill in life was driving a fucking car a few miles on a dirt road. Damn. If her old man was there right now he'd bust the bastard up.

Unclipping his belt, he shifted near her and put his arm around her shoulders. A couple of fingers curled under her chin lifting it.

"You did a great job, Rebeka. I am very proud of you," he leaned in and seized her mouth.

The kiss was so hot so fast he felt his body sizzle, when she didn't stiffen, didn't fight him, at first, the heat shot up ten notches. He ground his mouth against hers, if he could chew her up, climb inside her he would.

Then her body stiffened in his arms, she turned her head from his mouth. He dropped his hands.

Moving back from her, he said, "I am glad you liked it, Rebeka, truly. But there are lessons you need to know if you ever drive again."

Her eyes curious with interest she asked, "What are those?"

"Not only do you never take your hands off the wheel, you absolutely never close your eyes," he said it with a teasing grin.

She smiled back. "Yeah, I know. I just kind of reacted. I'm glad you took over and saved that poor bunny."

"Hmm," he smiled. "I was not looking forward to scraping fur off my tires."

"Oh!" she slapped his arm. "That's gross!" her giggles bubbled up.

"*Bine*, baby." He got out of the car and went around to get in the driver's side. "Scoot over, little pet."

She obliged and he brought the car back on the road.

She said, "I bet I'm the worst experience you've ever had with a woman in your car, huh?"

Forking a few fingers through his hair he replied, "Actually, you are the only woman that I can ever remember being in my car."

"Oh? That's hard to believe. Come on," she reached over and batted him on the shoulder. "You trying to tell me that you never, you know, did stuff in a car with a girl?"

At his shrug, she went on, "The girls at the school, the ones who came later when they were older, and the ones who went home a lot on holidays and birthdays and stuff, talked about necking in a car with boys. They said it's like a tradition, a rite of passage."

Jeph contemplated her words. Yeah, he had, had sex in cars. Mostly whores he picked up in bars, sometimes he just did them fast and hard and dirty and went back inside to drink more. But he wasn't about to share that with the prim miss sitting so demurely next to him.

But, then again, she wasn't prim, she was a whore too. He had to keep reminding himself of that. She just looked so pure and sweet and innocent, and that boarding school shit, what was that all about?

Even when he kissed her, she'd responded as if she had no experience kissing, her reactions were sweet and shy. Hell, his dick was growing hard. "*Bine*, okay, maybe I've done that."

With great interest she said, "Really? It must have been really difficult, you're pretty tall and those big shoulders," she shrugged studying him. "It must have been pretty uncomfortable."

For the women, he thought, it was mostly them on their knees pleasuring him. Black brows joining, he thought about her story about boarding school. Her report said she was a street-wise thief, a slut that did drugs. That was at great odds with being in a female boarding school in another country her entire life.

She'd said she'd only been home infrequently over the years. Did she make up for lost time in those six months she said she'd been home?

Shaking his head at the incongruity of it, she really did not know how to drive a car, no one could pretend her ineptness. His eyes on the road, he said, "Rebeka, tell me what you studied in your boarding school?"

She accepted the change in subject and told him bits and pieces of her life at school. It had been mostly miserable; and often painful when the guardians punished them.

Which was sometimes just for the fun for the guardians inflicting pain on the girls. She skipped lightly over those parts and told him funny things that happened.

Jeph could read between the lines. Again, if her fucking father was there- he kept his mouth shut and sat and listened to the pleasing lilt of her voice as she told him cute girlie stories.

The drive was companionable. She asked him. "Your friends, your captains, you all seem so close?"

He nodded while glancing off to the left side watching a cloud of dust spiraling to the south.

"*Yah.* I met them in prison. My country was so wretchedly indigent; many children lived on the streets. The only way to survive was to steal food, mule drugs for money, worse things. My friends were all orphans, they all ended up on the streets."

"That's awful," she said with sad incredulity.

"They had to do what they had to do to survive. Eventually, they were caught, imprisoned. That is where we all met. We learned to have each other's backs. The bastard I was enslaved to, when I took over his... organization, they came with me. Our loyalty is a steel bond between us. They are my brothers."

She nodded while listening, watching the trees and open land pass by.

He glanced over at her briefly, the sun lit up the side of her pretty face. "Sure, we are in a nasty business, but my captains, my friends, are not really bad men, Rebeka."

Bunching her lips, she turned to face him. "No? You kidnap people and sell them to abhorrent places with no futures as if they were not human, just chattel not even as valuable as moths.

"You murder people without qualm that are of no use to you. The transvestites, some were full transgenders, you said they had no value, that your buyers didn't want to *purchase* one thing and get a surprise. I've seen you kill with your bare hands, Mr. Kajic. That's pretty bad in my book. And your morals, I mean, you let women touch your privates right in public, that woman-"

"*Bine*, enough, Rebeka," he growled sternly, gruff enough she closed her mouth and faced out the side window.

When the silence grew, he said, "Listen, I told you we will be together for a while. I," he had enjoyed talking with her, it surprised him. He seldom conversed with females unless forced to for business. As far as he was concerned, women had one value.

"Anyway, let's try to not fight. I cannot change what has happened, but we can make this time together to not be uncomfortable. *Bine*? Ah, I mean okay?"

"You can't change the past, Mr. Kajic, but you can change the future. You can pull over right now and let me out and drive off. All you have to tell your employer is that I escaped."

Both his hands curled over the wheel, he quickly glanced at her with a dry smile. His sarcasm made snider with his accent, "Sure, Rebeka. I will just pull over, out here in the fucking wilderness and drop you off, sure, no prob. I think I saw a lion a ways back, no point in depriving him of dinner, eh?"

Her arm on the door handle, Rebeka leaned against the back of the seat, laid her head back on the leather, and turned to look at him.

"I know, you paid an absolute fortune for me. But, Mr. Kajic," she sat up straight. "I swear, I will find a way to pay you back, every dime. My father, he has money, I'll tell him it's a reward for rescuing me. Please, just stop the car and let me-"

"Fuck, Rebeka," he snapped, scowling darkly at her. "Fucking stop it. I am not leaving you in this fucking landmine of a woods, in a fucking foreign country with no money, no ID, no food, no weapon." He dragged his hand angrily over his head digging his fingers in his scalp.

"Maybe you could drop me off in a city, I can call my dad-"

Scrubbing a hand down his face, he spoke so ominously, the fury crackled in his voice although he spoke very quietly, "Stop." It was short and brutal and cold.

Her lips shut and she didn't speak again.

Chapter Nineteen

The next two days passed the same. They drove all day, and then exhausted, bone weary they stayed over in a hotel.

The first night he never went near her.

The second, after dinner at a small restaurant, when they got back to the hotel, Jeph grasped her wrist and sat down on the bed.

Ignoring the trepidation and fear congealing on her soft face, he pulled her down to straddle his legs facing him with her knees on the mattress. She was in a position that would be impossible to get out of, if he didn't want her to.

The fact that she still flinched when he touched her, and he had thought, hoped, they would be fucking like rabbits by now needled him. He could hardly sit still or sleep for his aching craving for her.

"Rebeka, relax, you act like I am going to pound on you," and sighed irritably when with her arms rigid, she pressed her palms against his chest pushing at him, her rejection vivid on her face.

When she opened her mouth to object, he gripped her face with both hands and slapped his mouth on her parted lips, instantly taking control of her. He was happily surprised when after only a moment she stopped pushing at him and reciprocated the kiss.

He could definitely feel the inexperience in her kiss. It confused the shit out of him, but also made him hot as hell. It was incredible, he could do as he wanted, and she would follow his moves, his body blazed, his dick was burning up in his pants.

Wrapping his big arms around her tightly, he moved a hand down to clutch her butt, pulling her harder against him so that his hard raging dick could rub her sex. "*Yah*, fuck yeah," he groaned into her mouth.

His mouth dominating, mesmerizing hers, it was as if he hypnotized her with his lips, his tongue. His hands holding her hard to him, Jeph pulled her up so their chests rubbed together, her soft breasts against his steely slabs, their warmth shared through their clothes.

Then he dragged her hips in so her pelvis felt the brunt of his erection, it practically burrowed into her cleft. He was tough and manly, frighteningly strong, but not hurting her.

Falling under his skillful spell, Rebeka's mind went blank as her body pinged and tingled. She felt dampness between her legs from his thick manhood pressing on her.

His kiss was so rough, harsh and hungry, like he wanted to eat her up. Dizzy with the desire he was building in her with his clever mouth, Rebeka couldn't think. She needed to stop him...for some reason, she couldn't remember.

His hands rushed up her ribs and claimed her breasts. Crushing them in his large palms, a spontaneous, unstoppable moan oozed up her throat, and that seemed to spur him on.

Feverishly devouring her, ravaging her mouth so fiercely, kneading and squeezing her breasts in his rampant lust, his strength was rough and out of control, now he was hurting her.

It took all her strength to push from him, she gasped, "You- you're hurting me, please."

His burly arms were made of iron, his hands hard and rugged, his mouth possessed.

She shoved and wrenched her head to the side, gasping for air.

With a pained groan, his head fell forward, hanging in frustration.

Panting as she was, it was like he had to mindfully force his hands to open, release the fierce grip on her tender breasts. He dropped his arms.

When he didn't move or say anything, without looking at him, Rebeka squirmed off his legs and hurried into the bathroom.

She locked the door but knew it really would be no defense if the bear of a man wanted in. Slamming her back against the wall, her chest heaving, Rebeka tried to gather her wits and catch her breath.

She had to keep reminding herself, he was a thug, a criminal, a murderer. He kidnapped her, bought her and was giving her away to a strange man, a worse beast than Kajic himself. He was only going to screw her and then hand her over.

Nonetheless, her heart raced, thumping madly in her chest, she held a hand over it as if she could stop it. Her sex between her legs literally burned, gushes of desire flooded it, making her want to put her hand on it, and do...something. She didn't know for sure, the girls that were caught touching themselves at the school, or each other, were beaten so badly no one took the chance.

Washing her face, she did her business, cleaned up and combed her hair with trembling hands. Terrified to go back out to the bedroom, she stalled as long as she could. Would he jump on her the second she stepped foot out there?

Slowly opening the door, she peered out. He was sitting on the bed, in his clothes, his boots off, and was calmly watching football on the television.

Unsure what to do, Rebeka trod over quietly and sat down in a chair and silently watched with him.

Neither spoke the rest of the night until he said, "Go get changed for bed." He didn't sound angry, that encouraged her.

She scurried back into the bathroom. When she came out this time he was standing by the side of the bed with the cuff and chain in his hand.

Her heart fell. If he chained her she had no hope of fighting him off, not that she could anyway, and she knew her time was likely running out to escape.

The next day they were on the road again. They'd eaten a silent breakfast at a diner where the waitress did everything but dance naked on the table to get Jeph's attention, but he didn't lift his eyes from his eggs.

Back in the car, Jeph slouched against the driver's side door with his right hand draped over the wheel. He didn't look at Rebeka, just aimed his brooding attention to the road.

Rebeka cleared her throat before she spoke, suppressing her propensity to sound timid. "Um, Mr. Kajic?"

His eyes on the road, he mumbled, "Hmm."

Not very encouraging, she sighed. "How much further are we to travel?" Her time had to be funneling close to where she would be handed over to a butcher.

One broad shoulder bumped up, he replied, "A few more days on the road, then we will take a jet."

"Oh." He wasn't more forthcoming, or specific. "Why didn't we just go to the airport all the others went to? It was only a half a day away..."

It made no sense to her for them to travel through the rural countryside for days when it wasn't really necessary. Not that she was in any hurry to get to their destination.

"Tis none of your concern," he said flatly. The vein bounced against his temple, his thumb started tapping on the wheel.

The silence stretched. She asked, "Why can't you tell me? It's not like I can do anything about it or tell anyone."

He partially turned his head, his gaze stroked down her quickly then he faced the road.

She didn't think he was going to tell her, then he let out a heavy sigh.

"Because of what I did. I purchased you. Tis unheard of for a participant, anyone having anything to do with the auction, like the, ah, abductors, the soldiers, the auctioneer, me, to buy a prisoner. To keep control of things for a variety of reasons, they made a rule that a person deigning to try to do so can be...executed."

At her shocked gasp, he glanced at her again, his lip lifted wryly.

"I concocted a sort of loophole, but it is completely legal within the guidelines of the auction contract. The problem is, like those men that came to my room before we left," he shut his mouth for a second, thinking about how much should he tell her. He didn't want her scared to death, but it might make her more compliant with his orders.

She prodded him to continue, "Yes? The men who came?"

Jeph scratched at his jaw; he had felt like shit this morning and hadn't shaved. Her shutting him down was killing him. Maybe he needed to pick up some local talent to get some relief.

"Those men had come on behalf of some buyers who wanted to bid on you, quite badly apparently, and were pissed that I bought you. They had come that day to take you from me and bring you to their bosses."

His eyes shifted over to her, saw her cheeks pale. "We took care of them, but, they might send others, there could be other buyers that would consider coming after us. I chose to take you this way to keep them off our trail."

He waited for her to say something, express her fear, or ask more questions.

She sat stiffly, pulling at her fingers. Her chest was rising and falling rapidly with shallow breaths. "The...those men. What happened to them?"

He was not going to lie to her, he turned to look out his window to avoid facing the accusation in her eyes.

Not answering her question, his eyes flicking to her fidgeting, twisting fingers, he said, "Rebeka, I don't think we have been trailed. You don't need to worry."

Looking to her again then back to the road, he said softly, "I will not let anyone take you, Rebeka. I will protect you. I promise, you do not need to be afraid."

Blinking back tears, she said softly, "You'll protect me up until you hand me over to some sociopathic cutthroat."

He had no answer for that. They rode without speaking.

The terrain seldom changed. They passed wild open fields, traversed through some forests and then foothills, but it all looked pretty much the same.

Jeph had gotten a lunch packed from the diner. After hours of driving, he pulled off the dirt road and parked under a tree. He asked her, "You want to eat in here, or get out and get some fresh air?"

"Out," she muttered and was out the door before he had a chance to get to her. Hearing her cut-off scream, he rushed around to find her sitting on her butt.

"Rebeka, what the hell?" He stood over her.

Giggles perked out of her. "I didn't really realize how high that step was."

"Ah, fuck, *nishka*, I keep telling you, you must listen to what I tell you. You need to wait for me to come and help you out," he bent and offered his hand.

She took it and he hauled her to her feet. She brushed dirt and leaves off her bottom then wandered around looking for a nice place to sit while he got the food.

She found a wide fallen tree a few feet out in the field and waited for him to come to her.

Jeph handed the sack to her.

Rebeka noticed he always did that. It was like he always wanted her to have first choice of everything. For such a roughneck, he oddly had a gentlemanly side to him. He held doors open for her, helped her up the high sides of the truck, carried her suitcase.

As she bit into a sandwich, Rebeka said, "Mr. Kajic." Sitting on the tree, she kept both knees together facing the field. The noon sun warmed up the cool day.

"Hmm?" He chewed and washed the sandwich down with a soda. He had one boot planted on the grass, the other leg bent slightly on the fallen tree, he was turned so he was facing her.

"When you're not kidnapping, selling, beating or killing people, what do you do?" She bit her lip at the scowl that darkened his face. Every time she said those things he got angry. But, it was the truth.

Chapter Twenty

Shoving in the rest of the half a sandwich he'd taken one bite out of, Jeph licked his fingers before wiping them on a napkin. The black scowl lightened.

He said mildly, "You mean what do I do for fun when I am not raping and pillaging and slaughtering?"

At his droll humor, the curve of her lips increased with her nod. Holding her soda in her hands, Rebeka tilted her face up to catch the heat of the sun and closed her eyes.

Jeph watched her, seeing the sun stroking over her fair skin bringing out the few smatterings of freckles that crossed so child-like over her pert nose.

The blonde hair shimmering brilliant in the bright light, it waved down her slender back in fat curls almost to that shapely ass of hers he wanted to bite like a crisp apple. Her breasts pushed against the soft t-shirt she wore, he forced himself to look away.

"Ah, in the summer, my friends and I like to go up in the high hills and go hang gliding, mountain climbing. Ride our Harleys anywhere and everywhere as fast as possible. The winters we snowboard. We enjoy going with the snow dogs on sleds through the roughest trails as far north as we can get. Fish, hunt, outdoors stuff."

His gaze drifted over her again, the way her lips just curved again in a sweet smile, he felt goose bumps on his arms, he forced himself again to look away.

"What about you, Rebeka, what do you like to do when you are not being abducted, manhandled, bought and sold?" He tried to keep his tone light, teasing, they hadn't really spoken to each other since last night.

Rebeka pulled her legs up so her feet set on the tree and she wrapped her arms around her knees. "Hey," she said excited, "look, deer, over there," she pointed to the west.

Jeph turned, the sun washed over his face as he squinted across the field and smiled. "Those are gazelles."

"Oh, they are beautiful, Chief, whatever they are." Her face scrunched in a frown. "You wouldn't hunt them, would you?"

With a smile he turned back from the gazelles that were now bounding out of sight alerted from Rebeka's excited shout and motion. "You should not ask questions you do not want the answers to, *nishka*." He stood up and dumped their trash back into the sack.

"Come, we should take a small walk and stretch our legs," he held a hand to her.

Her lips pulled in, she regarded his hand, then, she put hers in it and he helped her up. He didn't let go when they started walking.

Aware he could easily break her dainty little hand if he desired to, he was careful to keep his grip light, but tight enough she couldn't wriggle out, and he could absently stroke her soft skin with his thumb.

Their feet shuffled through tall grass smashing it down, the breeze ruffled her curls and the top of his wavy hair. The wind stirring through their shirts was on the chilly side, but the direct sun kept them warm.

Jeph glanced occasionally at Rebeka watching her enjoying the outdoors. The unusual trees and wildflowers she'd never seen before, and another type of antelope that bounced far across the open filed.

He scanned the area constantly keeping an eye out for predators. He didn't want to break her tranquility telling her to watch where she stepped, that she could disturb a basking snake, he rotated his gaze to scan the fields and sweep the ground as they strolled.

"So, Rebeka," Jeph said, "you did not tell me what you do for fun." He looked down at her. The wind kept her hair swirling around her back, tendrils tickled her face and sometimes caught in her lashes.

When that happened, he stopped them briefly and gently plucked the yellow strands out of her long lashes with strong thick fingers.

"Mmm," she considered what she liked to do.

"Well, I'm not really sure, Mr. Kajic. Most of my life has been spent at the school; they didn't allow for too much downtime, we had endless chores to do. I took piano lessons there, sewed clothes, knitted, I like to read."

"Hmm. So, when you were at home, did you do anything different?"

A soft smile lifted her pretty lips. "Since I've been home I've mainly baked. I enjoy cooking. Especially making cakes and breads and things like that. The past couple of months my sister has taught me how to play some video games. They weren't allowed at school. On weekend nights we were allowed two hours of television as a reward if we had no demerits that week."

Jeph kept walking, stuffing his ire. She said it all cheerfully as if she hadn't been a virtual prisoner in that cruel, fucking prison of a school her parents had forced her into.

"You have a sister?" he asked. "Is she the only one? Do you have brothers too?"

"No, Que- uh, my uh, sister, she's older, she's my only sibling. Actually, we are stepsisters."

"Does she watch out for you? Take care of you, teach you cool things?" He didn't show it, but he was intently studying her while she spoke.

She'd been lighthearted, speaking gaily about things she used to do. When she mentioned her sister, her tone changed, saddened, but she worked to hide it.

One shoulder shrugged absently as she replied, "No, not really. My being home so rarely, and now only for the past six months, we barely know each other."

"Ah." Gaze intent on her he asked, "Is she like you? Soft, sweet, shy as those graceful gazelles, is she as beautiful as you?"

Does she have the same blossoming scent of the freshest wildflowers that makes a man want to shove his face all over every inch of your body to inhale you, and lick you?

"Beautiful? Me?" Snorting a deprecating laugh, shaking her head, without a stitch of jealousy, she said, "No, I am obviously not beautiful, but she, my sister, she is beautiful. She won some pageants when she was little.

"She's tall like a model, and has a much stronger build than me, and she is definitely more confident than I am. She has gorgeous red hair, hazel eyes and lots of curves. The boys just love her."

"Boys? Surely if she is older than you she dates men. Grown men." Jeph watched her lemony brows draw down in thought, she nodded.

"You're right, Mr. Kajic. I've spent my life in school, I forget that we are adults now."

"Uh huh. So how old are you, Rebeka?" he asked casually.

"I'm-" her eyes canted to the side. Jeph knew people's behavior, and she was about to lie to him. He's seen her lie before, and for such a streetwise person she's piss poor at it. She stammers and turns red, and can't look the person in the eye, and just gives up.

Then she smiled. "You know how old I am, you said you knew everything about every prisoner. You're playing with me," her laughter was nervous yet oddly sincere.

"*Yah*, sure. So, you did not answer my question. Is your sister, what is her name? Is she like you? Her behavior, I mean."

Rebeka ignored the part about her sister's name. "No, not at all. She is...adventuresome, sometimes too much so and gets into trouble. She goes out and has fun, dances, drinks, dates. Not like me, I'm just the little house mouse, you know?"

He kept his long legs even with her shorter strides. A genuine smile lifted his hard face. "*Na* one would describe you as a mouse, *nishka*. Sweet shyness, kindness, being polite and courageous are not mouse-like characteristics."

Keeping her pace, on the terse side he said, "And you are beautiful, Rebeka, I don't know who has told you differently. Or why. I find that unnecessarily cruel."

She tipped her head up to him with a cautious smile, "You think I'm brave?"

The sun turned her milky skin to warm honey, he wanted to kiss her, suckle her, do more. So much more. "*Yah*, very. Too brave for a little girl like you."

Rebeka strolled quietly beside him absorbing his words. She frowned, "I am not a little girl, Mr. Kajic."

"The way you call me Mr. Kajic makes me think of you as a little girl. It makes me feel old. Maybe we would both feel better if you called me Jeph, like my friends do." He glanced down at her to catch her pulling her lips in, as if trying not to bite back her words.

When she didn't say anything, he said, "Well? What do you think?"

Looking at him then away, sadly, with a hint of anger, she said, "You are holding me prisoner, we are not friends," and tugged her hand from his clasp.

His chest rose with the deep breath he inhaled, then he let it seethe out slowly. He abruptly stopped walking and grasped her arm to stop her.

The hard face cross with irritation, he said sternly, "*Yah*, maybe not friends. But, we will be lovers, and lovers do not call each other by their last names."

Her lips parted in surprise and he caught up her jaw to kiss her- Rebeka swung from his hold and quickly turned back to where they'd left the car.

Her head down, she hurried across the tall grass ignoring him calling to her.

Eyes on the car, she wasn't watching where she was going- out of nowhere a jungle cat, a mountain lion vaulted from a row of dense shrubs and leaped on her- slamming her to the ground so hard the wind knocked out of her, she couldn't scream.

Trying to suck in a breath, Rebeka rolled into a ball expecting the huge incisors to slash into her head, its claws lashing her body, instead she heard a roar as Jeph hurled himself at the big cat.

He barreled into the cat hard enough to stun it and dislodge it off Rebeka.

When the cat landed on its side, on his knees, Jeph had his gun in his hand and he emptied it into the lethal feline.

Roaring and howling, throwing its head back with snarls and mouth wide exposing huge, curved sharp canines, the cat slumped but still threw out clawed paws trying to scrape at Jeph as he knelt between the animal and Rebeka.

Covering her head, Rebeka screamed with the deafening bang of each bullet that slammed into the yellow fur.

The cat steadily grew quieter, struggled less, until it fell still and silent, but Rebeka's screams still rent the air.

Jeph moved carefully to the lion. When he was sure it was dead, he crouched beside Rebeka.

Her hysterical screaming didn't stop, he wrapped her in his arms holding her to his chest. He spoke in his language, then realizing it, he switched to English, murmuring, "Tis *bine* now, *nishka,* shh, he is gone, he cannot hurt you."

Her terrified body vibrating like a tuning fork, Rebeka shoved her face into his chest, gripping his shirt in her fists, she sobbed.

Jeph stroked her hair and continued murmuring that she was okay.

When she eased, he cupped her face with both hands lifting it. Her lashes wet spikes over eyes swimming with tears like blue pools. Lips quivering, she turned to look at the animal, but he held her head firm.

"*Na, nishka,* you do not want to see it." He pressed a kiss to her forehead, then set a light one on her lips. "Let me see, are you injured?"

He set her back so he could check her over. "Ah, a few scrapes and bruises, but no broken skin or bones." Combing his thick fingers through her messed silky hair he asked gently, "You all right now?"

Her lashes swept down making fringed shadows on her red cheeks. Unable to speak, she nodded with a hiccup.

"*Bine*, come." He stood up and pulled her up with him.

Cupping her chin he chided quietly, "You learn your lesson, Rebeka? You stay by my side at all times; you do not run from me."

Confusion muddled her eyes. Still shaking, she kept her retort to herself.

Rolling his arm around her back, Jeph kept her turned so she wouldn't see the dead mountain lion as they made their way back to the SUV. He stopped briefly at the fallen tree and picked up the sack that had held their lunch.

He hated to have had to destroy the beautiful wild animal just doing what it needed to, to eat, but Jeph was not going to let Rebeka be the beast's lunch. Now, the cat will be someone else's meal.

Jeph opened the door and lifted her inside and tossed the sack of their trash into the back before climbing behind the wheel.

"Buckle up, *nishka*," he said quietly, firmly.

Sniffing, staring unblinking out the windshield she did as he said.

Back on the road, Jeph's fingers clutched the wheel. Seeing the huge cat leaping on her, taking her down, Jeph's own had breath caught in his throat. It took a lot of effort on his part to not pound the wheel with his fists and curse a blue streak to alleviate the pressure from the terror that had gripped him.

He glanced at her, she was still trembling all over, sniffing back the tears. A hell of an experience she'll never forget.

Feeling his glances at her, Rebeka gave him a watery smile. "I'm okay, Chief." A shaky laugh, she said, "It'll be a heck of story to tell, huh?"

Smiling in relief that she wasn't terribly traumatized, he patted her knee. "See? As I said, courageous."

Her laugh genuinely gleeful, shaking her head she said, "No, I was the screaming crybaby, you were the brave one."

He patted her knee again and faced the front. "*Na, níshka*, it was all pure reflex."

Shaking her head again she started to say something but they hit a severely rocky terrain and the car jounced and rocked like crazy. Rebeka grabbed the door handle to keep herself steady.

They didn't stop again until they reached the hotel for the night. Jeph got a room, carrying their bags, he walked her up a flight of stairs.

Unlocking the door, as always, he made her wait outside while he checked it out first.

It only took a moment. "*Bine*, come in, Rebeka."

When she gingerly entered the room, on edge, as if another cat waited, lurking, ready to pounce, he said, "Go ahead and clean up, I will get us something to eat."

She nodded wordlessly and went into the bathroom.

When the bathroom door shut and locked, Jeph hurried out the front door and downstairs.

They had reached a larger city and the hotel was much nicer. It had a restaurant and a bar. He strode straight to the bar ignoring the interested women watching him.

"Yes, sir, what can I get you?" the bartender, wiping his hands on a white towel greeted him with accented English.

"Give me a double, make it a triple bourbon, neat, make it fast," Jeph ordered, and pulled out a pack of crumpled European skinny cigars. Lighting one, he sucked hard on it.

As soon as the bartender brought the drink, Jeph set Euros on the counter and downed the alcohol in one long swallow. He wanted to order another drink, hell, he wanted to take the entire bottle to the room, but he couldn't be drunk and keep Rebeka safe.

Stubbing out the cigar, he left the bar and trudged back up the stairs. Pushing the door open, he stopped dead in his tracks, dark eyes wide and lit with sudden fire.

Rebeka was standing by her suitcase, wearing only towels. One wrapped around her hair, the other around her body. Water drops glimmered along her bare shoulders and half exposed mounds of her breasts still pink from the hot shower.

Jeph's stunned gaze dropped to where the towel hit at her thighs. A slow swallow, he gulped down the lancing lust that squeezed his balls and hardened his dick in seconds. She was stark damned naked under that towel. One move and he could-

Her head flew up when she heard the door open, hand paused midair at the open case. "I, uh," she grabbed up the shirt he'd leant her to sleep in and a clean pair of panties.

"I forgot to get, um, stuff, before I, you know, I saw you were gone so I…" turning bright red, clutching the clothes in her hand she turned and fled back to the bathroom.

Jeph stood frozen. The vein palpitating madly at his temple, his erection clawing to get out of his pants and at her, pink silk panties danced in front of his eyes. He closed them, shook his head to clear the vision.

When he opened them, she was gone.

Letting out an aching sigh, he thought, *I should just fucking chain her up and go bang some bitch, there were plenty that eyed him with lurid invitation downstairs*. But, he sighed, tasting ashes in his mouth at the thought, his stomach curdled. He only wanted Rebeka.

Sex had always just been a meaningless release to him. But with this girl, he was consumed with thoughts and desire of her. It was time. Soon. He would have to take her whether she was ready or not. He was a man, not an angel. And sure as hell not a eunuch.

He was still routed to the spot when she came back out dressed in his long shirt. The fact that she only wore the shirt and those pink panties made his head spin. "You done?" he asked casually.

"Um, yes."

"*Bine*, get in bed," he said.

He waited until she drew those shapely slender legs up into the bed with the covers pulled up to her chin before he came over and bound her wrist to the bed frame.

Keeping his eyes on the wrist he was cuffing, his mouth was a tightly pressed line.

"Mr. Kajic," her voice wobbled.

"Hmm?"

"Thank you. Thank you for- for saving me."

"Ah, sure," he mumbled, as if throwing oneself at a jungle cat in the wild was an everyday occurrence. He snapped the cuff closed.

A small yawn rolled out with her sleepy words, "I mean, I know you did it because of the money, but still, thank you."

His lids low over dark eyes hid the ire that struck them. Setting her cuffed hand on the bed, he grabbed some clothes and went to take a long, long shower.

Pink glistening skin floated through his mind, actually, it might not be that long.

Chapter Twenty-One

The drive the next day was quiet. Jeph brooded, and Rebeka's brain churned with wondering how much time she had left, and what exactly would happen when Kajic took her to his employer.

He would bring her in, hand her over to the fiend, then leave. He would get his money, wipe his hands of her, and she would never see him again.

The city they drove through was large, teeming with people and buildings, yet the structures didn't appear so modern.

Rebeka still didn't know what country she was in because everything she'd seen was written in a different language, and he kept her away from other people.

The buildings were beige and white, and made mostly of brick and stone. A few onion-domed structures in the distance led Rebeka to think they were near the Middle East.

She had originally thought Africa, and still, she really didn't know. At least there was more to look at now than just endless fields and hills.

People in loose pants and jackets strode quickly down the streets. They were all shades of brown, some olive toned. Dark hair and dark eyes, most had heavy features.

There were signs in stores, but again, she couldn't read what they said. Apparently Jeph could, because he parked at a building.

The more he spoke, the better his English was, he managed to toss in contractions here and there. They had been traveling all day and both were tired, and quiet.

When he got out and came over to retrieve her, wearily she asked, "What does that sign say?"

He looked to where she pointed. A sign posted near the road had writing and a picture of more onion-domed buildings.

Jeph answered, *"Blizhniy Vostok."* He gripped her waist and lifted her out.

"Oh," she said when he set her down. "Mr. Kajic, I feel like a child when you pick me up like that, and," she peeped over her shoulder at an elderly couple watching them from the street. "It makes people stare."

A corner of his lip cut up in an unaffected smirk. "I don't care, Rebeka, what other people think. You almost hurt yourself last time you got out on your own, tis not going to happen again."

He closed the door and clicked the remote locking the vehicle. A big hand on her lower back, he urged her towards the entrance of what appeared to be a hotel.

"I know, damaged goods can't bring in a decent price."

Exhaling harshly, he said, "Do not start shit, Rebeka."

"You can just give me a hand out, Mr. Kajic, not carry me," she chided mildly.

His fingers dug into her back holding her, making her stop walking.

Quizzically, the blues eyes turned up at him with raised brows.

Frowning down at her, his mouth bunched with irritation. "I told you, Rebeka, I don't like you calling me Mr. Kajic. I am not your professor or an old man. Knock it off." Annoyed, his gaze rolled peeved down her body.

She wore borrowed jeans and a white cotton blouse that had a bunch of pink bows all over it. A bow was attached to every button, on the sleeves and a few along the bottom. It was very feminine and childlike at the same time. Just like her.

The sun lowering behind her lit her blonde hair making it glow a curly golden halo, the breeze tossed glinting wisps around her face.

A twinkle in her eye, she swung from him starting to walk away and tossed over her shoulder, "Okay, Chief, whatever you say-"

He caught her arm, swinging her back to face him. Perturbed lines etched around his mouth stiff with annoyance, and unsatisfied desire, his brows twitched with pique.

She took a step back from the anger crackling in his eyes. Holding her taut, he snapped, "Not funny."

The twinkle banished from her eyes, her own anger replaced it. "Okay, fine. How about Owner then? Or Master, or maybe Jailer?"

Fingers squeezing her arm, he lowered his face closer to hers. Low voice threatening, he glowered, "How about we talk about respect again when we get in our room? Remind you how you are to do as I say while my hand is meeting your ass?"

They glared at each other. She dropped her eyes first and said, "Calling you mister *is* respectful."

"Not when I tell you not to." Onyx eyes steely under crocodile hooded lids, voice silky and dark with suppressed fury and impatience, he said, "You do it to keep distance between us. I told you to stop. You will do what I say. When we get inside I will reiterate it for you if you wish, while you are bare-assed over my lap. Does that suit you?" He was getting hard thinking about it.

Rebeka tugged at her arm but he held her firmly. Nose in the air, she sniffed, "I don't understand why you care what I call you or if there is distance between us. We have no relationship, not even friendship. You are my jailer and that is all."

His long fingers wrapped around her slim arm stiffened, tightened as his lids lowered leaving only black glittering at her. His rigid shoulders were wrought with tension.

Letting out a breath lowered them slightly. "It doesn't matter what you think, you will do as I say. My name is Jeph, you will use it from now on."

He pulled her closer and up on her toes, the heat of his breath wafted against her face. "You have not yet seen me truly angry, *níshka*, I suggest you stop provoking me. I have had a lid on my temper, do not push it off."

Yellow lashes fluttered up and down as she was forced to look directly into his angry face. When she said nothing, he set her on her feet and released her.

"Come," was all he said, his hand on her back again to walk her to the entrance.

Under her breath she mumbled, "Sure, Mr. Dictator, I would love to see this lid you claim-"

"What?" he barked, squeezing her back. "What did you say?"

"Uh, nothing," she said quickly. "You were going to tell me what that sign said."

He glanced back at it. "*Blizhniy Vostok,* it says Middle East in Russian. Tis an advertisement for travel."

217

Inside, he paid for their room and they went upstairs.

The room was large, a suite actually, and softly comfortable. Colorful tiled floor with throw rugs, cushioned chairs, small divan and satin comforter on the bed, all in gold with gold drapes made the room appear pleasant and warm.

Unlike the man who prowled by the window with his cell phone in his hand. He grumbled, "I cannot get reception here."

Seeing her standing awkwardly, he grunted, "What is the problem? Why are you not unpacking? You have the iReader I bought you to read books and listen to music, watch movies, why aren't you using it?"

The last town they stayed in they had hit a few shops to update their personal toiletries and get a blow-dryer for Rebeka.

Jeph bought her the iReader with an account to purchase what she wanted, and for some reason, Rebeka couldn't fathom, he had bought her a watch. A beautiful gold watch, slim for her small wrist, with flashing diamonds.

When she asked him why he bought it, he had only shrugged noncommittally while he fastened it on her wrist.

He had to show her how to use the iReader, she'd never seen one before. The boarding school was kept deliberately stark to keep the girls simple and out of trouble, as well as limit their contact with the outside world. Even television was forbidden except as a reward on the weekends.

She crossed her arms and cocked her head at him.

He glanced around. "Oh."

Due to their argument he had forgotten to bring their cases up. Grabbing up the keys he'd tossed on the desk, he started for the door, then stopped.

He turned and walked back to Rebeka, biting back his vexation at her shrinking from him. He pulled the cuff out of his pocket and saw her face fall.

Jeph contemplated locking her up while he was gone. He worried about leaving her abjectly vulnerable if he wasn't there and a fire happened, or a robber broke in.

Holding the cuff in both hands, he lowered his head and looked up at her through a lock of black hair that flopped over one eye. "Rebeka, can you promise me you will not leave this room if I do not cuff you?"

They had discussed this before, and she would not lie and promise him so he had kept her confined.

Watching the conflicting emotions pass over her face, he said, "I do not like leaving you vulnerable. Please, swear to me."

Her arms still crossed over her chest, her eyelids lowered briefly, then rose presenting the bright blues beaming with honesty and vitality. "Okay, yes. I promise I will not leave the room today if you do not cuff me."

Through slit lids, he studied her for deception.

Except for a few paltry terrible lies she'd made when answering questions about herself, most were just avoidances, he had found no deception in her the entire time she'd been at the camp and on the road with him.

She had attempted escape, but she never said she wouldn't, and had refused to promise she wouldn't.

His head snapped in a sharp nod, "*Bine*. I will be a while. I have calls to make and I need to find reception." He set the cuff and chain on the bed and started for the door.

Opening it, he paused, looked back at her with that hard, ruthless face and said, "I am trusting you, Rebeka, if you run, I will catch you, count on it. I will be beyond pissed, you will suffer my wrath. Those little smacks on your pussy will be nothing, you understand me?"

Face reddening at his vulgarity, arms crossed, she nodded. Then said out loud at his brows dropping, "Yes, I understand, Mr. uh, Jeph."

She was rewarded with a softening of his face, his eyes on her mouth when she'd said his name.

His hand on the door handle he said, "Do not open the door to anyone. No one but me. Got that?"

Rolling her eyes, she smiled. "Yes, yes, I understand, go already, I have a book I want to finish."

He almost smiled back at her, then he shut the door.

Rebeka went into the bathroom to wash her hands and face.

"Wow," she exclaimed stepping into the enormous marble palace. A huge hot tub with swirling jets overlooked a big window.

"As soon as he brings me my clothes I am getting into that," she promised herself. Bath salts and bubbles along with the basic cotton balls, ear swabs, body lotion etc. lined a glass shelf.

She spent a long time thinking about the bath she was going to luxuriate in. After a while, she left the bathroom and wandered through the rest of the place to check it out.

Eventually she returned to the living room and went over to the window.

There was a small balcony with a table and chairs overlooking the city. She thought, *the room must have cost a fortune.*

Out loud she murmured, "Why would he spend the money like that when they had passed numerous lesser hotels?" When they had shared personal history stories, he had told her he'd slept in caves, on rocks, in marshes, in deserts, it never mattered to him where he laid his head.

Her hand on the handle to the balcony, she was just about to open it when there was a knock at the door. Puzzled, she turned her head to the door. Who on earth could that be? Maybe Jeph had lost his key.

She hurried to the door and peeked through the peephole. A face was in the hole but it was so close she could only see a blur.

Stepping back, she called out, "Who is it?"

"Room Service, Ma'am. Your husband ordered wine and food to be brought to the room."

"Oh!" How considerate of him. He had ordered food for them before, but he was always in the room when it was brought, with his gun tucked in his waistband at his back, and had made her wait in the bathroom.

Opening the door, she said cheerfully, "This is so nice, but I don't have any money for a tip." Jeph always tipped the attendants. "You will need to come back later when he is here-"

The door slammed into her knocking her backwards.

Just as she hit the floor, a hand grabbed her blouse, jerked her to her feet and a fist bashed into her jaw stunning her.

Rebeka was barely conscious as she was hauled over a shoulder. Her body flopped, hair swayed as she was carried down the hall with a quick stride.

By the time they went out a side door, she was regaining her faculties. As they hit the outdoors, she yanked a pink bow off her sleeve and dropped it.

The man hurried down the street.

Kicking her legs, Rebeka punched his back and screamed. A hand slapped her bottom so hard it stung and brought tears to her eyes. "You fight me, bitch, I'll give you a sock in the eye you won't never get over," and he pinched her leg until she cried out.

He threatened, "Don't fuckin' scream or I'll peel the skin right off ya," he pinched her hard again.

As he carried her down the street pinching her and slapping her legs and butt apparently now just for fun, she yanked off bows and dropped them.

They went a few blocks, he stayed to the alleys to attract less attention, although at the time of day, evening was settling over the city, the streets were emptying, shops closed. When he turned down another alley he came to a stop.

A man was waiting there. He exclaimed, "Fuck me, Joey, you got the bitch! Good fucking job!"

A third man said, "What about him, the chief? Where is he? How the fuck did you get her away from that bruiser?"

The man carrying Rebeka answered, "We been watchin' 'em for days, Brooks, he finally left her alone. He had to go down the street to use his phone."

Shifting her over his shoulder, he was a big man with broad strong shoulders and a tough voice. He asked, "Where's the fucking car, Dempsey?"

The man named Dempsey said, "He's comin'. All these fucking one-way streets it takes forever to get anywhere. Just hold onto the bitch, he'll be here in twenty or so."

Joey, coughed then spat on the ground. His huge hand moved to cover Rebeka's butt. Squeezing it hard enough to make her whimper, he said, "I got somethin' we can do while we're waiting, huh?" His voice held a leering grin.

The man Brooks grabbed a fistful of Rebeka's hair. Jerking her head up, he got in her face.

Onions blew up her nose, she looked at the thug breathing onions and cigarette smoke in her face.

His jaw was unshaven, stubble days old covered it. His nose was long and hooked, his eyes greedy, voice a sneer, he smiled at her with crooked teeth. "There's a couple of closed stores we can break into to take our turn wit her. Let's check 'em out, see which ones don't got alarms."

The others agreed and trotted down the alley, Rebeka still flung over Joey's shoulder, his big hand groping her butt.

Chapter Twenty-Two

*J*eph knew she was gone before he got there, the fucking door was wide open.

He rushed inside and checked out each room just in case. His presumption was correct, she was gone.

Racing down the hall to the stairs, he felt his heart pounding against his ribs. He was struck with a more profound terror than when the mountain lion had sprung on her. At least he could see her, do something tangible to save her.

His brain scrambled with fear, he couldn't form a thought as he hit the bottom of the stairs and flew across the room to the front desk.

The bitch had no idea what danger she was in. People were after her, although the hotel was swanky, they were in a considerably dangerous city. She would not get out alive.

Hurrying up to the desk, he beckoned the attendant to come to him.

The young guy was tapping on a computer, he said in broken English, "Yeah, be right there, sport."

"You get your motherfucking ass over here- now- or I am coming over that fucking counter."

The kid turned to look at Jeph.

Jeph's face was dark and scrunched with fury. Fists clenched, he appeared to be about to hop the counter.

The kid hurried over to him. "Yes, sir?"

"A petite, beautiful young woman with blonde hair almost to her ass, have you seen her?"

"Uh, uh, uh," the kid's lips flapped uselessly.

Jeph was a terrifying sight, hulking, enraged, the kid couldn't speak.

Jeph reached over the counter, grabbed the kid's shirt in his fist and hauled him over the desk onto his stomach.

"I asked you if you have seen her? Answer me before I knock out every one of your fucking teeth."

"Uh- uh," the kid could feel the piss running down his leg. "I ain't seen her, sir. Just a guy come in, described her, sounded like your wife. He- he said he was her brother and was there to hook up with her. Wanted her room number."

"So you fucking gave it to him?"

"Uh, uh," the kid nodded, wheat colored straight hair flipped up and down over his petrified eyes.

"How long ago? Did you see them leave?"

"N- n- no, didn't see them leave, he was here like about 15 minutes ago-"

Jeph shoved him so hard back over the desk the kid slammed right on his ass on the floor. He didn't get back up until he heard the entrance door open and close.

Livid with blind rage, Jeph tore around the building thinking of how he was going to beat her ass when he got his hands on her.

Thinking they had to have gone out a side or back exit, he sprinted around the hotel until something caught his eye.

A pink bow lay on the ground. He crouched and picked it up, held it in his palm. It was lying outside a side door under an alcove.

225

Grousing furiously out loud, he snarled, "The guy must be someone she met at the camp. Must have somehow contacted him, told him where she was."

Fuming on super high, he was on the verge of exploding. "Bitch must have been so excited to be with her lover they made out right fucking here."

Picturing Rebeka and some guy making out so hot and heavy the bow got torn off her blouse, he crushed it in his hand. Then saw another one a few feet away on the sidewalk.

He went to it, bent and picked it up.

It was a match to the one in his hand, he shoved them both in his pocket and started searching for more.

Jogging down alley after alley, he would almost give up that direction then he'd see another bow lying on the dirty ground.

He was imagining Rebeka and her guy making out so furiously that next he'd find her blouse, then bra, then-

Thinking he heard glass breaking, Jeph slowed his step. Stuffing the latest bow in his pocket, he crept down the dank, brick-lined alley to the next one.

Passing dumpsters against the walls, and traipsing on litter covering the broken-up tar walk, he heard the rumble of male voices. Stealthy steps to the end of the alley, Jeph leaned up against the wall to listen.

"You snatched her, Joey, you get first fuck," a man said. "I'll climb through, go inside and unlock the door. You guys go around front and wait for me."

There was a scuffling, shuffling sound, more tinkling of glass hitting the ground.

Jeph carefully rolled his head around the edge of the brick building to look.

He saw three men. One was standing looking down the far end of the alley, opposite to where Jeph was. Another was opening a door from inside a building, and the third had Rebeka up against the wall, his body pressed against her, their heads together, Jeph couldn't see her face.

She wasn't screaming, she must be fucking loving it. The whore she was, she was doing all three of the fuckers.

His eyes on the guy not with Rebeka, Jeph watched for a weapon as he sprinted towards them.

When the man realized there was someone there and turned around, his mouth dropped open, Jeph roared- his boots hitting the tar like a snare drum he launched himself at the man.

The man yanked a gun from the back of his pants, before he could get it up and aim it, Jeph was on him.

Jeph bashed his fist straight into his nose. With his other hand he grabbed the arm the man was reaching for the gun with. Jeph put both hands on the man's arm and slammed it over his knee.

The bone breaking was a sickening sound in the close brick walls of the alley. He hit him again silencing the man's scream, knocking him out cold.

Jeph turned to the man holding Rebeka against the wall, but at a sound behind him, he swung around as the man who had opened the door leaped out at him.

The man's weight hurled both men to the ground. The thug pulled a knife out and slashed at Jeph, Jeph sucked his stomach in to avoid the blade and smashed his fist into the man's face.

They shared a couple of punches before Jeph wrestled the knife from the man and stuck it in the thug's chest.

The thug stared down at the knife, his eyes wide, watching his life blood pouring out, down his shirt to the tar road.

Jeph jumped up as Joey flung himself at him, he dodged him pitching his fist into his stomach as he hurtled by. Road-burn scraped Joey's face as his body scuttled on his belly across the tar.

Jeph followed him, bent over, grasped his head and slammed it a few times on the road until the man stopped moving.

Then he stomped over to Rebeka. She was leaning against the wall, hunched over, her hair covering her face. Jeph roughly grabbed her arm and without a word to her, dragged her down the alley.

"Jeph," she sobbed as he more carried her than she was walking on her own two feet.

A string of non-English curses roiled from his throat in a fierce guttural growl, he snarled, "You need to shut up."

"Jeph-" her voice catching in her throat she winced at his vice-like clutch on her arm.

He stopped so short she fell into him. Jeph stuck his fingers under her jaw forcing it up.

Her big blues were awash with tears, he wasn't buying it again. Snarling the ferocity of his rage at her, he said, "You need to fucking shut up, Rebeka, or I will make you and it will not be pleasant."

Glaring at her for a heartbeat, he tightened his hand on her arm and dragged her back to the hotel.

He took her in the back entrance and up the stairs. When they reached their room, he shoved the door open and pushed her inside.

Without looking at her, he plopped down on a chair and removed his boots.

Rebeka stood by the door, her arms wrapped around her shaking body.

His head lowered, Jeph stuck his fingers in his hair and clutched his head to calm his raging body. Hearing her sniffle, he slowly raised his head, his furious eyes clouded with wrath narrowed at her.

Getting to his feet, he moved to her, stopping a few feet away.

"Jeph-" she tried again.

"Shut. Up. You promised me, Rebeka, I fucking trusted you. What a stupid, gullible asshole I am, huh?" His head shook side-to-side with a wry smile. "Joke is on me, huh?" he took a step closer to her.

So close she could see he was past control, the rage slit his eyes, grit his teeth, darkness seethed in his skin.

"Wait, Jeph, please-"

"Wait? Why Rebeka? So you can do some more stellar acting? You have finally shown your true colors, *Queenie Benani*, you have finally shown me the whore you really are. You would not give me a fucking kiss but you were going to fuck some slug on the street. Who was he? How did you contact your lover to come here and get you?"

Eyes wide as saucers she gaped at him, her mouth open. "But- but, no, I didn't know-"

He crossed his arms over his chest, biceps bulging under the long sleeved black shirt. His accent so thick in his rage he was almost unintelligible, he snarled, "*Yah*, sure honey, tell me some more lies. Keep it up and I will slap your lying face."

"Please listen to me, Jeph-"

"*Basta*! Enough" he barked, coming towards her. "I have listened to the last of your lies. I was patient, tried to give you time, let you get comfortable with me, my touching you. I waited patiently for you to come to me, but *na*. You stick your nose up at me and go fuck like the slut you are with some other prick."

Seeing him seething, eyes almost completely closed with his fury, his arms up to grab her, Rebeka gasped and started to run.

"Hell no, bitch," he grabbed her arm.

Frantically, she tried to wrench from him. Fear and panic gutting her voice, she cried, "No, please, Jeph, listen to me!"

"Done listening. I am going to do what I should have that first day I saw you. You are going to fuck with anyone, *Rebeka*," he said her name with sneering sarcasm, "it will be with me."

Jerking her to him, he gripped her blouse with both hands and tore it open. She shrieked and hit at him. Ignoring her puny punches, he jerked the blouse off her then deliberately tore it into pieces and threw them on the floor.

His fanatical eyes avid on her breasts mounding in the silky pink bra, he reached for them.

"Stop! Jeph, please-" Crossing her arms protectively over her front, she edged away from him.

Jeph clamped his fingers around one of her shoulders while he reached behind her and ripped her bra open then forced it off her.

Shrieking, Rebeka caught the torn silk and held it up against her breasts to hide them.

Jeph suddenly bent and lifted her in his arms and stalked through the living room to the bedroom where he dumped her on her feet.

Before she could react, he ripped at her belt, tore the button on her jeans open and shoved them down her body. He crouched, and pushed her over his shoulder while he dragged her jeans off then her shoes from her kicking legs, leaving the matching pink silk panties on.

Sobs wracking in her chest, clogging her throat she pleaded, "Please don't, Jeph, please listen to me."

Jeph mocked her, "Why the tears, sweetheart?" He said bitterly, "You that sorry tis me here about to fuck you and not your lover?"

Using his powerful chest, he pushed her up against the wall, snatched her wrists and held them over her head, then besieged her mouth.

All his fury and jealousy and sexual frustration came out in the assault on her mouth. His chest pumped with adrenalin and desire, he blew up hot fast. Boiling lava tore through his body like a volcano on the verge of explosion.

Bending his knees slightly, he shoved his burgeoning erection between her legs, forcing it hard against her core.

Lowering his hands to hold her upper arms with her hands still raised above her head, he consumed her mouth, her tongue, her air. Devouring and biting and sucking like the mountain lion would have done, Jeph was in a frenzy to possess her.

Taste and touch and demolish every square inch of her, outside and in. He should hate her, despise her for rebuffing him and giving herself to another, but he could not make himself stop. He had to have her under him, he needed to sink inside her, dominate her, feel her soft fresh body squeeze him, milk him, make her forget there ever was another man.

Huffing growls, grinding breaths roaring in her ears, his fingers cut off the circulation in her arms he gripped them so tightly. His body engorged with desire and rage fiercely mashing her into the wall, his chest crushing her breasts, erection pressed so hard into her he was practically lifting her off her feet, his bruising mouth ravaging hers.

Her sobs went into his mouth, her cries rained down his throat.

His breathing a roller coaster, Jeph leaned back from her, chest heaving, hair falling over eyes blind with his rampage. His face was wet with her tears.

Furious, he commanded, "Stop fucking crying, Rebeka, your act is over. You almost had me convinced I was wrong about you." His burning gaze bore into her terrified eyes blurred with buckets of tears, then they lowered.

He was going to fill his eyes and hands with her bare breasts, but something caught his attention on the way down. Loosening his grip a shade, he moved back from her a fraction, then growled, "What the fuck is that on your neck?"

An ugly red mark wound around the front of her neck, bruising smudges were starting to appear. He released her and stepped back, reached out and brushed the marks with the pads of his fingertips.

Rebeka covered her breasts with her hands.

"Rebeka?" his voice stunned and quiet, "they look like...fingerprints." His confused gaze rose to her face. For the first time he really looked at her.

A bruise was turning purple on her cheek; he traced it with his fingers. Her arms covering her bosom, she turned her head from his touch, the tears streaming down her cheeks, chest gulping with her crying.

Throat constricting in confusion and concern, he growled "What the hell, Rebeka? Tell me what the hell happened."

She dropped her head and moved so her hair would cover her face and her chest.

The fury vanishing from his face, Jeph said gently, "Tell me, Rebeka." He raised a hand to touch her, but dropped it when she turned from him.

Rebeka dashed at her tears with a hand trying to keep her front covered.

Taking a deep shuddering breath she said, "There- there was a knock at the door. This man called out he was from room service. Said you'd ordered food and wine to be brought to the room. I- I looked out the peephole, I saw his face. I didn't know, I didn't think-" tears poured, her voice broke off with a staggering sob.

The wind of his rage instantly vacuumed from his body. "Ah, Rebeka," Jeph moved to her, put his arms around her and drew her against the shelter of his strong broad chest.

He asked her softly, "What did he do, baby?" God, she was so fucking naïve, trusting, her view so childishly narrow of the wicked world. It was his fault, he should have warned her.

"I left my pink bows in case, maybe you would come for me, I left a trail of them," she cried against his chest, her breaths coming in sharp little surges.

She felt him move, he stuffed his hand in his pocket and pulled it out then opened his fist to show her. In his palm were the bows she'd dropped.

Jeph kissed the top of her head. "You are as smart and resourceful as you are beautiful." Another light kiss, he said quietly, "Tell me what he did to you."

"He," shifting her head to look up at him, hiccups cut up her words, "he hit me, stunned me. Then he threw me over his shoulder and took me. He..." she gasped for wobbling breaths.

"He met up with those other two men. They said they were going to...you know, assault me before they took me to someone. He was…strangling me to subdue me when you came."

Tears blurred then tumbled. Drawing in a raspy deep breath, she said, "You were there, miraculously, but then," she lowered her head back down. "You- hated me. Instead of being relieved, I was so scared when you dragged me back here. I thought…"

His hand covered the back of her head nestled against his chest. "You thought what?"

Another hiccup, "That…you were going to beat me, then…kill me."

He said on a sigh of remorse, "Ah, *nishka*," cradling her head he set his lips on top of it. "I am so sorry. I was," what? Consumed, insane with jealousy? He couldn't admit that to himself much less her.

Murmuring against her head he stroked her hair, "I thought you ran from me to be with another man. I…"

Sighing roughly, he said, "I did not, would not, ever strike you, Rebeka. You are so small, one hit and-" he wouldn't tell her one punch could kill her, that wouldn't make her feel too safe being with him.

Rubbing her face on his shirt, it was damp with her tears, "I hate this, Jeph. I hate being taken from my home, being held prisoner, being molested, you, everyone wants to hurt me. Those men…" a shudder ripped through her, shaking her so violently he crushed her to him, held her tight until it dispelled.

Exhaling pained air, Jeph curled two fingers gently under her chin, and raised it. "Did he say who they were taking you to?"

Wordlessly she shook her head and laid it back on his chest.

His growl ground through his chest vibrating against her cheek, "Motherfuckers." He bent and lifted her in his arms and carried her to the bed and set her on it.

"Get in, Rebeka, get in and stay there."

"But, I have no- no clothes. You tore my blouse and didn't bring the suitcase." Her arms and hair covered her nakedness like Godiva.

"Just get in, under the covers, and you fucking stay there until I get back. I mean it, Rebeka."

He bent over her, pointing a broad finger in her face and ordered, "You do not get up, you do not answer the door, if there is a fire you wait until I come back before you leave the fucking burning building."

He loomed with thick hard muscles cordoning across his back, his big hand in her face, dark eyes glittering the promise of punishment if she didn't do as he said.

Sliding under the covers, she asked, "Where are you going?"

He pulled the blanket up over her, said, "You don't need to know, just do not leave that fucking bed." Stroking his hand over her hair, he kissed the top of her head, then turned to leave.

"Jeph, you are not going to go hurt them more, kill them?"

"Do not get out of that bed," he ordered, and stalked out of the room.

As the door slammed behind him, he heard her call out, "Please don't kill them, Jeph, please!"

Her pleas fell on his deaf ears. If he had known when he was beating the shit out of them that they had taken her by force, had hurt her, he had to take a deep breath to calm himself. Had to force his fists to unlock.

As soon as they tell him who sent them, they were dead, and when he got Rebeka settled, he would go after the guy that sent them.

She would not need to know any of it.

Chapter Twenty-Three

$\mathcal{J}$f he chose to, Jeph could creep without a sound through a jungle, sneak up on the enemy, man or beast, and slit their throats, and they'd never hear him coming.

At least when he returned to the hotel room the door was closed this time.

Sighing, he dragged his sleeve across his forehead clearing the sweat that dripped in his eyes, and he slipped silently in the room.

Relief swarmed him when he saw it appeared the same as he'd left it. He set her suitcase and his duffle down. The room was dark, the sun had set, he hadn't left a light on.

The tiny kitchenette was dark, he crept down the brief hall, there were also no lights on in the bedroom. Either she was asleep, or gone.

A harsh breath filled his chest, if she was gone, fuck, he'd kill her when he found her. He would always find her. He could find anyone, that was a skill he'd honed from the military and the other work he did besides controlling the auction.

That made him think of when Rebeka was up on that goddamned stage. Drugged, half out of it, bound helplessly to the scalboard, the buyers gawking at her half-bared flesh, her tits and cunt scantly covered with a tiny bit of silk, and that bastard pawing her.

He still owed that fucking auctioneer, and he would also pay him a visit once he got Rebeka settled.

Hovering in the doorway, he could see her small body, a curled lump under the covers.

A quiet exhalation of relief expelled lowering his taut shoulders, and a smile spread over his hard face. Jeph trod silently to the bed and looked down. He had trusted her and not cuffed her, and, he let out a pent-up breath, she was still there.

Of course he'd made sure she had no shirt to wear. Her head on the white pillow, blonde curls a tousled mess around her head. He wanted to sink his hands into that hair, grab handfuls and crush them in his fists.

Bring them to his nose and inhale her scent as deeply and as long as he wanted, then, rub the silken locks on his face, his chest, his dick, his balls.

Through the tiny bit of illumination from a nightlight strewn in from the bathroom, he could see the soft outline of her gorgeous face.

The long lashes curled on her round cheeks, perfect pouty lips closed as she breathed gently. His emotions had run the gamut from terror finding her gone, fury seeing her with that other man, jealousy and lust and rage blinding and deafening him to her pleas for him to listen to her.

He had only seen pure crimson. He had been seconds from throwing her on the bed and violently taking what the fuck he'd wanted from the second he'd laid eyes on her.

Even now the desire for her raged through his body, he was hard as iron. Jeph didn't kid himself, he knew even after he finally fucked her this mad obsession for her wouldn't leave him. Ever.

His goose was cooked as they say.

She stirred slightly as if she could feel the lust and emotion emanating palpably from him.

He went to touch her and saw the blood covering his hand. Damn. Taking one more look at her, he went into the bathroom to scrub the blood of four men off his body.

The one man he had killed when he took Rebeka. The two others, unfortunately, didn't put up much of a fight. He'd wanted a vicious brawl to release some of his rage, but they'd died too quickly.

The driver they had been expecting had shown up at the most opportune time. Jeph was able to extract the information he wanted before slaughtering him.

He dumped the bodies in the building they had broken into. Judging by the shit section of town and the many boarded up shops, it would be a while before they were discovered. He had time before he and Rebeka took off. He needed to change their direction.

Since those fuckers had found them, it was likely someone else knew they were there and would come looking for the dead men when they didn't check in. And then they would come after him and Rebeka.

Running his fingers through his wet hair, he trod in his jeans and bare feet to the knock at the door. The top button undone on his jeans, gun tucked in the back waistband, he wore no shirt. He didn't give a fuck what the room attendant thought.

Peering through the peephole, he saw the attendant he had insisted the manager introduce him to earlier. He wanted to know who would be coming through the door.

Turning on the light, he opened the door and stood to the side as the man in uniform of black and gold entered with a silver tray on his shoulder.

The man asked, "Where shall I set it, sir?"

"On the table." Jeph nodded to the coffee table and moved to stand between the attendant and the bedroom doorway with his hand behind him set on the gun. With Rebeka mostly naked in his bed, he was taking no chances.

"Yes, sir." The attendant set the tray down. It had covered dishes, a bottle of champagne in a bucket under a cloth, and champagne glasses. Reaching for the champagne, he said, "Sir, shall I-"

"*Na*. Get out," Jeph said curtly. Rudely, Rebeka would have said as she scolded him, he thought with an inner smile, like she had every time he'd been discourteous to someone.

Again, he thought of how his timid shy little girl had the spine of a warrior. She didn't take any shit even though she knew she could, would, get hurt for it.

The attendant froze bent over with his hands out. He was already nervous to come to the room. When he'd met the occupant earlier he'd felt faint with fear. Tenterhooks of alarm raised hairs on the back of his neck. The man was one of the most dangerous looking men he had ever seen.

It was in his fearsome face, unfettered violence gleamed from his hooded eyes. When Jeph turned, the attendant saw the gun and about wet his pants.

He snapped straight up. "Yes, sir, of course, sir," he pivoted on his heel and quickly strode to the door.

Jeph got there first and opened it, he handed him a hefty tip. That would assuage his rudeness Jeph figured.

Making sure the door was locked, he turned out the light and headed to the bedroom.

Silently opening the drawer on the nightstand, he stuffed a box inside.

Then he folded the blanket down, shoved the gun under the mattress and climbed into the bed in his jeans. Knowing she wore only panties, he needed some kind of barrier between them.

That thought sent a surge of blood to his dick. He wanted to fuck Rebeka so goddamned badly his brain fried along with his burning, throbbing body. However, he would control himself for now.

Between the damned mountain lion and now those assholes, not to mention his own shitty behavior towards her, she needed some peace and a sense of security to get over all the trauma she'd been through. Fighting him off all night was not going to help.

Here, he had been working on getting her to feel safe, comfortable with him, enough she'd let him get between her legs, and he'd fucked things up with the way he'd horribly manhandled her, stripped her, yelled at her, calling her names.

But, he needed to touch her, hold her, he wasn't going to sleep on the couch away from her. He would just have to suffer. Jeph shuffled across the bed and reached for Rebeka.

She took up so little space in the big bed. Rolling his arm around her, his hand on her stomach, he pulled her sweet body against him.

Knowing she was topless and wore only the silk panties was killing him, but he was careful to keep his hand tucked around her belly.

Even through the matting of hair on his chest, he could feel the satiny warmth of her back against him.

Tucking his knees up under hers, he lowered his head on top of the blonde fluff and put his nose in her hair.

Inhaling deeply, with the biggest hard-on he'd ever had in his whole damned life, he eventually fell asleep.

Chapter Twenty-Four

*J*eph woke before the sun rose. Of course he had huge wood. He could not wait any longer for her. He pushed the covers down and gently shifted Rebeka to lie on her back.

Brushing her hair aside so he could see every part of her, he knelt on the mattress sitting back on his heels, and drank her the fuck in.

Lying on her back so innocently, helplessly vulnerable, bare breasts rich mounds begging for his hands, his teeth. He gently took her ankles and opened her legs, spreading them apart. She wore only the tiny panties, nothing else. She was a goddamned goddess.

God, she was breathtaking. Her naked tits were more beautiful than he'd pictured in his mind. Plump and round and high. Soft damned pillows tipped with pink nipples also soft in her sleep. Her ribcage narrowed to the tiniest waist he'd ever seen.

She was the daintiest, most graceful female he'd ever had naked in his bed. His dick strained at his jeans, he gripped it while gazing at Rebeka's beauty.

He could sit and stare at her and those luscious fucking tits all damned day long. His fingers twitched and itched to grab them, feel her full flesh between his hard fingers, knead the hell out of them and suck his mark all over her creamy skin. Nip and bite and suckle those sweet little nipples. But, he wanted to use her sleep to arouse her.

His discreet seduction had worked, albeit briefly, before. She had thought she was dreaming and therefore didn't fight him, just let her body feel and respond. Now, he needed to up his game.

He had to keep her out of her head or she would shut him down. And, this time, he would make sure she knew who the hell it was making love to her, not some imaginary dream lover.

Huh, he grunted. He would be making love to this petite beautiful woman, not fucking her. His eyes fell to the tiny panties and he wanted what was under them. Now. See it, feel it, taste it, fuck it. Now.

Jeph carefully grasped the panties and pulled them down her legs and off. Tossing them to the floor, his gaze flamed instantly on her soft pink cunt.

Mouth watering like Pavlov's dog, he lightly stroked one finger over her tender woman's slit. His dick screamed in his pants. Soft, God, so fucking soft and supple, man, he was dying here. But he needed to stick to his plan.

He had seen and fucked a lot of women in his lifetime, but none drew him like this one. None made fire burn in his pants like this one, she sucked his self-control right out of him.

Jeph gently pushed her legs further apart and moved to kneel between them, the thick mattress barely moved under his weight.

Shifting down on his stomach, he put his hands on her thighs and held them while he lowered his mouth to that intoxicating pinkness. Waiting no longer, Jeph lightly drew his tongue up her slit and smiled when her body trembled. He raised his head to look at her, she didn't wake up.

Placing his thumbs on her feminine folds, he held them apart and licked her slit, bit her folds, tongued her sweet bud until it bound into a swollen bead.

Smiling, he glanced up her body and saw her nipples tighten just like her clit. When he set his mouth to her again, her hips moved and a tiny moan oozed.

His tongue on her sex, he tasted the honeyed silk that was slipping out of her as her body responded to his touch. Moving up, Jeph nipped her belly, licked it then settled back down between her legs.

Licking his way all over her pussy, he licked her folds, her slit, stuck his tongue deep inside her, and her hips squirmed and another moan rolled softly from her.

Peering over her body, he saw her shoulders ruffle in her arousal making her chubby breasts jiggle, *fuck*, he thought, *so fucking hot*. Her fingers moved slightly on the mattress.

Pressing his thumbs hard on her folds, he sucked hard on her clitoris and she bolted upright with a gasp.

He didn't stop.

Her mouth open, drowsy eyes widening, curls like yellow ribbons rolled over her beautiful tits. "Jeph! Oh my gosh, what are you doing?"

Elbows bent, her hands braced on the mattress behind her, she tried to close her legs, but that was impossible with a huge, broad shouldered man between them.

He kept licking her flesh, his thumbs pressing on her folds, he moved his thick fingers in a V to push them closed together and kneaded them. He nipped her clit before he sucked it back into his mouth to swirl his tongue around it.

"Uh," her head fell back with her gasp. Her entire body shuddered, shoulders rippled, hips jumped up at his mouth.

Coming fully awake, Rebeka tried to sit up and move her legs but he held her in his iron grip. "Jeph, please, what are you doing? Stop," she struggled to move back up the mattress away from him.

He clamped his hands down on her thighs and forked his tongue up her silken hole. Her neck arched, her head dropped back again with a gasping shriek as her body undulated with a mini orgasm. She fell back on the bed with a choked huff.

Lifting his head, he smiled, his jaw was covered with black scruff that was reddening the soft fairness of her thighs. "Rebeka, *nishka*, just lay there, feel what I do to you, do not fight me."

Breathing heavy, pushing her body back up, she tried again to break free from him, then he chomped down sudden and hard on her entire sex.

Another gasping shriek as another mini-orgasm roared through her. Her chest billowing with frantic shallow breaths, she cried, "Jeph, gosh, what are you- ohhh," she gurgled as he sucked her clitoris deep into his mouth.

Even as her hips wriggled against his mouth for more, she cried, "Please, you need to, ahh," gasp, "st- stop, uhh," groans whimpered up her throat.

Lathing her sex hard, rough, like a giant tiger, whipping his tongue fast over her bud, he nipped it and she about came off the bed.

"Jeph!" her shriek could be heard down the block.

Jeph grinned against her flesh. "Good girl, say my name again, baby, and again, I want to hear you fucking scream it."

Rebeka writhed at his mouth until she gathered her wits again and started struggling again to get free. She cried, "No, Jeph, you can't do this, please, I won't give into a murder-"

He set his big hand on her stomach pressing her down, holding her down and now worked her nub with his thumb.

Circling her clit, pinching it, his eyes on it, he said, "You fight me, Rebeka, even though you want me, you want this. You struggle because of who I am and our situation." He glanced up at her.

Her huffing breasts were flushing pink, her eyes transfixed and hazing.

He growled, "I will take the control out of your hands, you will not have to say yes and feel guilty, *Yah*?" Squeezing her clit, he bent and sucked quick snapping pulls at it.

Her struggles changed from trying to get away, to writhing against his fingers, his mouth. She tried to suppress the moans that roiled up her throat but they gushed out when he pinched her beading sensitized clitoris.

"Oh, Jeph!" she shrieked.

"*Yah*, baby, go with it, *yah*, good." While licking her woman's blossom, he pushed a thick finger inside her.

Shocked at the intrusion, she fought to move from his grasp again.

"What- are you, no Jeph-" Her breath was trapped in her tight lungs. Fear gripped her at his violation of her body.

"Please Jeph, I've never, please," she begged frantically wriggling from him.

Fire and electric pulses throbbed and stung in her sex. Unfamiliar with the sensations, she struggled for breath, trying to halt the desire that stormed through her body, making her head spin.

"Relax, Rebeka," he soothed, moving his finger in and out, gently at first, getting her used to it. He was surprised, and a bit uneasy to find her so small and tight. She was a petite girl, but her female channel was seriously small. So tight to his finger it was like she'd never been with a man before.

He had long concluded that the stories about her being a harlot off the street were clearly lies. He had an inkling so he'd put a plan in play, but until it all came to fruition he wouldn't know the complete real truth until it was revealed.

But for now, this was all about them. "Just feel me, honey, I will not hurt you, just feel me."

"Jeph-" her body gave a small spasm, she croaked in surprise. "Jeph, I-" a groan whittled up her chest and she could not stop her body from responding to him, she dropped back on the mattress.

Rebeka found herself grinding her hips at his hand and groaning louder, her breathing hastening. Her fingers found their way into his hair and tangled in it.

Plunging his finger in and out, fast and now harder, he bent his head, licked her slit then bit her clit.

Her cries turned to wheezing gasps, her hips writhing in his hands, a scream was flying up her throat then it exploded as her channel tightened on his finger. She doubled-up, folding forward as her body convulsed with her shrieks.

Her orgasm struck her, the climax grabbing her body and shaking the living hell out of her as she wrenched and buckled and cried.

Jeph pushed in a second finger, stretching her, curling them both inside her while pumping them in and out, relishing the silk that poured out, in his mouth, on his hand.

Her spazzing body uncontrollably jerked back and forth. He held her down, loving her gasps and groans as her tender sheath clutched and squeezed his fingers.

When she started calming, he withdrew his fingers. Rebeka flopped back on the bed like a boneless kitten, panting hard, crying, lungs hitching for air.

Wiping the back of his hand across his mouth, chuckling, Jeph tugged her spastic fingers from his hair and got on his knees.

Her chest heaving, Rebeka laid back with her hands up next to her head. Glassy eyes fogged with her climax, in a heady daze she looked up at him.

Kneeling between her legs, he unzipped his jeans, stuck his hand inside, rearranged then stroked himself. Then he leaned over her reaching for a bare breast.

Fighting to clear the orgasmic fog, Rebeka held her hands up to him. "No, wait-"

Expecting this, Jeph dropped down over her, resting on his forearms next to her shoulders. Still in his jeans, he maneuvered to lie between her open legs.

Their faces inches apart, he sucked at her lips until they were puffy and red. Their eyes connected, his storming with need, voice rough he reminded her, "You said anything I wanted, Rebeka, anytime."

Hair spread around her like a yellow cloud, big doll eyes teeming with agitation, her hands were pressed against his chest, body still twitching from her explosive orgasm. "I…" her mouth closed, eyes lowered.

"How about I make you beg me for it, will you do it then, *nishka*?"

Her eyes narrowed in bewilderment.

A smile curved his full, hard-carved lips. He murmured, "I think you are ready for another one, eh?"

Her confusion was huge in her blues. Her body was tingling, everything she was feeling was unfamiliar, strange, new, amazing.

Jeph said, "I am not sure what is going on, Rebeka, you are seriously small and tight, you act so green." His eyes raked over her, he said, "You never fucked King Martin, did you?"

Eyes wide and unnerved, she didn't answer him.

He lay atop her but braced his weight on his forearms. "I think you are a virgin, Rebeka." A brow arched, he asked, "Am I right?"

Her face bloomed with an embarrassed blush, she turned her head from him with her eyes averted.

He cradled her face, turned it to face him.

When her large eyes rose to his, he said softly, "I will go slow, baby, I promise. I will stop if you tell me to. But give me a chance, *nishka*." He moved his big hand down between her young legs and expertly stroked her sex.

She wriggled away from his touch, but didn't say anything.

Holding her down with his weight, keeping their eyes connected, he dipped his fingertip inside her to gather her silk. Spreading it on her clit, he circled it very, very slowly, and smiled when her hips moved slightly with him.

Her hands still pressed against his chest, but less rigidly.

While caressing her sex, he whispered, "You have never had an orgasm before, have you?"

Her eyes glued to his, she shook her said.

Smiling, he said, "Good. I have much to teach you, with the greatest of pleasure, *nishka*." He brought his mouth down to hers, licked her lips before sucking on them, then plunged his tongue inside and took her over, never ceasing moving his skillful fingers on her responsive body.

As her nerves relaxed, her body tensed with desire that he was slowly building in her. Her head lolled back, she closed her eyes.

Jeph thumbed her clit then penetrated her tiny channel with his thick finger. She didn't tell him to stop yet she resisted, but he persevered until his digit was completely buried in her.

Withdrawing it slightly he added the second. Moving them in and out, he searched around, seeking her hot spots. When she moaned and curled her legs, he grinned. The more her body squirmed and sinuated under him, at his hand, the faster he moved his fingers.

Soon, with a long spiraling groan, Rebeka shivered, her eyes opened then rolled back in her head. She was on the precipice, about to soar off again, and Jeph paused his strokes.

Huffing, her lashes flittered, chest heaved with fast shallow breaths; clouded eyes peered up at him.

He smiled. "You want more, baby?"

She nodded.

"*Bine*," and he built her up again and again only to stop each time as she was about to detonate.

"Jeph," gasping, a slight whine, "please..."

"Ah, my little baby, please what?" Heat burning in his dark eyes scoured over her face.

Whiskers a black shadow on his strong jaw, thick ridged brow low with desire and the strain of not plunging his manhood right into her, his harsh lips curved up slightly as he watched her dying for release but not knowing how to get it, how to ask for it, afraid of it.

Croaking, Rebeka cried breathlessly, "I- I don't know, help me, Jeph." Rasping whimpers jostled up and down her throat.

Heating her up again, he murmured, "Do you want me, Rebeka?" His fingers slid inside her, leisurely pumping. His thumb swirling her clit, driving her to the edge and then backing off until she was ready to scream in frustration.

"Answer me, baby, do you want me? Inside you? I will take you into orbit when I bury my dick inside your beautiful pussy."

He kissed her, feeling her soft full breasts press against the rocky muscular slabs on his brawny chest. He had slept shirtless, his undone jeans chafed their rough material against her soft thighs.

Groaning, Rebeka squirmed against him, rubbing her bare skin on his, her pointed nipples grazing over his flat ones. His own groans throbbed on her lips.

"I- I-" gasping, she pushed her body into his begging him for release.

"Tell me, baby," he whispered, his deep voice coarse with need. "Tell me yes. Tell me I can come into your body. I will stop if you say, but please, Rebeka, say yes."

Damn, he cringed; he had never begged anyone for anything ever in his life. Even when he was being whipped, his skin being stripped off his back, his legs, his chest.

He could force her, so easily, but he wanted her to want it, want him. Cupping her jaw, driving his fingers insanely inside her, he growled, "Say yes, baby, say yes."

Her head tipped back, eyes wincing in pain at his withholding her release.

Gripping the sheet in her fists, lips parted, her voice a bare whisper, "Yes, Jeph."

Chapter Twenty-Five

*H*is throat bumped at his hard swallow. Low, husky, he said, "Yes? You are saying yes to me burying my cock in your beautiful pussy, and taking us to heaven, Rebeka?"

A tremulous smile tilted her mouth, her eyes pleaded with him. Her burning body jerked urgently at his, trying to make him let her come, she uttered, "Yes."

"Oh fuck, *yah*, baby." He climbed off the bed, jerked the drawer next to the bed open and took out a condom from the box he'd put in there. He'd done it every night in hopes of her saying yes.

Shucking his jeans and boxers, he put his palms on the bed, got back on it, and stretched out beside her.

Her eyes rounding huge at seeing his thick rigid erection, her skin paled.

He netted her face with his long fingers, kissed her gently. Softly, he said, "Don't be afraid of me, Rebeka. The second you say stop, I will, *bine*?"

Curly lashes blinked at him. Her chest still heaved from the heat he'd fostered in her, leaving her hanging, her sex weeping, her body quivering for release. She nodded.

He wanted to make sure she was ready and willing, but he knew if he took too long she would remember who he is, how she got here, and where she was going, and she would shut him down.

Moving between her legs, he nudged them wider, and rolled the condom on then lay down just barely touching his body to hers. He covered her breast with his palm and his groan sounded like agony, his eyes scrunched in ecstasy.

Wrapping his long fingers over the big soft mound, he kneaded it, caressed it. His thumb raked over her nipple then he pinched it and she cried out in surprise.

"Ah, you like that, *yah?*" Bending his head, he sucked the nipple into his mouth. Catching it between his teeth, he batted it with his tongue while feeling her supple flesh, squeezing her breast until she was squirming under him making little hitching sounds.

Switching to the other breast he quickly licked her skin, sucked all over it before biting her nipple. At her yelp, he blew air on it.

She shivered in his hands, goose bumps rippled up her arms. The color rushed back into her cheeks.

Bracing on an elbow, he reached down to fist his shaft and pressed it at her opening.

Her nervous sharp inhale sounded in his ear. Rubbing the head of his shaft around her wetness, stroking her sex with it, he whispered, "Trust me, *nishka*, trust me to take care of you."

He had never fucked a virgin before, that he knew of. It was an honor and something that will set how Rebeka feels about sex for the rest of her life. It was his duty to make it wonderful and special for her.

To know he was the first, and only man to be with her, in her, made his heart quiver and clench, his cock pulsed like crazy. She was fully his to claim.

Slowly, he pressed inside her, pushing carefully, stopping to let her adapt to his girth. He was a big man and she was a small woman. She was frighteningly tight, small, so fragile in his strong hands, he had to be so careful not to hurt her.

"*God, baby*," he moaned hoarsely. He'd waited so fucking long for this moment, and as her soft sheathe wrapped around his hard shaft, it was heart-stopping magical.

She took his breath away. The shattering intensity of how she made him feel, how she felt, radiated from his exhilarated ebony eyes into her shaky blues.

"You *bine*, sweet? Ah, I mean are you all right?" He brushed her hair from her damp face.

She nodded. With a tiny breathy sound, Rebeka whispered, "Yes."

Then she smiled awkwardly up at his face so close to hers. "I'm…I mean you are filling me up so…uh," she groaned as he pushed deeper. "I'm…you're stretching me, Jeph. I'm so full."

Her face winced slightly; she wriggled under him to try to take him in more comfortably. Thank God for tampons or she'd have to suffer his breaking through her maidenhood. It was so long ago she'd torn her own hymen she hardly remembered the stinging pain.

"*Nishka*, it will be uncomfortable, at first, it will get better, I promise." He lowered his body more on her, he was dying to feel all of her skin on all of his.

They had a lot more things to do later, he wanted time to play with her tits, eat that pussy again, he had things to teach her. He pushed harder, further, deeper, letting her silk ease the way until he finally buried himself all the way inside her luscious body.

His iron hard dick wanted to slam into her like a wild man, but he couldn't, not until he got her used to him, his size, his strength. So tender, he would tear her up if he went at her like he wanted, like the savage that he is.

Pausing to let her woman's satin purse adapt to his thickness, he brushed her cheek with his thumb, then pushed it into her mouth.

She smiled around it, then sucked it.

"Oh shit, Rebeka!" He felt her sucking his thumb right down to his manhood, it swelled inside her, throbbing at her walls.

She rubbed her body against his with a shiver. Smiling, she told him, "It feels better, Jeph, it doesn't sting as much."

"Hmm, I do not just want feeling better, I want to send you over the moon, drive you fucking insane, little girl."

He wanted her to love it. Love him fucking her, to beg him to take her, not just now, but always, every damned fucking day. Fuck her so good she would never think of being with another man.

When he didn't move, a hint of rejection in her uncertain voice, she asked, "What's wrong, Jeph? Are you not...pleased with me?"

His smile warm, eyes shining satisfied, the top of his hair brushed her forehead when he lowered to kiss her tenderly.

Lifting his head to join their gazes, he told her, "Baby, you, this, is a thousand times more amazing, incredible, mind blowing than I had imagined."

He kissed the tip of her upturned nose. "I have dreamed of this moment, prayed to be buried deep inside you since that very first day."

He hadn't noticed her at first that day in the field at the auction grounds. She was so small and delicate, hidden by the bigger prisoners around her.

It wasn't until the soldier had put the spotlight on her by shouting at her to open her blouse that he saw her. Before the soldier ripped it apart, Jeph was already on his way to them.

The soldier was lucky he didn't die that day, Jeph was too intent on the new female prisoner to suffer him his wrath.

A few minutes later in his cabin when Rebeka lay unconscious in his arms, his mouth on her breast, he knew he was in trouble. His addiction for her flamed at that moment and only burned more intensely every minute of every day since.

"I," he looked slightly embarrassed. "I have wanted you for so long and you feel so extraordinary around me, under me, I am afraid I cannot hold back. I, ah," his dick pulsed against her walls causing her vagina to squeeze him, he jumped with a groan.

"Damn, Rebeka," his breath stroked her lips. "I needed to stop for a second or I would have exploded." *And gone nuts and hurt you with my out of control violent rutting.* His palm caressed her soft face.

Smiling up at him, she skimmed her hands over his chest, sifting her fingers through the masculine hair. When she wound her fingers behind his neck, pulling him down to kiss him, he started moving.

Jeph grinned into her mouth as he drew his shaft slowly out of her sheath, then pushed back in with her silk covering him, making the way slicker, slightly easier up her tight channel.

She had finally touched him in desire. Not the pressing her palms on his chest to push him away touching, but sexy strokes up his body and now she was combing her fingers through the hair at the sides of his head making him purr like a fucking cat.

"Ah, my *nishka*," he murmured a string of foreign words as he rocked into her, slowly starting a rhythm.

As she relaxed, the slight pain and discomfort diminished and her little hips rose to meet his.

His rhythm started to speed up as he dug deeper with each thrust, her sultry sighs inspiring him to plunge with more strength, faster.

He moved his heavy manhood all the way out then slammed back inside her so hard he pushed her up the bed forcing a grunt from her.

Bracing on an arm, he bent to suck at her breast. He cupped it, squeezed it up so he could clamp his mouth on it.

She made soft hungering sounds as he lathed her flesh, massaged her plump tit. His thrusts were slow and shallow then they picked up. Pistoning faster, he drove into her, unleashing more of his strength with each hard plunge.

Rebeka whimpered, gasped with the results of his rough strength. He bored into her so hard, thrust so fast she couldn't keep up with his drilling stabs into her tender body.

Her fingers clutched his shoulders, she could only hold on as he started rocketing. The friction, the way he forced his shaft over sensitive spots inside her sheath, and levered over her clitoris, she was bursting into flames, her body was literally screaming from the inside.

"Jeph," she gasped as he pinched her nipple, digging her fingers into his shoulders. "Oh- my- gosh, *Jeph!*" she wailed.

He pinched her nipple harder and drove into her with such tremendous power screams were forced out of her.

His mouth clenched, forehead furrowed, face contorted in his strain to hold out.

Biceps bulging, Jeph growled, "Fuck, baby, take it, take me deep, shit," he cursed blustering, puffing, slamming again and again into her like a crazed jackhammer.

Jeph wished they could last like this all damned day, but that wasn't happening.

Hitching cries gushing in his ear, Jeph reached between them to squeeze her clit, and again harder, circled it while shoving in her.

Growling, he grunted, barked at her, "Go baby, let go, babygirl-" Deep roars rumbled in his chest as he felt the heat building in him. His balls cramped, his dick burned, sizzled with his craving for release inside her.

Feeling her sheath clenching him, Jeph leaned back and caught her chin, moving her to look at him.

"Open your eyes, Rebeka, see the man who is claiming you, taking you, owning you, making you a woman, look at me," he commanded.

Her body shoved violently up and down, the enormous shaft roughly, aggressively forcing its way in and out of her virgin's body, slamming her so hard against the headboard he had to wrap his burly arm around her shoulder to hold her from hitting it.

It was the most amazing thing Rebeka had ever felt. Stars danced in her spinning head, like her entire body was stuck into a light socket. She felt an electric flush warm her entire body, cauterizing her skin, searing heat burned in her woman's channel, her belly, her breasts.

Jeph's voice low, quiet, squeezing her jaw he demanded, "Open your eyes, Rebeka, look at me."

When she didn't, he gave her chin a commanding little shake.

It was a struggle to force her heavy, drugged lids up. Delirium glazed in her half-mast blues, she raised them to see the fire blazing in Jeph's black discs. She could see the strain in his face, the scar white in the vein jumping at his temple.

When she looked at him, he unleashed his restraint and started powering hard and fast, so fast, her eyes turned white as they rolled back in her head with the scream wailing in her throat before it burst from her lips.

"Jeph!" she screamed. Her body thrashed wildly under him, the blistering flush raced up her chest to her face.

He cradled her head with one hand and shoved the other under her hips, gripping her bottom so he could raise her up. Jerking her to meet his thrusts like he was using her to masturbate, he hammered mercilessly into her while her orgasm bulleted like fireworks through her body.

Her body contorting, convulsing around him, her sex contracting, milking his cock, his name squealed from the pouty lips he loved, he finally let go.

His manhood swelled, engorged with blood and seed, driving into her, his eyes crushed closed. Grinding against Rebeka, the blinding heat railed up Jeph's body, his seed burst from him in torrential spasms.

All thought fled his brain as he vibrated inside her. He was nothing but a raging nebulous, pure raw, stinging primitive sensation.

He hissed her name, "*Rebeka*," as he blasted his everything into her again and again, until he paused deep inside, feeling his seed gushing from his body. Then he pumped until he was completely empty.

Even then, he never wanted it to fucking end. He collapsed with a beastly growl on top of her.

Big powerful chest heaving, Jeph struggled to catch his breath. His heart raced, veins cranked scorching blood through his beleaguered body.

A weary smile softened his face, he could feel her still pulsing around him, still gripping, wringing his dick as another orgasm rode her. Her ragged breathing chuffed in his ears.

Her body simmered, undulating more slowly as the climax spent, humming a satiated sigh in her release.

After a minute of them catching their breaths, he could felt her struggling under him, trying to move his big body off her.

Smiling, he rolled to his back pulling her with him. Her face rested on his chest, her dainty little hand settled so beautifully on his heaving chest.

Her hand so fair against the dark hair under it, he laid his own large hand over it. Folding his fingers around it, he clasped it over his hammering heart.

Their panting decelerating, he growled, "You fucking slayed me, Rebeka."

Snuggling against his big body, yawning, she asked, "It was okay, even though I didn't know how to please you?"

His hand cradling the back of her head angled it up to him. He gazed tenderly into her still dazed, amazingly sultry eyes.

"Baby, you fucking pleased me beyond this fucking stratosphere, you are fucking phenomenal."

Shifting self-consciously against him, she asked quietly, "Your women, your other women, did I please you almost as good as them? That girl, um, Patrisia, you liked her-"

Still holding her head, he shook it gently with a frown. "Rebeka, there are no other women in this bed, our bed. Do not be bringing anyone else, no one else in here. I never had one speck of sand as much desire for anyone ever as I do you." His eyes closed, he swallowed hard.

Remorse filled his deep voice as he admitted, "I…used Patrisia trying to wipe you from my brain. I regretted it the second she touched me. And, I was so disgusted with both her and myself I barely touched her. I raced to finish, the entire time it was your face in my brain. It didn't, won't, happen again. Ever. I want no woman but you, only you."

Splaying his hands on her back to press her down on him, he sighed. "Baby, I fucking love your lush tits on my chest, sends me out of space, come, straddle me so I can play with them." He ran his hands over her back and to her sides to lift her.

"But your women-"

Sighing with irritation, he groaned, "Stop, Rebeka, do not ruin this, what we just did. Do not ruin it with shit I have no interest in. This is all about you and me, no one else."

"But, when you drop me off, you'll go back to them-"

He shook her more roughly. "I said stop. Enough of this shit."

His voice softened seeing her sudden fright, uneasiness tightening her brows. "Rebeka, do not worry about something that has not yet happened. Just," he kissed her gently, "concentrate on me, us, our time right now. *Bine*?"

Blinking in confusion at him, her mouth turned down. She said, "But, how can I relax when I know what tomorrow will bring?"

He kissed her more thoroughly. When he'd taken her breath away, he said, "I have protected you so far, Rebeka. I have told you, I will not let anyone hurt you. Trust me on this. Let us take one moment, one day at a time, *bine*?"

But now that the lust fog dissipated, everything came hurling back to her. "I- but I, oh my gosh, I'm just a- a what do they call it, a notch in your bedpost! What have I done-" wrenching from his grasp, she pushed to get off the bed.

"Dammit, Rebeka." He flung out a husky arm and grabbed her, hauling her back to nestle on his chest. He spread a tough hand on her back to hold her down when she fought to get away.

"No," she cried, "you only used me, you only wanted to have sex with me, have someone right here available until we get to that man."

Pushing on his chest, she squirmed to get loose. "Then you'll throw me to him and run! I am so stupid! You tricked me, se- seduced me-"

"Goddammit, Rebeka," he cursed words she didn't understand, and held her immobile.

"If I just wanted sex I could have taken you any goddamned time I pleased from day one. If I wanted easy sex on our journey, there are plenty of women I could have. I could go downstairs right now and pick up half a dozen women without even leaving the building."

Tears dampened the hair on his chest. "Then go," she cried, "go get one, go get all of them, it's great you can have your pick of women anytime you want. Good for you. Just screw them and let me leave."

Her fists punched at him. He caught them, held them still. Slipping his hands under her arms he lifted her to lie on top of him and tipped her face up to his.

"Stop it, Rebeka," he commanded severely. "What we just did was beautiful, amazing, I have never experienced anything so incredible. I have wanted you, dreamed of you, craved you until I could think of nothing else. I do not want, desire, anyone else. Just you. I said I could get another woman easily enough not to brag, but to show you how much I want you, only you."

"But-"

His kiss firm to stop her, then he said, "*Na* fucking buts, Rebeka. I always take what I want without a second thought. I wanted you so badly, and for you to truly want me that I waited. Instead of pouncing on you, forcing you, I waited until you said yes. You have any idea how fucking hard that's been for me?"

Still uncertain, she shook her head.

One hand on her head, the other cupped her butt pressing her pelvis into his penis. "Baby," he said so gently, his eyes dark spheres of tenderness. "Trust me. Let me take care of you. Please." Third time he'd said that word with her, please, it tasted so unfamiliar on his tongue.

When she opened her mouth to protest some more, he fisted a handful of her hair pulling her head back and covered her mouth with his. Kissing her softly, then the potent raw heat flared between them and he plundered her until they were both shaking with passion.

He moved to clutch her ass with both hands and crushed it with his long fingers. Smiling at her lips, he said, "Come, little girl, you need more lessons. Let me show you what tis like when you wrap your graceful little legs around my waist and I fuck you up against the shower wall."

Her eyes popped, lips parted in shock. "Standing up? Are you sure-"

"*Yah*, baby, I am sure. You know I am strong. You are so slight I can hold that elegant body of yours while I bounce you up and down on my dick. You want to do it?" One brow rose in a leer with his grin.

At her shocked expression, he laughed and said, "I will wash that dirty, dirty body of yours, get it all bubbly and soapy first. I think your tits are especially dirty, they will require a lot of washing. What do you think?"

"Uh, I...I don't...know." Her breath suddenly whooshed out as he rolled out from under her, moved off the bed, then bent and picked her up.

Carrying her down the hall, he said, "I will take that as a yes. Later, I have more lessons for you, my *nishka*, and we have champagne and food waiting for us when we are totally sated. You see, my little sweet, I will take care of you," he bent to capture her plush lips.

Chapter Twenty-Six

*J*eph had them on the road before the sun rose. He started early mainly to keep Rebeka drowsy so she wouldn't think.

He had kept her up most of the night, she was well-fucked. His harsh mouth turned up in a pleased yet not satisfied smile. He knew once he took her sweet, sinful little body he'd never get enough of her. Every time, just as he came he'd wanted her all over again.

One time she was barely awake when he reached for her, and ejaculated so quickly she was asleep almost before he pulled out of her.

They ate breakfast while driving.

Rebeka's head was against the corner of the seat as she napped on and off.

They stopped at a café for lunch in a pretty city. White and pastel buildings shimmered in the sunlight.

When they got back in the car, and Jeph started driving, Rebeka turned to face him.

"Jeph," she said, to get his attention.

Here it comes, he glanced at her then back to the road. "Hmm?" But his stomach churned, her beautiful face was marred with worry and shame.

Louise Furley

"You…" Her eyes shuttered holding back the fear, the guilt. Taking a deep breath she started again, "You got what you wanted; can you please let me go now? Just pull over and let me-"

His phone rang, he didn't hesitate to pull it out and answer it.

To Rebeka's chagrin, he spoke at length, in his language, and when he finally disconnected, he called someone. And it went on and on like that the rest of the day.

He finally put his phone away when he pulled in front of a hotel.

Everything in writing was still in a different language. Rebeka stared wide-eyed at the lavish hotel.

Jeph said, "I will go in alone, I do not want you seen." He loped off to the entrance and disappeared inside. His gaze scarcely landed on the clerk as he paid for the room, it remained focused on Rebeka. He had called ahead to make a reservation so he returned fairly quickly.

Opening her door, he reached for her, but she moved back, away from his hands. Frowning at her resistance, he said, "Come, Rebeka, it will be dangerous for us to linger out here in the open."

Unhooking her seatbelt, he gripped her arms and though she still resisted, he pulled her out and set her on the paved parking lot. He took out their luggage then cupped her arm to usher her to the hotel.

Digging her feet in, she said, "No, Jeph, we have to talk, now, right now."

His fingers tightened around her arm as he forcefully moved her along. "Inside," he muttered, bringing her around to the back of the hotel to enter.

They had already been compromised once, he was going to be more careful now. He walked her up the back staircase to the second floor and to the suite.

Unlocking the door, he checked inside first as usual before allowing her to enter.

Jeph took her case and his duffle into the bedroom, when he returned she was standing by the door.

Her gaze skimmed his strapping body, rippled top and bottom with solid muscles, then rose to his face. As hard as ever, sharp angles and tough expression, yet his dark eyes were warm on her.

Her gaze lowered to his black jeans, and her cheeks blushed. His erection strained at his fly. Her eyes flew back up to his face.

He shrugged with a crooked grin. "What can I say, *nishka*, you do that to me without my even touching you." And it burgeoned larger as he prowled towards her.

Rebeka's hands came up. "Stop, please, Jeph, please."

"Ah," he sighed and shoved his palm over his erection. "*Bine.*"

Gesturing to the sofa, he said, "All right, we will talk. But, I will tell you, *ma nishka,* it will be quick. I am burning for you."

Yellow brows arched in incredulity. "Jeph, we did it like, I mean," the blush darkened, "so many times last night I lost count, how can you-"

"I will show you, *nishka* right now, come." Sitting on the sofa, he held his hands out to her. She avoided them and went and perched on the big cushioned chair much to his frowning annoyance.

"What? I cannot touch you while we talk?"

One side of her mouth edged up. "I know you by now. If you are near me we won't do any talking, and we will talk or I'll be sleeping on the couch tonight."

His brows furrowed with his patronizing smile. She's delusional if she thinks they would not be sleeping, or otherwise occupied, in the same bed tonight. He'd finally gotten her where he wanted her and he will be damned if anything changes it, including her shame and resistance.

Letting out a disgruntled sigh, as if he didn't know, he asked, "*Bine*, what is it you wish to discuss?"

The heat boiled in his eyes as he watched her settle herself in the chair, wondering in his head how soon their talk would be done and he would be taking that blouse off her back.

Smiling, pleased that he was giving in, she said happily, "Okay." Then the smile evaporated into a sad, desolate, grimace. Twining her fingers together to steady her agitated heart, she set them in her lap. "I…" she started then faltered.

"Rebeka," he went to get up and go to her.

She held her hand up. "No. Please," and waited until he reluctantly sat back down.

"I am asking you, please, tell me, be truthful, tell me everything. How much longer before we are to get to…that man's home where you will deposit me? And- and, tell me what I can expect from…him, this…my new life. Please be straight up with me, Jeph, please." Tears gathered in the corners of her eyes, she struggled to keep them there.

Seeing the tears, Jeph's heart compressed with the sting of knowing he caused her pain. The air in his lungs deflated in a long whoosh. He sat back against the cushions and folded his hands in his lap.

"*Bine*. I have not told you, Rebeka, anything, because I have a plan in the works, and I don't know if tis going to work or not. If not, I have Plan B. I don't want you pinning your hopes on something that may not happen exactly as I planned."

His sigh harsh, the dark eyes studied her, they rolled over her from head to toe then settled on her frightened eyes.

"Baby," his deep voice soft with his feelings for her that had burrowed deep under his skin and in his heart, his mouth turned up in an absorbing smile.

"I wanted you the second that I saw you standing there, so fucking beautiful, so foolishly prudish, refusing to lift your skirt that day even knowing you would be hurt for it. Hell, baby, your blouse wide open, those luscious tits, I could feel them in my mouth, my hands, from across the grounds."

Her face staining with embarrassment, she said, "Jeph, please."

His smile widened. "When you tried to save the trannies from execution, I was signed, sealed, and bought, baby. I would have never let you be sold on that fucking block. I could tell right in the beginning you were not the criminal described to me.

"The only thing I thought about the rest of the time was how I was going to get you. I planned on keeping you from the start. I could have just taken you, but then I would have to look over my shoulder for the rest of our lives, waiting for them to come after us.

"I came up with the loophole of buying you for another person outside of the auction, and made sure it was legal and viable within the auction rules. I never had any intentions of leaving you with Rumân Braşov. But, I have to get you to him to make the buy legit, to wait to make sure my men brought-" he broke off.

He couldn't tell her his entire plan, she would go bananas objecting. He would do it anyway of course, but it would go smoother if she didn't know ahead of time.

All their conversations, and he had finally realized something and he had his men researching and setting things up.

"Anyway," he said, "then I would take you from him. If that did not work for whatever reason, my last resort, I would have taken out the five men at the top of the auction chain. Without them pushing for sanctions on me, people would be too busy scurrying around trying to take over their positions with their greedy avarice, no one would care about who killed them, or why."

Her mouth dropped open. She started to speak but he cut her off.

"Except, they could have top lieutenants that might care and try to find out who did the hits, but, they would never be able to trace them back to me. I do not ever leave evidence that can be traced back to me. We would be clear to live out in the open as we desired."

Of course, that was predicated on the fact that, that was what she wanted. If she didn't, his head tilted back as he viewed her from under his hooded lids, he would have to deal with things differently.

Regardless, she was staying with him. But they weren't talking about that now. He was gravely unsure about her feelings for him and if she wanted to stay with him, and he feared addressing it now.

At her horrified look at his casual talk of murdering people so he could have her, he nodded, and said, "That is why I did not go that route right off the back. I already knew you, your soft heart, it would have made it even harder for you to come to me, be with me, if you thought I had killed for you. Even to save your life. Trust me, they are not nice people, there would be many suspects in their demise."

He calmly watched her process what he said.

The thoughts knotted over her face, darkening her eyes with renewed fear of this deadly force sitting there so coolly talking about murder.

Jeph could not change the man he was. Leaguing years of his own brutal slavery and prison, and worse, could not be gouged out, if so there would be nothing left of him. Yet, studying her, his eyes softened. She was so innocent and pure, kind and compassionate, she was rubbing off on him.

He didn't kill quite so quickly without considering alternatives, or the effect the person's death could have on others, such as their family. And, when she begged for a life even though it deserved ending, it pained his heart to reject her pleas.

A bit of guilt and compassion were worming their way into his black soul, tempering his vicious, remorseless violence.

He leaned forward with his forearms on his knees, hands clasped, the dark hair falling over an eye that directed pure honesty to her.

"Rebeka, I swear on my life, I would never hurt you. No woman, I have never harmed a female, ever, least of all the one woman in the entire world I...uh, care for." The *only* woman he had ever cared for.

He thought of some of the women he'd been with, like Patrisia. He was exceptionally strong, an aggressive, brutish man. Yeah, he had hurt her during their violent sex, but she wanted it rough, begged him to do things...he shook his head to dismiss the memory. Rebeka wasn't Patrisia. Not even on the same plane.

Her brows slashed down, "Really? You wouldn't hurt a woman, but those auctions, they are an atrocity, a-"

His hands came up, "*Yah, yah*, I know women get hurt, that is why the rules of no sex without permission and other safety nets I have put in place. We can discuss that at another time. Right now it is about you and me."

He shifted to the edge of the couch. "Rebeka, my plan is devised so no one gets hurt. I," he broke off remembering one aspect of his plot making that statement possibly not entirely true. Sitting back, he dragged his fingers through his hair pushing it back off his forehead.

Leaning forward, his hands clasped, forearms on his knees again, he stared frankly into her eyes and stated, "I do not plan to be involved with the auctions after this. I had always felt it was justice and right, and my due to capture and sell the people because it had been done to me, and I was innocent and none of the criminals I ever brought to the auction were innocent. None even professed to be, until...you."

Rebeka sat unmoving, taking in his words, his tone, judging his sincerity. Her expression waffled between belief and disbelief.

He leaned forward again. "Rebeka, I almost committed a terrible travesty by selling you to a doomed horrific life. I have never captured an innocent person before, but I did when I took you. I do not want to ever take the chance of that happening again. I want nothing more to do with that life. I could not bear it if I ever made that mistake again, sentencing an innocent to a life of living hell."

They both sat silent, pondering.

Under the watchful hooded eyes, he held himself tight, waiting for her response.

After a moment, she said, "So, if that did happen, you quit the auction," the doubt in her voice pinched at his gut. "What would you do for...work?"

Sitting back, he crossed an ankle over a knee. His lips pulled in as he considered, again, how much to tell her. "Ah, I, my team, we also do mercenary work. However, with our skills we have long been offered legitimate jobs with the government and," he sucked in a deep breath; let it out slowly, "we are finally talking about actually agreeing to do it. My team will follow me wherever I choose to go."

A smile tugged up his rugged face at her surprised look.

"Regardless, my pet, I have enough money to live extremely comfortably for the rest of my life. I would work because I would become bored if not, and," he shrugged with a grin, "most of us get in trouble when we get bored."

She was quiet, her ruminations flexing her face, her eyes were lowered, mouth pinned tight.

One arm stretched along the back of the couch, the other resting on his thigh, he watched her struggle with her thoughts. Jeph knew he would never in this lifetime ever tire of her, he prayed she would feel the same about him.

But for the first time in his life, he was afraid. It scared the fuck out of him that she would not want him, and he dared not ask, not right now. Not when her fear of him glimmered again in her eyes, and her future was still unsettled.

He immediately regretted telling her he would have taken out the top men in the auction to save her. Reminding her of the man he was, the things he was capable of doing.

She would never understand or acquiesce to murder. She would never accept him if she knew he cold-bloodedly killed, got more blood on his hands even for a valuable reason. Her life.

Even the trannies weren't to be murdered but used to scare the others into cooperating. No one would have known they'd been spared. They would have been secretly sent to a different auction. It was a way of inserting control over all of the prisoners by using fear, not having to physically harm them.

She twined a curl around a finger. Her round cheeks pale, she didn't look at him.

It took every bit of his will power to not get up and stalk over to her and plunder the living fuck out of her.

He said softly, "*Nishka,* talk to me, tell me what is going through that gorgeous brain of yours?"

She was never quick to answer him, and she wasn't now. It was a characteristic of hers that drove him insane, and she only did it with him. It showed she didn't yet trust him, or feel comfortable with him.

Of course that was his fault, he was often a controlling beast to her, and discussing executions didn't help.

Still, he wanted the first thoughts that came to her head, not some that were processed first, or forced by him from her sweet lips.

When she didn't respond, he urged, "Rebeka?" He was about to get up when she spoke.

"What…" she blinked, glanced at him then at some spot on the wall. "What will happen if you are able to get me away from…that…man? Will you send me home?"

Jeph uncrossed his legs, shoved the recalcitrant hair off his forehead and set both big hands on his thighs. "Ah, tis not an if, sweet, it is a when. But, we should stay with one step at a time, *bine*? Let's get you free first, *nishka* then work on the…uh, later part."

He was scared that she would insist on going home, and that wasn't going to happen, and he sure as hell didn't want to talk about that now. It would get in the way of him getting in her pants.

"But, Jeph-"

He stood up. "*Basta*, enough for now, we can only take one step at a time. I have told you that no way in hell will I leave you with Rumân Braşov. Now," he paced over to her, slightly miffed when she leaned back from him. "Enough talking, I have to touch you, Rebeka. Now."

Chapter Twenty-Seven

*J*eph bent, slipped his hands under her and lifted her into his arms.

She wriggled to get down, protesting, "Wait, Jeph, we just got here, can we wait a second before you, uh, we have sex? We need to talk more, there is more to discuss."

Her flushed cheeks lightened when he changed direction from heading to the bedroom and carried her to the couch.

"Thank you, Jeph," she smiled as he set her on her feet then he sat on the cushion.

A tiny shriek eeked from Rebeka as he grabbed her, easily lifting her and set her on his lap to face him.

"Jeph-"

Mumbling, "*Yah*, baby?" He positioned her to straddle him while he crushed her breasts in both hands, emitting a longing groan.

His mouth seeking hers, as she started to try to talk to him, he buried her words with his needy, aggressive kiss. Groping her roughly, he kneaded her breasts in such enflamed desire she cried out at his roughness.

Pushing at his grabbing hands, she slipped off his lap, but he caught her wrist and pulled her back to sit back down on his lap, this time facing out.

He gripped her legs and maneuvered them so they were hanging over the outside of his so she couldn't get away, and reached around to the front of her and started on the buttons of her blouse.

"Jeph, please," she protested. Her squirming on his lap in her attempt to get away only rubbed her butt on his rigid erection, making it grow bigger, and harder. The buttons undone, Jeph moved his hands to her back to unclasp her bra.

"Jeph! Stop, we need to talk, stop-"

"Unless you are telling me I am hurting you, we are done talking, sweet." He thrust his hard fingers up under the loose bra to pinch and pull her nipples.

At her outcry, he released her nipples to caress her breasts, filling his hands with them as they swelled painfully from his strenuous groping. His rasping moans muffled against her hair, lustful heavy breaths stirred tendrils across her face.

She grabbed his hands to still them, but his strength overrode her vain struggles. "Jeph, we do need to talk more, please."

Muttering into her hair, he growled, "Cannot get enough of you, *nishka.*" His chin in her neck, he forced himself to let go of her breasts and worked at her belt.

Rebeka pushed her shoulders at his back to shove her hips off his legs while swatting at his hands. One burly arm wound around her holding her immobile as he unbuckled her belt. Ignoring her objections, he popped the button and unzipped the zipper.

She squawked, "Jeph, seriously, listen to me, we need to talk-" Then a torturous groan roiled from her when he shoved his hand down the inside of her panties and gripped her mound. Her struggles turned into a sensuous, heated furling mew.

Catching herself, she realized he was controlling her with sex, turning her on so she would get distracted. She twisted, trying to get away from his hand tucked inside her pants, which was absolutely futile; his huge hand was not leaving her sex until he wanted it to.

He curled his demanding fingers over her already throbbing pussy, cupping it hard in his hand while grinding the heel of his palm against her clit.

"Jeph-" she cried out as his fingers stroked her vaginal lips before stabbing a thick finger inside her. Her silk poured out. His triumphant growl at the wet soaking his hand made her mad. Grabbing his wrists, she twisted and jerked to get free.

He only tightened his bulky arms around her holding her taut, and slid her natural lube around her budding clit until her struggles ceased and her moans increased.

Her back rolled back and forth over his chest as her hips rose to meet his hand, pressing for more, harder. Her protestations melted into moans of arousal amidst squeaky heavy breaths.

Smiling with his mouth still tucked against her hair, inhaling her heavenly scent, he murmured, "Ah, that is better, is it not, my beautiful *nishka*?" He stroked her pussy lips, swirled and pinched her bud with one hand, the other skimmed back up to clutch a bare breast under her loosened clothing.

A groan of delight rumbled deep in his throat when she arched her spine, pressing her back against his chest writhing with whimpering moans and fevered exhalations.

When she stopped fighting him, Jeph pushed her off his lap and jerked her pants and panties down her legs then pulled them off. When she opened her mouth to demure, he grabbed her blouse, tore it off her and tossed it, her bra followed.

Her mouth still open with no words coming to her mind, Jeph pulled her back down with her back against his chest, pushed her thin legs over his thicker thighs, cupped a breast to draw her back against him, and thrust in a finger, then worked a second inside her.

Her surging gasps churning sinfully with her moans of escalating arousal were music to Jeph's ears.

"Baby," he cooed in her ear while fingering her sex, drawing her silk all over her swollen nub. Squeezing her breast, he tweaked her nipple with a twist and thrust his fingers inside her faster.

"You make me so fucking hot with those crazy sounds you make. I want more, baby, sing for me."

He latched his lips on her neck, and worked his fingers wickedly over her until the gasps elevated to cries of ecstasy and her body undulated wildly all over his lap. Arching against his chest, her bosom heaving with erotic rushing breaths, hot cutting cries broke from her.

When she was at the top, about to hurtle over into paradise, her gasping now painful jagged cries; Jeph suddenly wrapped his hands around her waist and lifted her off his lap.

He carried her to the sofa and set her down on the floor facing it. Pressing his hands on her shoulders, he pushed her to her knees.

"Jeph- what-" disoriented and whimpering with need, Rebeka fought him.

"Tis all good, baby. Bend over, put your arms on the cushions," as he spoke soothingly, he maneuvered her to bend over the couch and nudged her knees to spread her legs apart.

"That is perfect, sweet, now, do not move, wait for me," he stood up and quickly shucked his clothes, grabbed a condom out of his pants and slid it on.

Kneeling behind her, Jeph caught her wrists and pulled her arms behind her. Her head lifted, she cried, "What are you doing? Don't-"

He put his hand on her head and gently pushed it back down on the cushions. "Shh, just do what I say. Here," he nudged her legs wider apart and moved between them.

Raising her arms slightly behind her, he gripped her wrists with one hand, holding her arms like they were a rope, pushed her shoulders down, lifted her butt, and grabbed his dick.

Pressing his manhood against her opening, he murmured softly to her in his own language. When he realized it, he spoke in English, "Just relax, my sweet, enjoy us."

"I don't know, I'm not sure, Jeph," Rebeka cried, trying to free her hands. Yet she wriggled her bottom back against his bulging shaft that was prodding at her butt and then her sex, preparing to penetrate her.

"Tis *bine*, sweet baby," he assured her, and slowly pushed the head into her weeping pussy. Letting go of his dick, he nudged her thighs even wider, and thrust inside her deeper. He could feel her tighten in her anxiousness.

"Relax, Rebeka," he soothed, gripping a hanging chubby breast to knead. Still holding her arms back, pulling them like reins, lifting her shoulders up to him, making her back arch.

He pulled out then pumped back in deeper and deeper as her muscles relaxed and let him in and her silk made them both slick. "How is that, you *bine*, you okay baby?"

"Mmm," her face in the cushion she was muffled, but she started meeting his thrusts with her hips.

"*Yah*, yeah, baby, tis so good." Picking up his speed, thrusting in and out of her with more powerful strokes each time, he released her breast and plucked at her clit.

Her groans were of ecstatic pleasure. Her hips pounded back at him, his shaft engorged, filling her, stretching her. The friction sending them both huffing, peaking with an aching need for exquisite fulfillment, for that primordial release.

Rebeka's breasts bounced harder as he pulled her up, forcing her back to arch further, plunging rougher, his immense strength shoving her hips into the cushions with every hard thrust.

He grabbed a bobbing breast and kneaded her full flesh, groaning, "God, baby, God, I need you so bad, so badly, uh," he grunted and thrust so hard he knocked the breath out of her.

She sucked air in and cried it out when he rammed into her again and again, going as deep as he could, now moving so fast she couldn't keep up with him.

His chest billowing against her back with his heavy breaths, Jeph saw the goose bumps rising along her arms, her inhalations turning to sobs of agonizing, unleashing joy.

Holding her wrists, he stuck his hand in her hair and pulled both her arms and curly locks back, bending her backwards until she thought she'd break, the pain was flawless torture.

He leaned over her, his breath wisps against her face, he whispered, "You ready, my beautiful *nishka*, come with me, together, *bine*?"

A grunt forced out of her, Rebeka cried, "Yes, yes, please Jeph, please, hurry, take us there!"

"Ahh," he growled, a beast slamming into its trapped mate, he drove into her, riding Rebeka like a wild animal while wrenching her hair and her arms back. Plunging in and out, over and over, her screams blended with his roars, each other's name on their lips as they thundered off the cliff together.

Rebeka's body jerked with convulsions, frenzied spasms fiercely gyrating her under him, her shrieking vagina clenching, milking his cock.

Jeph pounded her so hard now she was getting mashed into the sofa. His big body slamming into her until he paused, deep, deep inside her as his seeds gushed from his balls, and his dick felt like it exploded into smithereens.

His body jerked and twitched as he emptied, until he was a hollow, shuddering shell, and he fell on top of her, his millions of fragmenting pieces crushing her further into the couch cushions.

It took superhuman effort for him to roll off Rebeka. He grabbed her as he collapsed to the floor bringing her down with him. Falling to his side, facing her, he cuddled her against him, putting her head on his arm, his other arm strew across her trembling body.

Rebeka lifted a shaking hand to caress his cheek. He forced his spent eyes open, and smiled. Because she was smiling at him.

Her eyes heavy with euphoria, foggy with delirious exhaustion and trained on him, were the prettiest things he could ever imagine seeing in his life.

He moved slightly to dispose of the condom in the small trash can near the desk and drew her back into his arms.

They lay, dozing, cuddling closer.

His stomach growled, stirring him. Jeph gently moved Rebeka off him and got up.

Padding to the phone, he called room service for food. Setting the phone down, he trod back to Rebeka and scooped her up in his arms. She murmured but didn't open her eyes.

He carried her to the bedroom and tucked her under the covers.

When the food arrived, he woke her.

They shared a delicious dinner with a good wine before returning to the bed for more...exercise.

Chapter Twenty-Eight

They stayed at the luxurious hotel for several days. They left occasionally to shop, have dinner out, stroll the streets, but spent most of their time in bed.

Until, Jeph's phone rang. It was the call he'd been waiting for. His men were ready.

Murmuring, "Baby," he leaned over Rebeka stroking a gentle finger down her cheek.

Her lashes fluttered over sleepy, contented eyes that opened with her soft smile. "Hey," she whispered, her voice husky with satiation and sleep.

His smile, genuine, he was smiling more in the past few weeks than he had his entire life. "We have to go, tis time." His smile wavered at the loss of hers.

The anxiety poured into her eyes pushing out the happiness.

"*Na*, baby," he said quickly, stroking his fingers through her hair. "I told you, I promised you, everything will be fine. You must trust me." He sat down beside her on the bed, the mattress sinking slightly with his weight.

"Do you trust me, Rebeka?" His voice strong, confident, held a hint of worry that she doubted he would take care of her.

Then her lips curved in a soft, more certain smile. With a nod, somewhat tremulously, she said, "Yes. I mean, I'm trying to Jeph."

Then, seeing the determination in his eyes, the strong thrust of his jaw, her smile deepened. She said firmly, "Yes, I trust you, Jeph."

"*Yah*, good, *bine*, baby." He leaned over to give her a mind-melting kiss. Reluctantly pulling back from her, he said, "Enough of that, my precious girl, anymore and we will be late." They needed to arrive at Rumân Brașov's before his men did.

"Come, I will shower then you can-" He broke off when he turned down the sheet and saw her glorious nude body.

"Ah, shit," he groaned as his dick swelled. "We can shower together."

It took longer than he planned, but soon they were packed up and on the road.

After hours on the highway, they turned off to follow a serpentine road that wound through the forest then up a mountain.

The road thinned to stone then dirt, so far out in the middle of nowhere they didn't come across another traveler.

Finally, they could see the estate, more like a castle. Perched on the side of a mountain the glistening cream-colored fortress nestled amongst vast greenery.

The closer they got, the more they could see the variegated stones that made up the three-story structure. Cars were sequestered off to the right in front of a twelve-car garage, and guards marched on patrol around the perimeter.

Before Jeph could get all the way up the long driveway, a jeep rustled around from nowhere and stopped in front of them. Two armed men got out leaving more men inside.

One strode up to the car.

Rolling down the window, his arrogant voice stern, Jeph stuck a hand out with his credentials, his accented voice cold authority he stated, "I am Jephunneh Kajic, we are expected."

The guard examined Jeph's credentials before swiftly handing them back. Jeph's reputation preceded him, and he had been there numerous times before.

The guard wanted as little contact with the dangerous chief as possible. He nodded briskly and stepped aside. "Please go on through, sir."

Without another word or look at the guard, Jeph drove past him up to the house. He parked near the other cars.

Stepping from behind the wheel, he left their luggage in the car and glanced surreptitiously at the vehicles to see if he recognized any. He needed to be prepared for anything.

When he felt assured there was little imminent danger, he helped Rebeka out of the car.

Jeph wore black jeans and boots with a dark blue, button-down shirt. Rebeka had on a dress and heels. He was second-guessing her attire. He had wanted her to wear the more protective slacks, but they had spent all their time in bed and hadn't gotten to the laundry.

The dress was pale green on the clingy bodice, with roses along the bottom of soft skirt that swirled femininely around her slender legs.

It was shorter than he would have liked, it didn't show her tits but the material cradled them, exposing their beautiful plump shape. When she was cold, her nipples pressed against the light material. Already he had glared threats at the guards gawking at her.

Tucking a hand under her hair on her lower back, he said, "We will leave the luggage, they will bring it." He guided her over the paved driveway to the double front doors.

One of the doors was wide open and two servants stood in the threshold. Guards hovered at attention behind them.

"Welcome, sir, madam." A butler in black bowed briefly then stood aside for them to enter the enormous building.

They paused inside an immense marble foyer with skylight shining sunlight down on the center of the room. A wide staircase rolled up to fork into hallways at each floor.

"This way, if you will, Chief Kajic, Mr. Braşov awaits you in the den." A female servant also in black held her hand out in a motion for them to follow her.

They walked down several corridors, Rebeka's heels tapping quietly on the tile as she and Jeph, the two servants, and a half a dozen guards, traipsed along.

When they reached the den, the maid and butler stood on either side of the huge doorway and gestured for Jeph and Rebeka to go in.

The room was decorated in various shades of brown. The drapes burgundy, the chairs with dark brown leather cushions, there were glass coffee tables, end tables, two austere bookcases that went from floor to ceiling and a fireplace.

Against a wall was a bar in gold and burgundy with a servant standing stiffly behind it.

There were men gathered inside, they all turned as Jeph and Rebeka were announced.

Glances went quickly from Jeph's hard-featured face to Rebeka.

Overwhelmed, her eyes were lowered to the floor. She didn't see the wolfish desire in the men's eyes. One of the men broke from the rest and trod over to them.

Holding out a hand, he shook Jeph's. "Chief, you finally made it. I have been waiting quite a while since our conversation," his narrowed eyes slid to Rebeka. Although he tried to hide the luridness glowing in them when he perused her, it utterly vaulted from his every pore.

"Ah, this is the infamous Queenie Benani." Rumân Braşov was a tall, well-built man in his forties. He appeared strong and vital. Power radiated from his dark brown eyes that matched the slick leather chairs.

Thick chestnut hair waved back off his forehead, he wore a cobalt blue suit jacket, oxford shirt and brown slacks. He oozed wealth and confidence. Also not quite hidden in those wolfish eyes was a vicious brutality that was above and far beyond Jeph's.

Jeph had a limit to whom he would hurt and why, whereas Braşov eschewed any hint of kindness, compassion. He was an unadulterated, pitiless monster. He hurt people purely for the fun of it. He held his hand out to Rebeka.

Although as innocent as the undriven show, she could discern the tainted evil glint in his licentious eyes.

Jeph's hand tightened on Rebeka's back at the shiver that roiled through her delicate body.

She stared at Braşov's big, thick hand and felt as if it wanted to grip her throat, throw her down and do hideously harrowing things to her. She gingerly raised her eyes to his and wilted.

Undisguised, cruel, sick interest in her blared clearly from the jaded eyes that traveled nonstop up and down her body, until they finally settled on her frightened eyes. His narcissistic smile steeped. Fear made him hot.

Rebeka's limbs froze, she couldn't make herself touch the fiend that stood waiting to devour her and spit out her gorged on, sucked clean, skinless bones.

Her tangible fear raised the depraved hairs on the back of his neck, and his cock stirred in his pants. The smile, sharp at the corners rose higher on his handsome face. A few lines crinkled around his eyes and full mouth, the wrinkles were created more from sadistic dissipation than age.

The smile shifted higher on one side of his mouth than the other as he leaned forward and took her hand. Bringing it to his lips, he kissed the top, leaving his mouth on it for several beats. The room was silent except for the anticipation in his heavy breathing.

Turning her palm over, he set his tongue on it. Not licking, just blatantly tasting her.

She tried to close her fist and pull it away, but using his other hand, he pressed her fingers open and held her still.

A rumbling growl bristled from Jeph as he moved to stand slightly in front of Rebeka, forcing Braşov to release her.

His jaundiced eyes glued to Rebeka, the grin lengthened, Rumân said, "Nice, Kajic, so fucking nice. The reports of her were understated. They said she was gorgeous. Fuck, she is so much more. Sirens of the sea got nothing on her, eh?" He reached for one of her blonde curls.

Another threatening growl rolled from Jeph as he moved more in front of her.

Frowning, Rumân's lips pushed out. "What the fuck, Kajic, why do you protect her like she's yours? You bought her for me. She will be my bride." He turned his rapacious attention back to Rebeka, the aberrant smile returned.

"I will hurry the paperwork along, my dear, I can't fucking wait to take you." He reached for her hand again but Jeph was now almost fully between him and Rebeka, bringing Rumân's frown to a scowl.

The men in the room cradled cocktails in their hands. Some had cigarettes, others cigars, all eyes were on the trio near the doorway. Not one of them said a word.

His chest puffing out, Jeph said, "I told you when we spoke there were some hitches to this entire event. On the way here I finally received confirmation of something."

Rumân raised a suspicious brow. "You said you purchased a bride for me, a Miss Queenie Benani. And, here she is," he nodded to her, "all wrapped up in a pretty package just waiting for me to unwrap her."

His eyes raped her all the way down her quaking body. The more he sensed, smelled her fright, the harder he became.

Partially behind Jeph, Rebeka folded her arms around her shaking body. The obviously morally corrupt, base man horrified the living heck out of her. Terrified he would leave her with such a monster; she stuck her trembling fingers in Jeph's belt and held on.

Feeling her, Jeph backed closer to her to comfort her. He said to Rumân, "The thing is, Braşov, this is not Queenie Benani." At Rebeka's shocked gasp, he turned slightly and winked at her.

Brows drawing down like daggers, Rumân snarled, "What the fuck are you trying to pull here, Kajic? You said you bought this Queenie girl and you were bringing her to me. Well?"

Rumân nodded to Rebeka with derision. "Obviously, here she is. Now step the fuck away and let me take my fiancée. You and the guys can stay here and imbibe," he turned his gleaming lusting eyes to Rebeka."

Smiling at her, Rumân said, "I want to get to know my impending bride. Come, my sweetheart," he held his hand out for her to take. "Let's go to my room where we will have privacy to…get to know one another, eh?"

Rebeka shifted further behind Jeph.

Jeph stood with his boots planted strongly akimbo. Crossing his arms over his muscular chest, his voice cool and commanding, he said, "I repeat. This is not Queenie Benani. This is her little sister, Rebeka."

A smile tilted his lips at her gasp again. She had no idea that he had learned the truth he'd suspected from one of his phone calls who she really was.

Forehead furrowing, Rumân's brows slashed down over his angry eyes. He sputtered angrily, "What the fuck is this, Kajic? What game are you playing? You said you bought her for me. You know you can't keep her, it's against the rules, they will hunt you down and-"

Jeph nodded. "*Yah*, I am aware of the rules. I bought Queenie Benani for you, and I took Rebeka Benani, for me. Queenie is the one that is on the auction records. She was the one for sale, not Rebeka."

His face a maze of confusion and anger, Rumân opened his mouth but there was a commotion outside the door.

Jeph glanced down at his watch and smiled. *Right on time.*

His sandy-haired ox of a friend, Ving Lankov, and smirking Hubbard Shaw strutted into the room.

They held a woman between them. Her hands were bound behind her back, a gag tied over her mouth. Her face was livid with rage; it was so red it matched her curly hair.

Rebeka stepped out from behind Jeph. Bewilderment parted her lips and widened her eyes. She cried, "Queenie? What on earth, Jeph-"

Jeph caught her arm and held her close to him.

Trying to push from him to reach her sister, she said in stunned awe, "Queenie, what are you doing here?"

Jeph wasn't taking the chance of one of Rumân's men snatching her, he held onto Rebeka with the grip of a vice.

She turned to him, eyes swimming with confusion, rounded in shocked question.

Queenie struggled in Ving and Hubbard's firm grip. They smiled and just held her like she was a puppet. Raging behind the gag, her muffled voice roared and screamed, hazel eyes bulged with fury.

Jeph said to Queenie, "If you calm the fuck down, we will remove the gag. If you are going to scream and yell," he shrugged, "we do not want to hear it."

Rumân's face filled with puzzlement, he stared from Queenie to Rebeka to Jeph. "Kajic, what the fuck, man?"

Nodding to Queenie, Jeph said, "How about I remove that gag, Queenie, and you stay calm while you explain to your little sister what you did?" He waited.

Queenie pitched a fit, screaming behind the gag, throwing her body back and forth to get free.

No one said anything; they were waiting with baited breath to hear what the hell was going on here.

Finally, wearing herself out, Queenie settled, the muffled screams ceased.

Keeping one hand wrapped around Rebeka's arm, Jeph stepped to Queenie. His gaze hard and narrowed in threat at her, he said, "I mean it, woman, one shriek, one lie, you tell the truth, every fucking bit of it, or the gag goes back on. You understand me?"

He waited until she nodded, tears of rage in her greenish eyes. He lowered the gag to hang loose around her neck. "Now, you tell Rebeka what happened."

"You bitch," Queenie spat furiously at her sister. "You fucking-"

Jeph slapped his hand over her mouth. His expression black with warning, he said, "That is your only one chance, girl. Calm the fuck down and do what I said or we will tie you to a chair and leave your ass in the corner facing the wall until you die of starvation." He waited.

Queenie blinked infuriated at him, to Rebeka, then back to him. Then she lowered her eyes and nodded.

"*Bine*, ah, okay," Jeph said. "Last chance Queenie, I fucking mean it." He lowered his hand and moved Rebeka to face her sister while he still held onto Rebeka.

Tall and robust, Queenie swallowed hard, glared at Jeph then down at Rebeka. "Fine," she groused sullenly. "Your stupid boyfriend, Curt McCain didn't rape me." She smiled at the surprised confusion on Rebeka's face.

"Yeah, you stupid cunt, I needed a fall guy-"

Jeph slammed his hand over her mouth and said roughly, "You speak respectfully to her or we are done here. Got me?" When she nodded, he moved his hand and stepped back.

Swallowing down her furor, her face ruddy with wrath, Queenie sighed hard. Rolling her eyes, she said, "I pretended that Curt raped me. Even had him knock me around some to make it look good. I mean, shit, he and I have fucked on and off for years. He's not the best, but certainly not the worse. If you weren't such a prude you could have-"

At Jeph's grunt and hard look, she spoke quickly, "Anyway, I had stolen King Martin's smack and he was after me. He and a few others I had, well, banged and maybe ripped off," a shoulder shrugged in mild abashment.

"So, King said he'd put out a hit on me, like a writ sort of, if I didn't bring him back his drugs. But," she shrugged again. "They were already cut and sold and gone, the money spent on...ya know, partying, travel, I needed these," she shook her huge tits, "enlarged. Daddy would only pay for a D cup, I wanted bigger. Do you like them?" She shook them again, her gaze roving over the crowd of men.

"Queenie," Jeph growled a warning to get to the point.

Her cunning eyes dashed around to each of the men, seeking one that she could entice to help her.

They all regarded her with disgust. Especially the big menacing man in front of her that was holding onto Rebeka, not as a prisoner, but more like he cared for her.

Queenie's eyes narrowed at her sister before she looked back up to Jeph. She said with a coy soft voice, "Honey, you have to be one of the most frightfully scary looking men I have ever met, yet," her gaze stroked down his long form to hesitate on the bulge behind his fly.

Cocking her head to him, her smile tipped up with greed. "Hell, Mister, you are one sexy foreign bastard, I would fuck you in a min-"

Jeph not gently slapped his hand over her mouth. Beside him Rebeka gasped at Queenie's vulgar spewing.

Jeph snarled, "I will not tell you again, you bitch, spit out what you did, nothing more, nothing less."

When he lowered his hand, Queenie shook her head trying to loosen the red springy hair, some of the coils stuck to her face damp with sweat. She couldn't move her arms, Jeph's men held her secure.

Glaring at Jeph, "All right," she said crossly. "I stole the drugs. King put out this note on me, it was all over the underground dark net. He wanted me caught and taken to these auctions, they are-"

Jeph cut her off, "We know what they are, go on."

Glaring bullets of hate at him, she sniffed then said, "Anyway, I couldn't pay him back and he couldn't sick the law on me because I had stolen his drugs, so he sold me to the auction. He would get his money off my hide when I was bought at the auction. I was to be sold to work in some shitty brothel somewhere. At least I'd be on my back, right? No hard work?"

Her snide grin rolled around the room. Some of the men now regarded her with lust in their dissolute eyes. Jeph's and his men only held disgust.

Rebeka clamped her mouth shut to keep in her disbelief and confusion.

"Anyhoo," Queenie shrugged, her gaze coming back to her little sister. "Of course I didn't want to go to the brothels. They chain you, beat you, you have to fuck swine sometimes, not that I wouldn't for the right price, but-"

At Jeph's glare she went on, "So, I remembered that story you told me about Curt. That he tried to abduct you to assault you," she noticed Jeph's fingers tighten around Rebeka's arm at her words.

"That when you got away, he had threatened to do it to me. You didn't know of course we'd already been, intimate," the coy smile was back.

"Queenie, I don't understand," Rebeka cried softly, "what-"

Jeph squeezed her arm. "Let her finish, baby."

At the baby endearment, Queenie, Rumân, Ving and Hubbard all looked with differing degrees of surprise at the harsh man.

Ving and Hub grinned openly at their friend.

"Uh huh. So, anyway," Queenie went on, "you are such a soft-hearted cun- uh, patsy, I knew you would fall for it." She drew out a laborious sigh.

"I pretended Curt raped me so you would feel bad and do anything you could to make it up to me. Anything. I knew these men were after me, they were closing in, it would be only a matter of days before they caught me and took me to the auction. So, I waited until the folks and the servants were gone and you were home alone.

"I had worn a blonde wig often when I was with King so there were descriptions of me as both a blonde and a redhead. So, when I learned King's men were after me I wore the blonde wig whenever I was outside.

"Then that one day I saw the van that had been stalking me and I hurried home, but slow enough to lead them there. I pretended I went home, but in fact," a sheepish grin twisted her lips.

"I snuck quietly in the door and right out the back. I saw them pull up in their van. I saw them take you."

Rebeka's lashes flapped at her in stunned disbelief. "You- you knew, you knew what would happen to me? You did nothing to help me? Warn me?" Her voice grew shrill, "Call the police? Anything?"

Queenie lowered her head. But when she raised it, there wasn't a shade of remorse or caring on her hard face. "Yeah, I did. You are a fucking sucker. You needed your life livened up for cripe's sake. You're a useless, cold, shriveled up little prudish virgin," a sneer snickered from her thin lips.

At the horrified look on her sister's face, Queenie barked out a harsh snicker. "Goddam, Beks, I got a kick out of picturing you chained down on a grungy bed in a seedy hotel with a line of nasty men waiting to fuck you blind.

"You can't fight them, can't even scream, you'd be so drugged up. Shit, Curt and me and my friends had some jolly laughs over what we knew would happen to you. Your little virgin body all torn up and blistered bloody-" she stopped at the look on Jeph's face.

He looked about to wrap his hands around her neck and crush every breath out of it. Within Jeph's black rage at her, Queenie saw the tender look he laid on Rebeka. Then Queenie glanced at her sister, her eyes narrowed with a frown.

Rebeka's cheeks were bright pink and her eyes were cast down, she chewed at the inside of her lip.

A vulgar smile curled up Queenie's face. "Oh my God, you slut, you. You got fucked at the auction. By who? How many?" She sounded jealous. Her lids lowered to slits when she saw Rebeka and Jeph look at each other.

Awareness spread across her ruddy complexion. "Oh, it's that way is it? I've heard of him, Beks. You are so fucking in for it. He's one of the most vicious, brutal men in the world. They say he's a rutting beast in bed, huge cock, honey, he will tear you apart, he-"

Ving slammed his hand over her mouth, hard. "We do not need to hear any more of your degrading filth. You are not one grain of sand of the worth of your sister."

When he removed his hand, Queenie sneered, "She is not my sister, you asshole. We have no blood relation whatsoever. Her father fucks my mother, that's it. You think I have any feelings for that pale, frail little bitch? Huh?" She snorted tossing her hair back and snarled with repugnance at Rebeka,

"A goody two-shoes. I couldn't wait until they took you. I wanted so many times to slap that pretty face, beat you into the ground. I had to hold back, your father would have had a fit. I am so glad you've been sold to the vile brothel in my place. You will die there, in filth and pain and disease, fucked and fucked every day and night-"

Before Ving could do it, Jeph slapped his hand over her mouth then shoved the gag back up.

Ving and Hub glowered at her with revulsion, their hands gripping her arms so tightly there would be bruises.

Shaking his head, Rumân stepped forward. "Hell, Jeph, what the hell is your plan?"

Jeph rolled his arm around Rebeka's quivering shoulders, pulling her against him. He said to Queenie, "Rebeka was not the only one you set up, right Queenie?" A brow arched over his knowing dark eye, he reached and tugged the gag down slightly.

Queenie's eyes shifted back and forth, then she shrugged. "Yeah, so what. I got a commission for turning in a few other girls, this blonde bitch named Jackie, another called Lily Taylor, and-" she stopped at Rebeka's dismayed choke.

Jeph's face as hard and cold as always, except when he was looking at Rebeka, glowered at Queenie, then he said to Rumân, "Rebeka was mine the second I laid eyes on her. That bitch is yours," he jerked his head at Queenie, "to do whatever you want with."

Rumân eyed Queenie with a strange look. "But the auction rules-"

Jeph said, "Like I said, it was her name on the auction contract, technically she was legitimately bought and paid for even if she wasn't present. She was the one King Martin made the writ for. And now, Rebeka and I and my men are out of here."

The rest of his team was secreted around the building in case of trouble.

His eyes gleaming with sadistic cruelty, Rumân turned to Queenie. "Ah, fine. I won't fight you for your bitch, it'd be a battle I wouldn't likely win. But I will take this one until

I use her up. She's not got the class and beauty of your woman, so marriage is off the table." He sighed, "Gonna have to wait until the next auction for my bride. Boys," he nodded to a few of his men.

They came over and Ving and Hubbard released Queenie to them. Two held her arms, the gag put back in place. She struggled, glowering at them all, cursing behind the cloth over her wicked mouth.

Jeph said quietly, "Say goodbye to your...to Queenie, Rebeka." His hand moved to grip her arm, he once again lowered Queenie's gag.

Rapidly blinking to hold back the tears, her voice creaky with sorrow, Rebeka said, "Queenie, I'll help you." She turned to Jeph. "Jeph, please-"

"Fuck you, you little skank," Queenie spat with venom, eyes streaming vile hatred at her. "I do not want your feeble-assed help. I will do just fine on my own." She cast an angled, alluring glance at Rumân who watched her silently under heavily hooded eyes giving nothing away.

Queenie turned her hateful gaze back to Rebeka. "I am so damned thrilled to be done with you, finally. I didn't need the money or attention of my parents taken off of me for one second for some scrawny little pretend sister."

Sniggering at the sorrow in her little sister's eyes, Queenie sneered at her, raising her nose in the air. Spite filled her face carving harsh creases around her nasty eyes and thin lips.

She snarled at Rebeka, "I have always hated you. I worked with my mother to keep you at that school. Whenever you were home when I did something bad I made sure you got the blame, took the punishment. Get the fuck out of here, I'm good, you bitch, you-" This time Rumân slung the gag back up to cover her filthy spewing.

Holding her clasped hands over her heart, tears springing, Rebeka said softly, "I am so sorry you feel that way, Queenie. If you ever want to get in touch with me, I will always welcome it. Goodbye, be well." Jeph forcefully turned her away from Queenie as the tears fell.

Ving leaned in and whispered in Jeph's ear, "We got that Curt fucker tucked away when you're ready for him, bro."

Jeph's chin jerked up indicating his thanks. With a slight nod to Rumân, then to Ving and Hub, Jeph quickly ushered Rebeka out of the room. He had seen Rumân's sick grin while lighting a cigarette, his malignant gaze glowering luridly over Queenie.

Jeph and his people were out the door, they didn't see Rumân grab the top of Queenie's blouse and rip it straight down to her belly exposing her new, huge, bare breasts. Grinning with heinous lust, Rumân sucked on the cigarette getting it searing hot, while staring at her breasts.

Eyes gleaming with sadistic glee, he said, "Damn, big ruddy nipples, babe, I do love a little nipple burn, don't you?"

His men licked their lips and watched as he moved the red blazing end of the cigarette to her left nipple, grinning harder as he saw her eyes widen, and she felt the heat, then the burn, and she screamed through the gag.

Chapter Twenty-Nine

*A*fter meeting with his men, they parted from Jeph and Rebeka to go on their way.

Jeph lifted Rebeka into the SUV and they took off down the winding road away from the horror in the mountains to the fresh, clean forest. He drove to a small private airport where his personal jet waited.

As they entered it, Rebeka's eyes were big and round at the opulent interior of the aircraft.

Jeph sat down in a huge captain's chair and pulled her onto his lap. Cuddling her, he chased her mouth, but she kept her head turned.

"Jeph, what will happen to Queenie? I can't let her stay there and be tortured."

He captured her jaw to hold her to face him. "She will be fine, *nishka*. I have people on the inside there. If she is in real serious, I mean like *fatal*, danger, they will get her out. Now, forget about that wretched woman that I am sorry I had to ever lay my eyes on, and kiss me."

"Wait, aren't your men coming with us? Are we waiting for them?"

Sighing with frustration, "*Na*, my precious girl, they are taking a different flight. We are going somewhere else. I will

301

meet up with them in a while. For now," he licked his tongue across her lips, "I want to concentrate on us." He slid his hand down, inside the front of her dress to grasp a breast.

"See," he sighed more happily, "this is how we should be." Squeezing her plumpness, he pulled his hand out to slide it up her dress. His hand sifting inside her panties, he trickled his fingers over her sex then pushed a finger inside her soft channel.

Squirming with the wonderful sensations he elicited with his magical fingers, Rebeka moaned, "Jeph, we shouldn't…"

Covering her mouth with his hushing her, he murmured on her lips, "*Yah*, we should, baby, every chance we get," and shoved his other hand back down the front of her dress to clutch a breast. Gripping it in his big hand, he tried to lift it out of her bodice and right out of the bra.

Rebeka writhed all over his lap mashing his hard-on to his delight. Jeph leaned back in the captain's chair and moved her sideways so he could access her body better. Her skirt was all bound up around her hips and he was trying to get more fingers inside her tender sweetness.

"Sir," a reprimanding voice threw cold water on their building heat. "You each must be in your own seat and buckled up for takeoff."

The stern flight attendant inclined her frowning face at him until she saw Jeph had pulled out half Rebeka's naked breast and his hand was up under her skirt. Red lashed at her sharp cheeks and she quickly spun around.

Ignoring her admonition, Jeph said, "Bring us something to eat and drink, take your time."

"Uh," the attendant mumbled awkwardly. "I will see to it, immediately, sir," she muttered and stalked down the aisle snapping a curtain closed behind her.

Blushing herself, Rebeka pushed at his hands. "Let me up, you got us in trouble," her giggle took the rebuke out of her words.

"Dammit," he growled, giving her pussy a hard pinch. Tucking her breast back in the dress, he helped her off his lap.

Rebeka climbed into the seat beside him and buckled in. They turned to stare at each other, their eyes joining. Hers soft yet brilliant blue, his hard and brutal, yet so gentle when he gazed at her.

When the roar of the jet quieted and evened out, the flight attendant brought their food. They made light talk while they ate.

After the attendant returned for their dishes and left again, Jeph cleared his throat, looking at the woman he wanted above anything else in the universe.

He said with uncustomary uneasiness, "Rebeka," he reached over and held her hand. "I want you to stay with me, do you want the same thing?" Anxiously, he tried to read her expression. All sorts of emotions traveled over her face.

Her voice so soft it was almost inaudible, "Can we wait until we land to- to talk about this?"

His eyes dimmed with worry and anxiousness. Damn, he prayed he wouldn't have to keep holding her prisoner, but if she didn't want to- "Uh, sure, sweet. We can rest, we will be there soon."

He watched her as she settled in her seat and slipped off to sleep.

When Rebeka opened her eyes, Jeph was unbuckling her seatbelt. "We have landed, sweetheart. Time to go."

After thanking the small crew, they trod down the steps of the aircraft to a waiting limo.

Helping Rebeka inside, Jeph slid in next to her and held her hand. Raising it, he kissed the back of her hand and smiled at her. "We will be home soon, my sweet."

She peered out the window as the car sped past towns, again, everything was in a foreign language, she still had no idea what country she was in.

The limo drove down a long street compiled of mansions that had a ton of land spread between them.

It finally parked in front of an illustrious huge house. The mansion was made of brick and stone, two stories, surrounded by a variety of trees, and had several chimneys rising out of the roof.

Behind the house was a mountain. Below it, in a lush valley, an alpine lake glistened. Jeph's boat swayed with the rippling current.

Jeph helped her out. Rebeka exclaimed looking up at the big home in wonder, "Jeph, it's beautiful, is this your home?"

After Jeph's personal chauffeur brought their luggage into the house, he sent the limo on its way and led her up the steps and ushered her inside. The inside was as lavish as the outside.

Huge rooms with cathedral ceilings and skylights for bright illumination, white tile flooring with gold marbling and blush walls. Extravagant furniture and paintings on the walls exuded wealth.

Bringing her to the richly decorated yet comfortable living room, he paused, said, "*Yah*, tis my home. And," he bent to kiss her lightly, "yours too, I hope."

Surprise widened her eyes as she looked around then to him. "You want me to stay, here, with you?"

Nodding, his gaze glued to her lips, he said simply, "*Yah*."

"For...how long?"

He'd kept his hands to himself long enough. Jeph stepped in closer to her and drew his arms around her. "Forever, Rebeka. I want you to stay with me forever."

His heated gaze moved up to see her reaction to his words. "What do you say, baby, will you stay with me, marry me?"

The yellow lashes sprung up matching the dismay in her voice, "Marry you? You- you want me to marry you?"

Red crept into his face as he feared her saying no. He knew he was a foul villain and she was sweet as honey. Still, he hoped they could start anew, work on changing his occupation.

His head bobbed up and down. "*Yah*, sweet, marry me, have my babies, I..." His heart of stone had turned to mush. He couldn't believe these words were coming from his mouth, "I love you, Rebeka, I have from the start. Marry me."

"I...don't know what to say," she floundered.

"Then say nothing, for now, *nishka*. Give me some time to win you over, give us some time, *bine*?" He took both her hands and gently held them.

"I know tis a lot to take in. I've treated you harshly, allowed your abduction and let them flaunt you on that fucking stage. I'm a criminal and you're..." his smile lopsided, "well, you're you. Perfect. And, perfect for me. I would like the chance to try to be perfect for you."

"I..." she again hesitated, then smiled. "This is all so, you know, strange, what happened to my life. I feel upside down sometimes. But, I... don't want to leave you. I can't believe it, but I don't want to leave you."

At the light that sprang into his eyes beaming them with hope, she said, "But I also don't know exactly how I feel, about you, about us. I need that time to sort it all out. Is that okay with you?"

"Fuck *yah*, my princess, you take all the time you need. Just don't shut me out, let me in. Give me a chance, that is all I ask."

At least she didn't say no, he wouldn't have to keep her there against her will, which is what he would likely do if she refused him.

He never said he was a nice man. But, she did say she didn't want to leave him, relief squirreled through his body leaving it tingling.

"We need to discuss this, my beautiful *nishka,* down the hall, let me show you," before she could take a breath he scooped her up in his arms and strode through a warren of corridors.

He was so happy to have her there finally, safe and with him, he brimmed with excitement, it overflowed making his limbs feel like jelly.

Marching up a flight of stairs and down another corridor, he brought her to his bedroom. It was a huge, lavish yet masculine room of burgundy and blues.

He set her on her feet and immediately spun her around and pulled the zipper of the dress all the way down. Then he turned her back around then shoved the dress to her feet.

She was giggling when he crouched and took off her shoes and the dress, and stood back up to cup her breasts. The giggles dissipated into breathy puffs. Jeph was anything if decisive.

With little movement to spare, he divested her of her bra and panties and lifted her, laying her on the bed.

His eyes on hers, he removed his shirt, drawing it over his head and tossing it then removed his boots, jeans, underwear. His very ready cock sprung up ready for action.

A lot of it. He fisted it as he came to the bed, stroking his closed palm down, then up it.

Rebeka's eyes glowed from the dim light with the drapes closed. The faint illumination shone over her creamy skin. Lying on her back, golden hair a pool around her beautiful head, she raised her arms, hands out to receive him.

Climbing on the bed, he deliberately didn't grab a condom. He knew he was clean, he made sure all of the people at the auction camp were constantly tested, including himself, and he had never fucked without a condom.

His hope was that he would get her quickly with his seed, his child, she would stay with him then. He wouldn't have to ever worry she would leave him. If he treated her as the princess she was, she would never *want* to leave him.

Prodding her legs apart, he moved between them, his hand went right to her pussy. "Ah, baby," she was already wet. "That is good, because I am not going to last long, I have to have you before I explode."

His fingers stroked her slit, played with, clinched her bud until it was swollen with need, then he inserted one thick finger inside her.

When she was slightly stretched and soaking and mewling, he added a finger and curled them both stroking over her hot spots again and again until her body writhed under him.

"Oh, Jeph," she sighed with delight, "you make me feel so good." Her fingers groped in his hair and tangled in it.

"I need you now, Jeph, please, now, I want you inside me, fill me, fill me fast," her breathy pleas, and hitching breasts arching up to him pulled him under.

"*Yah*, baby," already breathless himself with his voracious hunger for her, he suddenly drove right into her, spearing fast and deep through her tender folds and soft sheath, and so powerfully hard she cried out.

When he paused to see if he'd hurt her, she grabbed onto his hair, pulled it hard, and commanded, "No, don't stop, Jeph, don't ever stop!"

He took her with savage expediency, his thrusts rages of strength, his cock hard as iron- a drilling turbine on speed ravaging her body, barraged in and out until they both peaked at the same time and flew off into space together.

Rebeka stabbed her nails into his shoulders as her body contorted around his and she shrieked his name again and again as the whirlwind tornado blew through her, tossing her into the air where she spiraled, then exploded.

At the same time, Jeph's body lit like a stick of dynamite. The flames scorching his insides he combusted, his seed erupted from his pistoning cock endlessly pummeling her.

"*Rebeka-*" his face a work of agony and excruciating pleasure, he roared until his throat was hoarse. His arms wrapped emphatically around her, clutching the breath out of her he held her so tightly, so close to his heart, and they plummeted back to Earth together.

Gasping, panting, their hearts throbbing in unison, they hugged until their pulses slowed.

Epilogue

Curling into Jeph's arms, Rebeka said shyly, "Jeph…"

"Hmmm?" His brain was a-buzz, he couldn't draw breath much less speak in full sentences.

"Um, usually when a man asks a woman to marry him, he, well, he has a ring, and, well, he gets on his knees, and-"

"Fuck baby." Gaining his wind in record-breaking time, Jeph lunged off the bed and raced to the living room.

He was back in a flash and skidded to his knees beside the bed.

Laughing, Rebeka inched to the side of the bed. Climbing up on her knees, her long curls dangling around her pink nipples, she said, "What are you doing?"

His voice as soft as rough velvet, he pushed the lid up on the tiny box he held, and exposed a diamond ring. "Rebeka Benani, love of my life, will you marry me?"

Mouth falling open, her eyes gawked like rubberneckers at the gem then up to his dark eyes glowing with love.

"What? I don't understand, how did you-"

"Hubbard got it for me. I called him, told him what I wanted. When he got done laughing, he agreed to bring it to Brașov's."

Jeph cradled the back of her head, holding her for a brief kiss. "Answer me, my beautiful girl, will you marry me, live happily ever after with me? With you at my side I can learn to be a better man. An honest one who never harms another person again."

He paused, then, "At least no innocent person. Let's build a family together. Give our children the love that was never given to us. Together, baby, we are strong, strong enough to withstand anything."

His head tilted as he smiled. "We will make the most beautiful children, I want them all to look just like their beautiful mama. What do you say, Rebeka?" His eyes lit with anticipation.

"Let me take care of you, love you, honor you, cherish you with everything I have, with everything I am." Brows rising in hope, he watched her, waited.

Her hesitation ground his stomach into dust, then, her face burst into a big smile.

Voice soft with tender caring, Rebeka said, "I realized as you held me in your arms right now that I was in a place I never wanted to leave. I know we have some work to do, but, yes, Jeph Kajic, I will marry you."

Growling, "Oh fuck, baby," he reached for her, she held a hand up.

"But," she stated, "no more stealing and selling people, and I won't be bullied by you. And," she giggled as he nodded and kept trying to capture her lips. "You must have a lawful occupation, and allow me to work, or go to school, or do whatever I want. Do you agree?"

"Hell *yah*, yeah, woman, anything you want, anything is yours. Just make me a happy man and marry me." *So I don't have to keep you chained to my bed.*

Rebeka paused, then smiled brightly. "Okay, I will marry you, Jeph Kajic. I love you." She was already pretty sure of her feelings for him before he brought her home. He had saved her from the auction at the risk of his own neck, and he had saved her from Rumân Braşov.

He had figured out a way to rescue her without having to kill people, or have them hiding and running for their lives forever. He had exposed Queenie for the treacherous, sociopathic, hateful creature that she was, and technically saved Rebeka from her as well.

Because the truth of it was, if Rebeka had managed to return home, Queenie would ensure some other horror would befall her little step-sister.

Realistically, Rebeka had no desire to return to her former home. Her step-mother hated her and would thwart her at every turn, and her weak father would continue to let her do it.

Rebeka turned a warm gaze on the man that stared so hard, so hopefully at her. When had he stolen her heart?

The days while waiting to hear from Rumân Braşov had been the best time of her life. She enjoyed Jeph's company, and thrived in his adoring arms. He made no mistake that she was everything to him.

Yet, he cared enough for her to let her go if that was what she wanted. Or, at the least, he said he would give her time to discover what she truly wanted.

Rebeka studied Jeph. His hard face, cold eyes, a very dangerous man. No doubt if she'd said no to him, even after time apart to think about it, he likely would not let her go.

He wasn't that kind of man. He'd been forged from battle and violence. No kind heart or compassionate soul had ever rendered him softness or benevolence.

But, it appeared he was actually learning kindness and gentleness, and it didn't seem fake at all. Jeph appeared to truly want to change into a better man.

He certainly wasn't the kind of man that asked women to marry him, or profess his love for them. Before Rebeka, she'd learned he'd never even spent the night with another woman. No, she was indeed uniquely special to him.

Smiling at his lips pressed grimly together as he waited to hear his fate, she told him, "I wanted to see if you would pressure me, or be mean to me if I told you I had to think about whether or not to stay with you."

The smile widened, she went on, "And, you stifled your normal bullying self and said you would be fine with me taking my time to think about us. I take that as a step in the right direction showing your willingness to change for me. And, I love you for it, I love you."

The color drained from his face. All he heard her say was, 'I love you.' He blurted, "You...what?"

He couldn't believe it. This sweet, innocent beautiful girl that he'd treated so horribly, so outrageously, couldn't possibly really care for him, not seriously! He'd prayed and hoped but deep down he never believed she would fall for him. His eyes lazy, glowed warmly at her.

"Say it again, Rebeka, say it again."

Her smile broad and happy and adoring, she did as he asked. "I love you, Jeph. I want to spend the rest of my life with you."

His throat clenched, heart throbbed, the backs of his eyes stung, "Oh baby," he slid the ring on her finger, then pushed her over so he could get back on the bed with her.

His grin naughty, he said with evil glee, "You wanna celebrate?"

She didn't get the word yes out and he was already inside her.

The End

Dear Reader, thank you for purchasing Auction Block! *I know you could have picked any number of books to read, but you picked this book and for that I am extremely grateful.*

I hope you enjoyed this novel, and if you did, please leave a review, *and look for other exciting titles in my name!*

About the Author

Louise Furley loves writing romance with a huge helping of suspense. She finds it exciting to study new lands and learn everything she can about the area and the natives that call it home.

Her idea of fun is researching ideas, studying enigmatic modes of science, archeology, and different ways to kill someone.
Her Significant Other finds the last to be particularly notable. He remains wary yet gives Louise his full support with her writing adventures.

Sunny Florida is home where Louise is a graduate of St. Thomas University with a master's degree in Mental Health.

This degree is essential for exploring the deviant soul, and understanding the mind of a killer, while finding it exhilarating, frightening and sad all at the same time. With artistic license, Louise can be judge, jury, and sometimes executioner!

Louise is the author of numerous published novels. When not researching or writing, she is dreaming of unique plots, and discovering fresh ventures she hasn't yet experienced in the world.

Ride along with her as she travels new and thrilling journeys!